A Dark Road Home

Volume 1

The Last Line of Hope

Charles E. Fredrick &
Lani La Verne

A Dark Road Home Volume 1
The Last Line of Hope

By:

A Dark Road Home Volume 1: The Last Line of Hope

Charles E. Fredrick &
Lani LaVerne

A Dark Road Home Volume 1: The Last Line of Hope

A Dark Road Home Volume 1: The Last Line of Hope by Charles E. Fredrick and Lani LaVerne Published by Brick & Mortar Entertainment Shoreline, Washington

www.brickmortarentertainment.com

A Dark Road Home Volume 1: The Last Line of Hope

Entertainment LLC

Cover Art by Leanna Judd

Ebook ISBN: 978-0-578-72929-9

Brick & Mortar Entertainment LLC seeks to bring the very best in entertainment to a diverse audience. We work closely with artists to bring their distinct vision to life.

www.brickmortarentertainment.com

A Dark Road Home Volume 1: The Last Line of Hope

Chapter 1

1

"There are other worlds," whispered a scrawny, dark skinned boy from the back of an overcrowded classroom. Boys and girls, nearly identical in light grey pantsuits, sat packed in like caged animals. Puddles of sweat pooled on desks across the tight space.

"What?" said the boy seated to his right. He was slumped over his desk. Long brown hair twisted down in knots and covered his face.

A box fan droned on in the rooms lone window. A repetitive thump mirrored the tick of the second hand on the wall clock. Time moved by at a sloth's crawls. Lead scratched on paper. Students struggled to keep their eyes open in the sweltering heat. The temperature inside the room had reached over 90 degrees before the woman looking over the students had finally agreed to open the window and turn on the fan.

"There are other worlds," the boy whispered again. "One that I know of for sure." He punctuated his words with fervent nods. The cracked ends of his dark black hair hung like a veil over the side of his face.

"Another world?" The other boy scrunched his nose up and huffed. Flakes of skin broke free from his lips and floated down from the corner of his mouth. "You must be joking. We live in an orphanage. There aren't any other worlds but what's right in front of us."

"No, Alex, I'm serious." The boy turned in his seat and his desk scraped along the green linoleum. The sound seemed to go unnoticed. "Behind the boy's dormitory. The lake at the bottom of the cliff..." Jackson trailed off. He glanced about sheepishly and spied the students sitting closest to them. If they had heard any of their conversation, they'd done a good job at playing coy.

"Come on Jackson," Alex urged, "spit it out."

Jackson shifted and leaned across the small space that separated the two boys. "I was being chased by Bobby Farber."

"Big Fat Bobby," Alex coughed.

"Yeah Big Fat Bobby," Jackson continued. "He had me pinched with my back to the cliff. Only place I could go was down. I scrambled down the path, towards the thicket on the far side of the water. He grabbed me before I could make it. He tossed me in."

Alex stiffened. "When did he do this?" He shook. "Why didn't you tell me?"

"I thought I was going to drown out there." Jackson ignored the questions. "I couldn't breathe. I'd swallowed so much water. But then, out of nowhere, I was pulled into something, a portal that –"

The room around them burst to life. Wild squeals bounced off the brick walls and echoed around the tight space. The two boys broke apart as a wood meter stick slashed down where they'd been huddled together. Bits of their brown and black hair landed on the floor beneath them as they shot back to avoid another blow.

"Jackson," a short, plump woman boomed. A beak like nose hooked down from the center of her round face. Her eyes narrowed and were barely visible. "You are here to study in silence. I would think a fifteen-year-old could understand basic instructions."

"Sister Margaret," Jackson stammered. "I was only trying to –"

"Silence," Sister Margaret said sharply.

All the sound in the room stopped. Even the box fan seemed to have listened and limited its thump to a dull beat. The dramatic shift of the energy in the room drew the last pair of eyes to the budding confrontation. Students, just seconds before working intently, came together to watch the spectacle unfold. They tried to temper their enthusiasm, but their eager faces betrayed them. Sister Margaret stepped forward; the corners of her mouth curled upward.

After a moment of silence Jackson continued. "Sister Margaret, I only just leaned in to tell Alex something. I was just about finished."

"So," Sister Margaret interrupted, "you were not just talking for the last three minutes before I came over?"

"I –"

"No," Sister Margaret boomed, "I gave you a chance to correct your nasty behavior but still you persisted." She inched towards to the two boys. "Yes, I, so generous and forgiving, can only take so much. And to think so little of your fellow students." She turned her head and surveyed the kids in the room. An abundance of smiles stared back. "Such thoughtless behavior must be punished."

Sister Margaret shifted her feet and turned her back to Alex. She pushed in against Jackson's desk and set the meter stick on the edge. For a second, she did nothing. The moment stretched and the other students squirmed. Pencils tapped the desks in earnest. Shoes began to shake. Hot breath huffed out and envelop the room with the odors of potatoes and eggs.

"I believe ten lashings should suffice." Sister Margaret pulled from the desk and straightened her back. She turned and cut through the desks towards the chalkboard. "Up with me Jackson. Quickly now we've wasted enough time today."

Jackson glanced at Alex. His eyes glazed over and he snorted. He shook his head from side to side and clamped his fingers on the edge of the desk. In one swift motion he pushed back and sprang to his feet. The white canvas fabric of his shoes nearly broke free of the sole from the sudden force. A piece of his trousers caught on a screw and tore at the seam. He fixed his eyes on the blackboard and started the short march to the front.

"Wait a second," Alex shouted. He shot up. "Ten lashings? That's ridiculous. That's barbaric."

"And that's the way we do things here," Sister Margaret said absently.

"Well give me five then." Alex started to the head of the class. He overtook Jackson and stopped. "That's only fair. I was talking too."

"I suppose you were encouraging his behavior." Sister Margaret tapped the end of the meter stick against the linoleum. The sound was drowned out by repressed shrieks of delight. "Very well. Five lashings each. Hurry up, we haven't got all day."

The classroom was suddenly alive with life. Chatter erupted from every available mouth. Sister Margaret ignored the rising volume and pushed a small black stool back to the chalkboard. She circled the spot and chuckled. With limited effort she nudged the stool a second time and tucked it right beside her desk. She created a void at the front of the class to carry out the corporal punishment.

Alex glared at the faces staring back at him. He stood stoic, rolled his shoulders, and lurched forward. Jackson followed on his heels. It was only a second before they were at the center of the space. The two boys shared a glance and turned back toward the group. They elevated their hands and clenched their fists.

Sister Margaret rounded

from the side. She laid the meter stick on her shoulder. "Noble of you, Alex, to protect your friend like this."

"I'd do anything for Jackson," Alex said defiantly.

"Noble, yes." Sister Margaret lifted the meter stick over her head. "If misguided."

The sound of grumbling from the hallway outside diverted the attention. After a moment of rapid conversation, the door swung open. A tall, lean man with a wisp of hair at the center of his head shuffled into the room. He put his hands on his hips and surveyed the situation from over his gold rimmed glasses. His eyes shifted. He examined each face before they finally stopped on the boys being punished.

"Mr. Smart," Sister Margaret said sheepishly. "What have I done to deserve this visit from you today?" She lowered the meter stick but kept it out.

"Jackson Howell." The man took a step but was barely in the room. "Leave your things and come with us. My assistant here will make sure anything important finds its way back to you."

Jackson didn't move. He didn't lower his fists. "What?" he muttered confused.

"Lower your hands and come with me. We have found a permanent home for you. Your benefactors will be here shortly to get you."

"What?" Jackson repeated.

"Move it," Mr. Smart cracked. "We haven't got all day."

The silence in the classroom had returned. Once eager faces were replaced with scowls. Barely audible grumbles reverberated through the space. Whispers of jealousy and anger manifested into sounds of outright contempt. Jackson moved in slow motion. He dropped his hands, turned, and fixed his stare on Alex.

"But sir," Sister Margaret pleaded, "I've yet to administer his punishment."

Mr. Smart pivoted. He passed over the threshold and out the door. "Continue with the other one. Jackson comes with me." He disappeared and a young woman rushed in. She weaved her way over and took everything off one of the vacant desks. In an instant she was gone.

"Jackson." Alex broke his stiff posture and grabbed for his friend. Sister Margaret snatched him by the elbow and wrenched back. "Jackson, no." He yelled even louder. Tears welled in his eyes.

"Knock that off boy,"

Sister Margaret barked. "I thought you would be happy to see your friend get a new home." She forced Alex back and positioned her body between the two boys. "Go now," she snapped.

Jackson didn't move. He stared at Alex. His lips twitched. He started to talk. Words formed but nothing came out. Alex struggled against Sister Margaret. He kicked her shins and wiggled to get free. Her grip grew tighter with every movement.

"Please," Alex pleaded. A hand suddenly appeared. Jackson was pulled backwards. "No," he yelled even harder.

Jackson went limp. He had nearly disappeared into the hallway. "It's real," he shouted as he vanished out of sight.

"No," Alex said dejected. He stopped struggling.

"Put your hands out,"

Sister Margaret said coldly, "this isn't a circus. Ten lashings for you now."

In the aftermath of the commotion Alex had forgotten about the punishment. "Ten," he mumbled solemnly, "I thought it was five."

Sister Margaret rolled her eyes and scoffed. "It's ten lashings for the pair. I don't care who takes them." She reached down and snatched his right hand. "See," she said, "misguided."

Alex trembled and fought back tears. He closed his eyes and pinched them tight. The air near him broke. Pain shot up his forearm. He clenched his teeth and let his focus drift.

Alex was sad. He was angry.

A dull pain resonated through him. He ignored it.

Jackson had a new home, a new family.

There was pressure on his knuckles, but the pain was gone.

And still he insisted the portal was real.

Liquid flowed through his clenched fist.

Alex knew he would have to look.

It flowed freely; the smell of iron overtook his senses.

If another world did exist, he would have to find it.

2

The week passed and Alex found himself the subject of nonstop, merciless, torment and ridicule. It started almost immediately in the wake of his split with Jackson. Word spread before they'd even left the classroom that he'd been weeping uncontrollably. By the time he'd made his way to the second-floor dormitory, he'd been weeping and peeing himself. In the dining hall that evening, it was fact that Sister Margaret had to be disinfected, her habit burned and buried. When he awoke the next morning, apparently he'd peed four or five gallons, because his clothes, bedding, and mattress were soaked through. Each day that went by brought uninspired acts of bullying. By the fourth day, he shifted focus and thought of nothing but his friend and the last words he said to him.

After the week, Alex relinquished any hope of seeing Jackson again. Lying on his cot, alone in a room built for twenty, he watched a tiny speck on the ceiling. The black dot jerked. It shot forward. It settled before it dropped and started to descend. It continued methodically until it was just above his brow. Alex swept his arm up and cupped the speck in his open palm. The tiny spider darted about in a panic before it froze. He examined the creature.

"Just like me aren't you buddy?" Alex said the arachnid. "Small and insignificant. Out of place in this stupid world."

He waited for a response. When none came, he dropped his arm to the floor and shook the spider free. The creature disappeared amongst the dust and dirt. Alex sighed and threw his arm across his body. He curled onto his side and pulled his knees up to his chest.

Alex had been at the orphanage for as long as he could remember. Worse still, he'd been devoid of any friends until just four years earlier when Jackson arrived. From what he could recall Jackson's parents had been killed in a car wreck. He didn't have anyone else. Like Alex he was alone. The people who should have taken care of him didn't and he'd ended up at the orphanage.

Their friendship was

instant and blossomed overnight.
Jackson had been lost, scared. He was
prey for the older kids and Alex sensed a
kindred spirit. It was the first time he'd
ever felt such a connection. When Alex
stepped in to protect him for the first
time, there relationship was sealed.
Since that day they were inseparable.

A gentle rain fell. The
patter of drops on the roof pulled Alex
from his reflection. He could hear
shouting in the distance, but he paid it
little attention. Classes were done for the
day and rest of the kids would be
blowing off steam. They paled it up
amongst friends. Groups squared off on
the baseball diamond. Some secured
poles from the Deacon and went fishing
at the lake.

The lake, Alex suddenly
remembered. "It can't be," he said aloud.
He lifted his head and made certain he
was still alone. "It can't be," he said

softly.

But why, Alex wondered, would he have continued with the ruse even after Mr. Smart came into the room? It was just a ridiculous thought. Jackson would never lie to him like that. They had been thick as thieves. Before Jackson, there was nobody. He was the loser who nobody wanted. He was the one who had been abandoned. He was the one whose parents left him to die out in the cold. Even the bullies who were bullied by other bullies bullied him. Why would Jackson use that last moment to lie? To Alex the answer was simple; he wouldn't.

"What did you find, Jackson?" Alex smiled and rolled off the cot. "You may have a new family, buddy, but you left me quite the little puzzle didn't you," he chuckled.

Alex planted his feet. The distant sound of shouting turned

into a panic. The gentle patter of rain intensified, and Alex realized how thunderous the noise really was. In a matter of seconds, the shouting overtook the rain. The door to the boy's dormitory burst open. A flood of young men trudged in and shook off like dogs. The first wave broke off in multiple directions and paid no attention to Alex. He waited for the onslaught of activity to fade. Another group stomped in and laughed. They smacked one another and moved across the room, straight for Alex.

One of the boys caught sight of Alex. He smirked. "Oh my, look at who we have here." The boy popped on his toes and skipped over. "The little baby can't play ball with us." He bent over and shook his coat off over Alex. "Afraid he might get hurt."

Alex huffed. He rolled his head to the side. The other boys in the group gathered around the cot. He tried to ignore the taunts.

"Come on Dean," another boy chirped from the back, "he should have known there was no way around that." They all laughed.

A blur passed through the edge of his vision. Alex was suddenly upended. His head just missed the frame and smashed into the floor. Water and mud rained down from above. Blow after blow struck him in repetition. Laughter echoed off the walls. The sound of heavy breathing and wheezing filled the space.

Alex bounced to his feet; fists clenched. He threw his elbows out and aimed for soft flesh. The group struggled to get through his guard. They buoyed in and out but could not get a grip on his flailing limbs. For a moment Alex saw daylight. A gap opened between two of his assailants and he lunged for freedom. There was one sweet second before a meaty paw snatched him from behind. It pulled him to a stop.

"Yeah, get him Arty," someone hollered.

"Why'd you do that?" Dean put a hand to his face. It came back covered in blood. In all his effort Alex made solid contact.

"Knock him good Dean," the same person hollered and laughed.

The room around them paused. The rain took a brief hiatus to watch the confrontation play out. A thick arm curled around Alex. A second pulled his other arm back and he was overpowered. Dean wiggled his arms at his side. He shook his fists at the wrist. He bounced up on his toes and wrenched his neck in a circle.

"You asked for this," Dean spat. He pulled his fist back and snapped it forward. Soft flesh buckled and bone crunched. Blood poured from Alex. A second strike followed in quick succession. Alex doubled over and spit blood from his nose and mouth.

"I think you broke his nose," Arty said. He tossed Alex on his overturned mattress.

"He deserved it." Dean wiped his knuckles on the blanket. "Shouldn't have hit me," he said as he walked towards the back of the room.

"I guess," Arty said. He turned and walked away.

In the aftermath of the assault, the group scattered. Alex touched his nose. He pressed gently with his finger and pain overwhelmed him. He touched his lip and it produced the same results. With one fluid motion he rocked to his feet, flipped his mattress, and snatched his blanket. In an instant he was back on his belly, desperate to clear the blood from his nose. For some time, he dared not move. Late in the evening, after the sun had long set and the rain receded to a soft patter, he got up and tiptoed to the bathroom.

Alex pondered his face in the mirror. His long, dark hair was matted with blood. It stuck to his forehead. A bulbous bit of bashed cartilage was where his nose should have been. Both of his eyes were more black than blue. A massive gash crossed from one side of his lips to the other. It looked as though he was a boxer gravely injured in a prize fight, not a 15-year-old boy.

Water ran warm out of the tap. Alex splashed in across his face. He cleaned the blood from his hair and pulled it over his shoulders. His nose was still busted but looked better without the dried blood. He quickly washed his lip and let it be. After he looked presentable, he slid out into the dormitory. At his cot, the blood turned his blankets into a mess. He clenched his hands and started to shake.

"One way or another," Alex whispered, "I'm leaving this place tomorrow."

3

Unfortunately for Alex, determination was useless in the face of constant authority. The days went by and there was nary a word from anyone about his condition. Those who knew what happened said nothing. Those who didn't know, didn't really care. Fortunately for Alex, the harassment he'd faced in the wake of Jackson's departure ceased. *Even a blind eye was better than an engaging one, Alex thought.*

As the teenage population at the

orphanage curtailed their aggressive behavior, Alex found no such respite from those in charge. Late one afternoon, as the sun pushed onto the horizon, Alex walked around the lake behind the dormitory. His eyes were fixed on his feet. He strolled around and around, deep in thought.

A portal in the lake. A portal to another world. It had to be a joke. He'd read stories. Fantasies about kids just like him. Kids with nothing who suddenly had everything. It was a joke. He'd always preferred the more grounded stories. There was no point getting your hopes up when life dealt you a bad hand.

A sudden shimmer pulsated from the depths of the water. Alex stopped in his tracks. He took a giant step back and the shimmer reappeared. *A trick of the mind.* He stepped forward and saw a distinct shimmer. *It must be the sun.* He took another step back and saw definition in the shimmer. He stepped forward yet again and saw it clear as day. *It was deep, but it was there.*

Alex reached down and tugged his shoe off. He grabbed the other and nearly lost his balance. The grass was cold beneath his feet. He waded into the shallows and the chill of the water sent goosebumps up his arm. His feet slid beneath soft sand. Alex made his way out, inch by inch. He bent over and inhaled as much air as he could manage.

A force yanked him from behind. Thick callouses grated against the base of his neck. He tumbled back on solid ground. The air burst from his lungs. His tailbone smashed into a rock embedded in the earth. Alex scrambled to his feet. He threw his fists out ready for a fight.

"Not thinking of doing anything foolish I hope," a woman said.

"What are you talking about," Alex

barked. He worked to keep his footing on the slick grass. When he saw who it was, he dropped his hands.

"Don't speak to me that way." The woman grabbed Alex.

"Sister Collins I," Alex barely managed to get out.

Sister Collins pulled him in and pivoted to the side. "You'll be scrubbing dishes every night for the next month for the way you have talked to me."

"I didn't know it was you," Alex stammered. "You've seen my face. I thought they'd come around to have another go."

The commotion caused a sudden stir. A group gathered at the top of the slope. Sister Collins kicked her foot out and Alex started forward. They moved slow. More and more people gathered above. Before they'd reached the trail, the entire orphanage seemed to have assembled. By the time they made the top, the rumors had already begun. One person said it was an attempted breakout. Another said it was something much darker.

Alex trudged on in silence, his feet black from earth and mud. Heckles and insults hurled at him, but he paid them no mind. His captor frowned but said nothing. They marched on until the spectators had their fill and dispersed. They approached the administrative building and veered off perpendicular to the entrance. They moved at a hastened pace. Door after door went by but they didn't enter the building.

"Where are you taking me?" Alex couldn't get free of her grip.

Sister Collins didn't break stride. "You have an acid tongue don't you," she said absently.

"You didn't answer my question," Alex spat.

"Yes, an acid tongue indeed." They

approached a small arched doorway and stopped. "There is someone here who is better equipped to deal with you than I am." Sister Collins leaned in and pounded on the door. "I'm far to forgiving for such a wretched child."

It took but a moment before the door opened. Sister Margaret blinked at the setting sun. She shook her head. She was dressed for bed and clearly hadn't been expecting any company. She saw Alex and her face dropped. She grunted. She took a single step back and grabbed at an overcoat behind the door.

"You'll never learn, will you?" Sister Margaret said. "I'll take it from here Sister Collins."

"Don't you want to know what he's done," Sister Collins asked. She failed to relinquish her grip.

"I'm sure I can guess." Sister Margaret shut the door and grabbed Alex around the collar. Sister Collins let go and backed away. "Being rude and interrupting my evening for starters." They started towards the rectory.

"And he threatened me." Sister Collins stayed back. She glanced around and saw nobody was listening. "He threatened me," she said softly.

4

It had been nearly a month since Alex was disciplined for his behavior by the lake and he hadn't had a chance to sneak away. He had been stuck in the kitchen every free moment of time; scrubbing dishes until his hands were chapped, peeling potatoes, going in and out of the deep freeze. What few moments of peace he could find were inevitably interrupted by one of his many tormentors doing what they do best. Even sleep had become a challenge. Some nights he would lie awake into the wee hours of the morning, waiting for an assault that would never come. Other nights he'd doze off under the guise of a restful slumber and awake to a volley of shots raining down on him. It didn't help that those who were there to protect him turned a blind eye to the abuse.

Over time, the constant harassment had the opposite of its intended effect. Instead of feeling like a victim, Alex was emboldened. The first Saturday after school had been dismissed for the summer, he was alone in the library. The room was a vast space crisscrossed from front to back with high shelves. Hard covered books were obscured in layers of dust. Large windows at the rear were lined with thick oak tables and matching chairs.

Alex sat down and dropped a large tome onto the table. There was a loud thump and an echo lingered for nearly a minute. He rested his elbows on the wood and waited for the sound to dissipate. The table wobbled under the pressure and settled on a slant. Alex rummaged through his bag. He secured a pen, pulled it out, and flipped open the cover of the book. The first few pages were editors notes and acknowledgments. He used the pen to flip a few pages in and stopped on chapter one.

Well this is my summer. He sighed and continued to read. Shadows crept across the floor. The lunch bell rang, he ignored it. Chapters one and two went by. Then chapters three and four were done. He flipped over onto chapter five when a metallic shriek pierced the silence. A deep baritone laugh filled the room.

"I saw him in the window," the voice said through gasps, "and you know he will still be in here."

"Little piggy trying to hide out in the library?" The voices moved along the edge of the room. They crept closer. "I'm ready for another go, how about you?" Dean let out a squeal.

The group was just out of view. Alex reached into his pants pocket and pulled out a small white bottle. They snuck around the last shelve and he popped to his feet. Dean was to his left. Tall, thin, and wiry. His curly brown locks were streaked with sweat. On his right, a massive frame was slouched over at the waist. A belly stretched the limits of a tight grey t-shirt. Dexter's lip twitched into a grin.

"You know, Dexter," Alex said, "I've always wondered how you could get so fat on the crap they serve us here."

The hulking giant labored forward. "What did you just say to me?" Dexter reached out and swiped.

Alex jumped around the table. "You're right, you're right. I'm sorry." He pushed with his left hand and created some distance. "I've actually got something for you. For the both of you really." He fumbled with the bottle behind his back.

"Oh yeah?" Dean inched closer. "What have you got for us," he asked tentatively.

"Yeah what have you got for us." Dexter took another swipe. He narrowly missed.

"Well," Alex hesitated. He glanced to his right. "I've got this," he shouted. His right hand flew from behind his back and squeezed. A stream of thick white glue arced through the air and splattered onto Dean's face. He shook from side to side and emptied the remainder of the contents onto Dexter's arm. "Ha," he blurted.

Alex spun on the ball of

his foot. He broke passed the two boys, shot around the corner, and nearly lost his footing. Once stable, he bolted along the outer wall of the library towards the double doors at the entrance. The pounding of footsteps joined the thumping of his heart. Beyond the librarian's desk, he chanced a glance over his shoulder. Dexter was still some ways back. Dean was right behind him.

"I'm going to get you for that," Dean huffed. He threw his hands down on the desk and vaulted over.

The doors to the library burst open and Alex tumbled into the hall. A young girl walked out of the bathroom beyond and they almost collided. She screamed in terror. Alex didn't wait. He shot off down the corridor and weaved through a group of students. Grunts and cries of distress followed him. He neared the end of the hall and went through another set of double doors. He turned left towards the boy's dormitory.

What could he do? It was fun in the spur of the moment. But now he was fleeing for his life. His nose had barely just healed. And it was crooked at that. If they caught him now who knows how steep the punishment would be. No, if he could get away from them now, they'd cool down.

He had to devise a plan. There was no way he could just hold up in the boy's dormitory. And going to anyone for help wouldn't get him anywhere. The only place they wouldn't follow him was the thicket of brambles beyond the lake. Technically it was off school property. Plus, the gashes those thorns caused were painful.

"You can run," a voice hollered from behind, "but you can't hide."

Alex shook his head. He ran passed the boy's dormitory and stopped at the end of the hall. He turned right and approached the door that led out to the field. He lowered his shoulder, dipped down, and elevated into the exit. The steel door flew open on its hinges and slammed into the brick wall. His shoes slipped on loose gravel, but he kept his footing. The stretch of grass before him was clear. It was nothing but air between him and the lake.

Alex hesitated. In an instant Dean was on him. Alex scrambled on his toes. He bolted for the path down the slope. He was there in a flash and took off down the steep incline. His momentum carried him at a rapid pace. Dirt and stone came free and he skied down on the flow. When his feet hit solid ground, he was off. The water was to his right. White crests rolled against the stiff breeze. The thicket of brush drew near.

A sudden shimmer at the corner of his vision caused him to slow. He wrenched his neck to keep focus and was crushed from behind. Both boys tumbled to the ground in a heap. Dean jabbed his fists out and connected. Air left Alex's body and he fell limp. The adversaries gasped and wheezed. They struggled to breathe.

"Got you." Dexter lumbered up. He dropped his hands to his knees and panted. "Didn't think you could get away that easy, did you?"

Alex rolled onto his side and coughed. "I got away from you just fine," he managed to choke out. "It was this prick who caught me."

Dean's face contorted. He lifted his arm and came down with an open palm. He slapped Alex across the cheek. "You don't know when to quit," he said. "Pick him up."

Dexter sucked in air. He reached down and picked Alex off the ground. "He is all yours," he said.

"Can't even fight your own battle?" Alex struggled to get free.

"Once again you are wrong." Dean moved over and positioned himself before Alex. "I have friends. My battle is their battle. Their battle is my battle." He smiled and his eyes narrowed to slits. "Your little friend is gone and you're never going to see him again." He laughed. "But me, you're going to see me every day."

Dean cocked his arm back and popped it forward. Bone crunched under the sudden impact. Blood poured from Alex as his nose bent to the side. A second pop and his vision blurred. After the third his knees buckled, and he fell slack. A final blow hit his belly and he tumbled to the ground like a pile of dirty laundry.

"Alright he's had enough," Dean said. "Let's dump him in the lake. Maybe he'll drown. Fitting. You started here and now you'll end here." The tormenters laughed.

They worked in tandem to hoist Alex in the air. At the water's edge, they swung him back and forth. They counted to three. On the precipice of the final arc they released. Grass and reeds rustled as Alex cut through foliage. The sun bathed his face in a warm glow. Gnats and water bugs paused midflight.

Alex hit the water and the surface shattered. Waves rippled out in every direction. Seaweed under the surface grabbed at Alex and he kicked. His legs didn't move. He reached down to free himself, but his arms were stuck. His eyes darted around for help. Dean and Dexter were already gone and would soon disappear beyond the rock ledge. He tried his extremities again, but they had disconnected from his brain.

Don't panic, Alex told himself. You know how to swim. It's just your clothes weighing you down, you'll be out of this in no time, he reassured his conscience to no avail.

Beneath the surface of the water the weeds tugged. Alex felt his chest tighten. His heartrate elevated. He clenched his teeth and started to shiver. Before he could take a breath, he was beneath the surface. Stagnant water filled his mouth and he inhaled. He coughed but inhaled more of the cold liquid. Fire shot through his body. Everything began to spin.

Alex started to descend. Water shot passed his face and forced his eyes open. Penetrating darkness permeated his vision. The fire in his chest gave way to the pressure of a thousand needles. Deeper and deeper he went. Euphoria overcame him. He felt a sense of peace. A blue halo shimmered before his eyes. He smiled.

Without warning, Alex

compressed. His legs and torso flattened into a single form. The blue glow that surrounded him penetrated his flesh. It continued into his body and overtook his soul. As it disappeared, the world flipped and his body was whole once more. Water flowed past him in sheets and he was thrust upward.

Alex ascended and everything around him brightened. Incandescent blues and greens rushed by. Bright white foam was visible through streaks of crystal-clear bubbles. Groups of tricolored fish swam by in unison. Something red scuttled into view and was quickly gone. Even the sky was visible from the depths of the lake.

The realization he was submerged returned and with it came an aching pressure on his lungs. Alex was desperate for a breath. He tried his arms and was relieved to see movement. His legs worked and he kicked. He pulled desperately towards the surface, but his efforts seemed in vain. The lack of oxygen took effect. He became disoriented. Black rings pulsated. They closed in on his vision.

Alex grit his teeth and pushed. He broke the surface of the lagoon. Warm air filled his lungs and he coughed. Buckets of dark sludge came out of him. When the fit subsided, he paddled like a dog towards the shore. The sun baked down. It was hot and humid. The water was thick. He worked slow and steady until he could stand in the shallows. He reached down and tugged off his shoe. He tossed it onto the bank and did the same with the other. Another fit overtook him, and he struggled to keep air in his lungs. After a minute, normality returned.

Alex reached his arms to the sky and stretched. He caught sight of some unusual things and gasped. A vast expanse of woods surrounded the lagoon. Vibrant colors of purple and blue dotted the shore. A doe and her fawn eyed him suspiciously but disregarded him almost immediately. And the orphanage was gone.

"I must have died," Alex said aloud. His voice intruded in on the serenity. "That, or I have just found the portal in the lake."

Chapter 2

1

Alex stepped from the water and his bare feet nestled into soft grass. He reached down and tugged at his polo. The heavy fabric clung to his body as he lifted it up and over his head. It came free and he tossed it on the ground next to his shoes. His pants were next. He stripped them off one leg at a time until he was standing in his underpants. He shook his hair out, flipped it over his shoulders, and dug the palms of his hands into his eyes.

Alex pulled his hands free and the glare caused him to squint. Streaks of light obstructed his vision before his surroundings came into focus. The lagoon was a rich turquoise near the banks and almost black near the center. Though deep, the light from above seemed to penetrate to the very heart of the depths. Far below, a blue halo shimmered.

The jungle around the clearing encroached on every side. Dark branches poked out from neon ferns. Thick trunks covered in moss towered into the sky. Bright hints of color popped amongst the shadows of the forest beyond. Somewhere high above a bird shrieked. A second call mirrored the first. Below the trees rustled.

In an instant Alex was scared. Where was he really? He was alone and nearly naked by his own doing. Wild animals roamed somewhere just beyond his sightline. His shoes were in tatters and probably not even functional. He had but one set of clothes ill-suited for such a warm climate. If Jackson hadn't mentioned a portal, he'd just have assumed he was dead.

Oh Jackson.

He snapped his head up. The euphoria of excitement gave way to a sense of dread. His eyes shot from side to side. Alex scanned the far side of the lagoon and saw nothing. He peered down along the ridgeline, but there were no trails or identifying markers. When he finally turned completely around, he stopped.

A small shack rose a few feet back from the water. The outer walls looked like flat sheets of tin studded with tiny rivets. The roof was lopsided and sloped towards the lagoon at a slight angel. There were no windows, but an oblong piece of wood appeared to serve as the door. In the far corner, a pipe stuck up through the metal. A steady stream of smoke poured into the air.

"How'd I miss that?" Alex said. His voice cut the silence like a knife. "Better than the orphanage," he said softly.

With a swift kick of the foot he had his pants in hand. He started off. The ground was slick, and he nearly fell as he covered up. His pace was brisk. He stepped on a sharp object that poked out of the ground and flinched. All the ambient noise from the forest dwindled away. He neared the shack, slowed, and stopped. He crept forward one foot at a time.

The door suddenly burst open. Alex jumped back. A man in a long, tan robe stooped over and exited. He thrashed about with a broom. Bristles flew from the end. Long white hair flowed down into his beard and obstructed his vision.

"Who's there?" the man shouted. A flock of birds shot up from the forest and cawed. "Don't make me use this." He moved forward and jabbed the broom out.

"I'm sorry," Alex stammered. "I didn't mean to bother you."

The man stopped moving and shook the hair from his face. "My my, a child." He set the broom off to the side.

Alex hesitated. "I'm hardly a child," he insisted.

"Well yes," the man said, "I suppose that is true enough." He moved closer. "But look at you. You are a mess."

Alex shifted. "Who are you?"

A smile spread over the

man's face. "The question, my dear boy, is who are you? This is my home you see." He nodded and his smile broadened.

"Fair enough," Alex conceded. "Name is Alex. And, believe it or not, I just popped up out of this lake of yours."

The man pondered for a moment and chuckled. "Oh, I believe you. You are not the first person to come out of the water."

Alex smiled. "My friend told me about this place. I thought he'd gone mad."

"Jackson," the man interjected, "where is he? Right behind you I suppose." He dipped his head from side to side and examined the clearing.

"Wait," Alex gasped. The words barely escaped his lips. "Jackson?"

"Yes, is he coming?" The

man strode towards the water and his smile vanished. "Is he coming?" he asked again.

Alex dropped his head and frowned. "He's not coming. He's with a new family now."

The man glanced about. After a moment, he started towards the house. "So, he is not at that orphanage?" He walked passed Alex and paused before going inside.

"No," Alex said softly. "I don't know where he is."

"Well that is a shame. I really did like the boy." The man snatched the broom up and turned. "Well," he said wryly, "are you coming."

Far above a hawk screeched in anger. Alex shuddered. "Yeah, thanks. What's your name by the way." He started towards the door.

The man dipped his shoulders and just made it under the

doorframe. "Name's Leviticus Cole," he said jovially. "It is good to finally meet you Alex."

2

Inside the shack Alex stopped. The room before him was a sprawling expanse. A large rectangular carpet of maroon and brown squares covered a first level platform that stepped down to an inner flat. Two dark stands on either side of the door were adorned with tiny white bell flowers. A fragrant mix of lilac and jasmine mingled with the savory aroma of roasting flesh. On the far side of the space, blue and orange flames danced inside a brick basin. Smoke wafted up towards the ceiling before it caught in the circulating air and flowed out a broken metal pipe.

"What is this place?" Alex went back outside. The structure was a patchwork of rusted tin sheets. He stepped inside and looked about. "Looks smaller on the outside."

Leviticus shuffled to a pile of linens stacked on a chipped bed frame. He swept them to the floor. He rummaged through the pieces that remained and nodded. "Appearances... deceiving." He tossed the clothing at Alex. "And all that," he added.

"What am I supposed to do with these?" The collar of the shirt was ripped into a ragged V. The pants were torn into shorts at the knee. "They look like rags."

"They are just temporary," Leviticus chuckled. He shifted a stool at the base of the bed and moved it towards the fire. "Don't just stand there, come and sit."

"Thanks," Alex shrugged.

He went towards the center of the

space and looked around. The room was minimalistic but well appointed. To the left was the bed and discarded pile of clothes. At the foot, a squat wooden chest sat open. Trinkets of silver and gold glittered in the light from the doorway. Near the fire, a pair of chairs bookended an oval table. Three clay pots were poised at one side. Steam billowed up from the dishes and disappeared. Close to the entrance, an ottoman was sloped to one side. Ragged, tattered books were piled around and upon the piece of furniture.

Alex reached behind him and closed the door. The light from outside snapped off and the room glowed orange. Leviticus poked at the fire with a long dark rod. Flames burst up from the coals and kissed the charred meat. Shadows cast a long silhouette across the wall. He nodded and wiped the ash on his pant leg.

"Come and sit." Leviticus speared the center of the roast. He pulled it from the fire and laid it directly on the table. "Don't really have any dishes but I think we will manage just fine."

Alex paged through a thick tome at the top of a pile. "You didn't answer me," he said absently. He slid the book to the side. "I mean what is this place. It looks like a tiny shack outside but…" he trailed off and mouthed a line of text. "Wait. These are in English."

Leviticus chuckled. "You're shocked? We've been speaking in English this entire time." He lowered himself into a chair and pulled the roast into chunks. "My manners are a bit outdated it would seem." He turned a pot on its side and potatoes rolled onto the table. "I hadn't planned for any company."

"What is this place?" Alex repeated. He left the books behind and his eyes wandered. "Where am I?"

"Sit and have something to eat." A second pot of bright green florets spilled onto the table. "You've had quite a shock to your system." Leviticus upended the final pot and a mixture of leafy greens covered the food.

Alex pondered a small brass broach. He bent down and picked it up off the floor. "Everything here is so different, yet somehow so familiar. I mean what is this place?"

"If you would sit down, I could tell you," Leviticus grunted.

"I'm coming." Alex slipped the jewelry into his pocket and looked up. "Holy crap! Look at all this food," he exclaimed.

"There should be enough, I believe."

"Should be? This could feed like, ten people, at the orphanage." The open chair raked against the wood flooring. Alex flopped down and inhaled. "Smells great too."

Leviticus pushed a pile of meat with the back of his hand. "It should. I have been working on it all day." He used his other hand to separate the remainder of the food into two piles.

"So, are you going to answer me," Alex asked again. "What is this place?" He reached for a potato but stopped before his fingers made contact. Instead he nibbled on a deep indigo leaf.

"This place," Leviticus paused. He picked up a piece of beef. His teeth gnawed a chunk free. "Well I suppose it's magic."

"Magic?" Alex coughed. Food flew from his mouth. "What do you mean magic?"

"Eat," Leviticus chuckled. "I will tell you over lunch."

3

The food disappeared and the table was nearly clear. A loud belch interrupted the quiet. Alex wiped his face with his shirt. He let out a long low groan and tipped back in his chair. His hands slid down to his naval and he rubbed in slow circles. After a few rotations, he patted his stomach and sat forward. Leviticus leaned in. He swept the leftover scraps into an empty bowl. He set them to the side and propped his elbows on the table.

"Did you enjoy?" Leviticus flicked a piece of gristle towards the fire. "It was just thrown together, I am afraid."

"Are you kidding? That was awesome," Alex exclaimed. "I've never had anything so good." He belched a second time and laughed. "That compliment is for the chef."

Leviticus smiled. "I don't

normally have guests around here. Aside from your friend Jackson from time to time."

"Wait… Yeah?" Alex pulled his chair tight to the table. "How did Jackson even find this place? How many times was he here? Why did he even come back for me? Where are we? Didn't you say something about magic?" He suddenly stopped.

In the quiet, the fire crackled loud. Leviticus grabbed a tankard from under the table and put it to his lips. He took a long, slow pull and held it out. Alex accepted the offering and took a drink. The liquid barely touched his tongue and he started to cough. A dark red mist spit out and he threw his hand to his mouth. He sucked in air but continue to choke. After a minute, his breath returned.

Leviticus rolled in his chair. "I should have warned you," he laughed. "It can be a bit strong." He took the cup and had another sip.

"What the hell was that?" Alex coughed out. "Tastes like medicine or something."

"I suppose you could call it that." Leviticus laughed. "Jackson came to enjoy it."

Alex dropped his head. "Jackson," he mumbled, "I miss him." The laughter subsided. A hand reached out and he ignored it. "I've missed him."

The levity in the room dissipated. Silence returned and hung in the air for a heartbeat.

"So," Leviticus broke the tension. He indulged in another drink. "You asked me a great deal of questions. What would you like to know first?"

"Where are we?" Alex lifted his eyes and gazed across the table. "Jackson seemed to come and go as he pleased yet I'm here and he's not. Why would he have even gone back to that place? He was free."

Leviticus downed the remainder of the tankard. He tipped it on its side and watched it roll across the wood. "As to your first point, we are in a forest. After that it gets a bit more," he pondered how to continue, "complicated. Your second question is simple really. He wasn't going to leave you alone in that orphanage. He went back for you."

Tears leaked from Alex. He heaved and sucked in air. His chest labored and he struggled to breathe. Streaks shot through his vision and the room began to spin. A series of repetitive huffs came out in gasps. It took some time before he regained his composure and the world came back into focus.

He wiped the moisture from his eyes but continued to cry.

"The Fates were cruel to separate you," Leviticus said softly. "But you are here with me now and I am grateful for their gift."

"I suppose," Alex paused. "You said this place was magic. What do you mean? Your house is way nicer on the inside than it is on the outside. Is that it?"

"That is part of it. But it is complicated."

"You already said that," Alex snorted. "I get complicated."

"Okay." Leviticus pushed to his feet and winced. He circled the table and made his way over to a stack of books. "That broach, the one you have in your pocket. Completely ordinary I am afraid. But what it represents, therein lies the value." A large volume nearly fell over and he snatched it up. He examined the cover and hurried back to the table. "We have a piece of copper pressed into a simple shape, that is all. But to some, that broach represents something dark, something evil."

Alex reached in his pocket and wrapped his fingers around metal. He pulled the trinket free and brought it to his face. The jewelry was deep bronze and covered in dirt. An outside ring encircled a rigid metal shield. Tiny spikes studded the side. Two daggers embossed with jewels crossed into an X at the center. He flipped it over. The back was absent of markings.

"I guess it looks kind of menacing. With the daggers and spikes." Alex set the broach on the table and pushed it away. "It doesn't look evil though."

Leviticus flipped from one page to the next. "That is a house pendant. It is a sigil that represents a specific family. Even those in servitude were born with a house sigil, but very few had the means to acquire a pendant." Halfway through the book he stopped. He jabbed his finger at a line of text. "Here," he said. He rotated the book so Alex could read it.

"The Law of Two's," Alex read aloud. "What does this have to do with magic?"

"It is –" Leviticus said.

"– complicated," Alex finished.

The fire started to sputter out. Leviticus stood and kicked at the ash. The flames rekindled and he gazed at the resurgent glow. "Complicated, yes. Magic in this world is born in The Law of Two's. It starts with a pair. Not three, not four, but two." He shook his head and returned to his seat at the table. "A mother thanks the Gods when she has a third child."

"Two?" Alex queried. He shoved the book to the side and leaned in.

Leviticus continued. "Always a pair of siblings. A bond so unique it forges an invisible current between them. A wave of power that can be harnessed and used to great effect."

"Are you a twin?"

Leviticus lifted his hand and Alex went silent. "As I said, it is complicated. Magic is all around us. But whether one can see it, or use it, is up to them."

Alex looked around the room but said nothing.

"It starts early. Little things. A joke on a neighbor. Revenge for an indiscretion. It escalates. Someone gets hurt. People demand reparations. One sibling acts out. The other tries to make amends. And here is where things get simple. Here is where The Law of Two's exists."

The fire died away. Leviticus got to his feet and walked across the room. He opened the door and Alex squinted. A stream of air swept through and dust swirled in the light. In the distance birds whistled as one.

"Gorgeous." Leviticus stepped over the threshold and inhaled. "Let's walk.

There are only a few hours of daylight left. Plus, the birds are out."

Alex jumped to his feet and the chair toppled over. He picked it up just as fast as it had fallen and bounced to the door. Outside, the pair walked along the bank. They listened as the birds crooned a harmonic song. Something jumped from the water and landed with a resounding splash. The sound echoed through the clearing and disappeared into the forest.

"The Law of Two's?" Alex asked tentatively.

"Yes." Leviticus looked up to the sky. "The Law of Two's. It is simple really. Good and evil. That is what it all comes down to. Twins are bound from birth to be good or evil. Early on it was viewed as an anomaly. As years passed, it became the rule. If a mother birthed a pair, they were immediately expelled from society. Entire families were cast out. But good and evil. They couldn't escape it. One was good and one was evil."

Alex stuck his toe in the water and shivered. After a second, he pulled his cuffs up and submerged his feet. "I don't get it," he said. He dunked his face. "How would they know who was good and who was evil?"

"That is a question even history can't answer. I imagine it is different for all of them."

"Were they all good or evil? I mean everyone?" Alex ran his fingers through his hair. He picked at the tangled knots. "They couldn't all be good or evil."

"Some tried to fight it. A few even did a good job for a time." Leviticus hopped down and cupped a handful of water. "But." He took a drink from his hand. "The Law of Two's. It never fails."

"What happened then?"

Alex waded into the deep and submerged his head. "To all the twins out there," he asked as he emerged.

"Well, now, that is where things really get complicated. That is where our history begins and ends." Leviticus climbed back onto the bank and sat.

"What does that mean? What does any of this have to do with magic?"

"That current that connects them. That is the magic. The necromancers, the bad twins, harnessed that power and used it against their siblings. They hunted and eliminated their counterparts. Good doesn't stand a chance in the face of absolute evil."

The air grew cold. Trees blocked out the remaining light. Alex got out of the water and sat on the bank. He ran his fingers through the grass and pulled a piece free. His eyes focused on the blade and he flicked it away. Time ticked by in increments as the sun descended behind the trees. It wasn't long before the air around them buzzed and flashes of yellow light lit up the forest.

"So, what happened? The good twins? What happened to them?" Alex finally managed.

Leviticus sighed. "There was a necromancer that started it all. Must be twenty years ago by now. He killed his brother and hunted down every twin he could find. One after another he vanquished the good and recruited the evil. After the twins were eliminated, he turned his anger on a kingdom to the west. There was nothing they could do. The necromancers killed the king, killed his family. He erased their bloodline and claimed the throne for his own. From that day forward, the Kingdom of Harwell ceased to exist."

Alex sat motionless. "What were the good twins called," he asked abruptly.

"What?" Leviticus got to his feet and stretched his arms to the sky. He rotated at the waist and his back popped.

"If the bad twins are necromancers what were the good twins called."

"It has been so long," Leviticus said. He put his finger to his chin. "Soothsayers I believe."

"Which one?" Alex leaned back on his elbows and closed his eyes. A smile played at the corner of his lip. "Which one are you?"

Leviticus turned his back and moseyed toward the shack. "You ask a lot of questions," he chuckled. "What makes you think I am a twin?"

"Well that's easy." Alex spread out. "You know magic."

4

A breeze swept through the clearing and the surface of the lake rippled black. Light from a crescent moon brought a single streak from above. A cadence chirped in rhythmic harmony. Something cried out from the darkness and the sound quickly cut off.

Alex sat bolt upright. He rubbed his eyes and shook his hair from his face. His breath labored. His head shot from side to side. The ground was slick with dew, but he wasn't cold. A warm flow kissed his skin and his breathing stabilized. Everything around him was cloaked in a shroud of mystery. Animals moved in the underbrush. Bugs crawled in the grass unseen. Unknown birds of prey circled overhead. A jarring screech pierced the air and the water splashed.

The commotion caused Alex to flinch. He rolled to his knees and jumped to his feet. His eyes shot about.

He saw the shack on the edge of the water and waited for his vision to come back into focus. Reality suddenly returned. The hair on his neck settled. Everything from the previous day came flooding back. Alex started to cry.

It took a long time before his sobs subsided. After his eyes dried up, Alex went to the shack and crept inside. The fire had been stoked and the room was hot. He left the door ajar and tiptoed towards the table. A faint orange glow illuminated the book they had been looking through. Alex folded the cover over and tucked the text under his arm. He turned and went to the ottoman.

"You were asleep," Leviticus sighed from the other side of the room. "I just left you out there."

"It's cool. I forgot where I was is all." Alex cleared the last few books from the ottoman and sat. "I'm going to read for a while, if that's okay."

"Call this place home. We will make a bed for you tomorrow," Leviticus said. He shifted to his side and yawned. "You can leave the door open if you'd like. Nothing will bother us. I just get cold is all. Grew up in the desert."

"Thanks." Alex set the book on his lap and brushed away a layer of soot. "You're being awfully nice." The cover was a deep emerald. A gouge ran down the spine. "Why?"

Leviticus laughed. "Purely selfish reasons I assure you. I don't get much company out here and I used to be a bit of a social butterfly, if you can believe it."

Alex flipped to the first page of the text. A pair of numbers were written out in looping script and separated by a dash: *850 – 900*. "What do these numbers mean," he asked. He flipped the page. "Eight hundred and fifty to nine hundred?"

"The dates," Leviticus yawned. "That is a history book. It is nine hundred and four now so that is all recent history."

The fire cracked. Leviticus rolled to his side. Alex shifted the book around on his lap until the pages were illuminated by fire light. There were no headings. The prose was delicately scrawled from one margin to the other. He read the opening line but stopped and thumbed ahead until he was halfway through. He went from word to word with his index finger. After a few pages he found what he was looking for a started to read.

The connection has been well documented for many generations. Twins share a unique bond between them. One child is not enough to generate the magical current and any more than two will pull the current into threads not strong enough to sustain a connection. In that connection the dichotomy of good and evil exists. It is very much like the opposing sides of a magnet, strong and completely at odds. But, when isolated, that force becomes tempered. The simple solution has always been social distancing. Twins left home to find their own way, to their own people. The practice was harsh but effective. This has since changed.

The problems began in 889. Necromancer Ulrich Flemming murdered his brother Vladimir and led The Revolt of One. Details are still scarce but The Revolt of One was much *larger than the name implies. A host of dark forces were involved in the plot to overthrow the King of Harwell. Far more than we are aware of to this day. The regicide started The Great War. As of current writing the kingdoms of Sparham and Matisse continue to lead the counter assault. Once again, details are minimal. Those involved in the action assure this author that the fighting goes on.*

The Great War began with the tip of a...

Alex shut the cover. The fire had died down to embers. His eyes began to ache. He set the book on the floor and stretched his body over the ottoman. The piece of furniture was a large square box covered in soft cloth. He rolled to his side and pulled his knees to his chest.

"How accurate is that book?" Alex asked. "Like, is this war still going on?"

The soft sound of shallow breathing answered back. Leviticus burped and started to snore. A draft pushed the door open an inch and the room cooled. Alex closed his eyes. The breeze came and went. His mind raced with a thousand questions. He flailed from side to side but couldn't manage sleep. The birds started to sing. Rays of golden light appeared in the sky and grew bright. Inside Alex waited, eager for his new life to begin.

Chapter 3

1

The next few weeks flew by. Alex learned to fish and cook, fashion clothing, build a shelter, track and hunt game, fight with a sword and dagger, dress wounds, and simply care for himself. Though busy teaching practical life skills, Leviticus made time for moments of levity as well. The new friends read books. They played a game called "Da'con," which Alex still hadn't gotten the hang of. They spent entire days foraging for berries and then cooling off in the lake. Every morning they would snack with wildlife by the water and every night they would feast.

Leviticus awoke early one morning and set out. Alex heard the door shut but paid little attention. He stayed tucked under a thick wool blanket and drifted off. It wasn't long before he awoke drenched in sweat. He threw the cover back and planted his feet on the floor. The ottoman had been moved to make space for the new bed, but the corner of the shack was still tight. Alex kicked a book to the side and found his clothes. He slipped his feet into a pair of hide moccasins with thick leather soles. Once dressed, he grabbed a handful of bright white tubers and made his way out the door.

The sun beat down from directly overhead. Alex finished eating and tossed the stalks into the brush. A small path weaved away from the lake and he followed it into the overgrowth. The forest was thick near the clearing and he bent to avoid the trees that encroached on either side. After a few minutes of walking he picked up the pace and started to trot.

A sharp bend took the trail back towards the lake. Alex dipped off the path. He bound 2 feet at a time into a dense patch of foliage. There was a small break in the cover. He leapt onto a trunk that had collapsed at a 45-degree angle and charged up the incline. The tree was splintered off at the apex. At the last moment, Alex planted his foot and launched into the air. He sailed over a large gap and landed on a small platform tethered to a trunk 10 feet off the ground.

The platform teetered. Alex grabbed a braided rope attached to a branch high above. The tree swayed under the weight. Leaves showered down all around. The movement subsided. He loosened his grip and slid to his knees. Vomit threatened to come up. Alex held the moment in check. He burped and his stomach settled.

It wasn't long before the ambient sounds of the forest returned. A bird landed on an adjacent branch and pecked at the wood. Two small creatures scurried by. They glanced at Alex and ran off. In the distance, an antler stuck out from behind a smooth rock face. The animal poked its head from cover and sniffed the air.

Alex stiffened. He eased to his feet and reached for the braided rope. He secured the line and yanked. The rope stayed taught; the branch didn't budge. He threw one foot over open air. He put all his weight out and leaned forward. The tree bent and the rope swayed. It settled and Alex inched his way down until he was just above the ground. He dropped and watched the brown and white fur on the animal's hindquarters.

A twig broke with a pop. The sound made the animal turn. His head swiveled and his ears twitched. Alex stood motionless. A light gust swept over his face and he crouched. The animal looked away and he took a step. Another twig broke. The animal jumped. He stared at Alex and bound off into the forest.

"Smooth," a voice chuckled from out of nowhere.

Alex shot around and fell to the ground. Leviticus laughed. He sat hunkered over on a small rock tucked behind a fallen tree. The two were only a few feet apart. He got up and put his hand out. Alex scowled at the gesture. His fist clenched into a ball and he hit the ground. When he pulled his hand back, a bit of blood was on the knuckles.

"You were there the

whole time?" Alex asked. He reached up and Leviticus helped him to his feet. "I scared the thing off."

"You were not exactly subtle." Leviticus turned and walked back towards the path. "Nice moves though," he said sincerely. "I could not have made that jump, even as a younger man."

Alex hurried to catch up. "How did you find me?"

"Again, you were not very subtle." Leviticus got to the path and turned away from the lake.

"Where are you going?" Alex looked around confused. "What have you been doing all morning?"

Leviticus moved at a brisk pace. "I have something I want to show you."

The forest thinned. They walked along until the path disappeared into a large clearing. Ragged stones and angular boulders ran around the circumference of the field. A thin cover of grass swayed against a light breeze. Leviticus took a hard left and Alex followed. He got to the base of the wall, stopped, and ran his finger along the outer stones. He started to count. When he got to 100, he dropped down and pressed a small mound in the soil.

A hollow thud rumbled from below. Two boulders suddenly split and a crack appeared between them. Leviticus held his thumb in place. The stones eased apart until the opening was the size of a small man. A second thud shook the ground and a blast of stale air belched out from the darkness.

"Where are we?" Alex asked. "I don't think I've been this far out before." He kneeled and poked his head into the void. A tunnel went back a few feet and plunged straight down.

Leviticus reached out. He

took Alex by the shoulder. "Inside here are the last of my family's possessions. The final remnants of a time in my life long passed." He got down on his hands and knees and backed into the entrance. "Just be careful. And follow me. There is a ladder here if you are wondering."

The tunnel was tight, but Leviticus managed to squeeze through. He inched back until he slid down and out of sight. Alex followed suit. He used his toe as a guide and felt around until the ground disappeared. His foot touched the far wall and he braced himself. He lowered his body and felt around for the first rung on the ladder. He tested all his weight. The ladder didn't budge.

After a short climb, Alex was at the bottom of the decent. The air was cold and smelled of damp earth. He turned and his elbow caught the corner of a wooden crate. Pain shot through his arm. Tears flooded his eyes and he winced. He his vision returned, and his mouth fell agape. He rubbed his eyes and gasped.

The candle flickered and illuminated a cavernous space. Crates of various size and shape were stacked to the ceiling. A dozen, or more, dull white statues were crammed in the far corner. Burlap sacks were piled at the center of the room. Near the far wall, Leviticus bent over a long rectangular box. He rummaged through the contents for a second and abruptly stopped.

"You are the first person I have ever brought down here," Leviticus said. He stood up and pulled a 3-foot chain from the box. "I have something for you."

Alex took a step forward. "Um, thanks." He bowed his head and looked up. "Seriously, thank you. I can't say I remember the last time I got anything. Besides a lashing that is," he added under his breath.

Leviticus pushed the lid closed and turned toward Alex. "This is a Manrikigusari. It has been in my family for as long as I can remember." He held the weapon out and caressed the steel links. "I have not seen it in a long time."

Alex accepted the gift and smiled. The chain slipped through his fingers. He caught it at the last moment and tightened his grip. Compact stones were twined on either end. The added weight made the weapon difficult for him to hold naturally. He tried it in his right hand and then his left. When neither felt comfortable, he laid it over his shoulder.

"A Manriki what?" Alex rubbed the chain between his index finger and his thumb. A sheen of oil made his skin slick.

"Manrikigusari." Leviticus shuffled across the room and pushed a burlap sack aside. "That weapon holds the strength of 1000 men," he said. He fumbled with a box perched atop an awkward stack of crates. "I have something else for you, as well."

Alex moved in. "You don't have to give me anything else. This Manriki thing is awesome. I don't even know what it is, and I love it."

Leviticus brushed the lid. Dust swirled into the light and fell away. "That is nothing really. This, this, is why I brought you down here." He handed the box to Alex.

The box was ordinary enough. A single piece of wood was secured in place with a bronze hinge. Etchings near the center formed a ring. Something was carved within. Alex scoured the dirt and grime with the hem of his tunic.

The image came into focus. "Hey," Alex exclaimed, "this is the same symbol that is on the broach you gave me."

Leviticus grinned. "I don't remember giving you that broach," he jibed. "But you are correct. It is, indeed, the same house sigil. Go on, open it."

Alex trembled. He held the box tight against his chest and bent the top back. Inside, a silver hilt stuck out from a rich brown leather scabbard. The metal was muted in the dim light. Ruby gems studded the circumference of the pommel. An identical sigil to the one on the box was barely visible on both sides of the grip.

"Seriously?" Alex whispered. He touched the weapon. The metal felt warm. "I'm guessing this is your house sigil," his voice was barely audible.

Leviticus nodded. "And you have guessed correctly." He looked around and walked to the back of the vault.

Alex cocked his head to

the side. "Didn't you say something about this symbol being evil?" He stared at the dagger.

"Why don't you meet me up top," Leviticus urged.

"Yeah," Alex said, "you called it evil incarnate."

Leviticus put his back to the wall and braced his legs. "Go," he said, "I will be up shortly."

"But," Alex protested.

"Go," Leviticus insisted.

Alex went to protest but stayed silent. He closed the box and felt the Manrikigusari on his shoulder. His fingers stroked the length of the chain. He felt the weight of the stone fastened to the end. A smile spread over his face. He spun back and skipped towards the exit. He grabbed the ladder with his free hand and started towards the surface.

2

Alex emerged from the tunnel and squinted. The heat from the afternoon sun roasted the open field. What little breeze there had been before was gone. Even the animals had vanished into the shade of the forest. Alex stood. Loose gravel slid out from under his feet. He threw his free arm back and braced against the stone wall.

"Crap," he exclaimed. The box slipped from his grip and hit the ground. The wood split in two. The scabbard bounced down the slight slope. "Crap," he said again.

The Manrikigusari fell from his shoulder. Alex caught the chain and wrapped it around his waist. He crossed the two ends together and cinched the tie tight. He scooped the two halves of the box up and examined the break. A pair of small nails had pulled free from the lid. A maroon linen lined the inside. It felt damp to the touch.

Alex set the box aside and retrieved the dagger. The scabbard was a rich mahogany. Horizontal cracks were strafed with deep gouges along the leather. Silver gleamed in the sunlight. On both sides of the hilt, the house sigil was scored with tiny striations. The identifying marks were nearly gone. Around the pommel, the rubies glowed red.

On the far side of the clearing, an oak cast a small patch of shade. Alex left the box behind and made his way over. Sweat formed on his brow and dripped down his face. Out of the sun, he plopped to the ground and rested his back against the tree. He pulled the Manrikigusari free and set it to the side. He tucked the dagger in his trousers and patted the added bulk. As time went by, he laid back. It wasn't long before his eyes fluttered shut. Alex fell asleep.

"Get up!" Leviticus kicked Alex. He grunted and kicked him again. "What happened to the box?"

"What?" Alex groaned. "Oh yeah, the box. I dropped it. Didn't see any reason to keep it."

Leviticus reached out. "Really?" He took Alex by the hand and helped him to his feet. "You are missing something," he said.

"I'm at a loss." Alex grabbed the Manrikigusari and tied it around his waist. "But please, feel free to enlighten me as to what I am missing."

Leviticus shook his head and turned towards the path they'd come in on. "The entrance is supposed to be hidden. You left the box right there for anyone to find. I returned it to the vault. Something you should have done after you broke it."

Alex pulled the dagger from his pants. He hurried to catch up. "Okay, I'll own that. I wasn't thinking," he admitted.

"I am impressed with you," Leviticus said. They entered the canopy of trees and started towards the lake. "It is always difficult to recognize one's own mistakes. Harder still to admit fault. A rare character trait indeed."

The air was thick. Alex struggled to keep pace. "I'm always wrong," he laughed. "One of my only faults though."

"It seems to me sloth is another one of those faults," Leviticus said matter of fact.

"What does that mean?" Alex scoffed. He stopped in place.

Leviticus continued in stride. It wasn't long before he was almost out of sight. "You were asleep," his voice was barely audible. He shook his head. "I give the guy my dagger and he falls asleep," he said to himself.

Alex ran to catch up. The trail moved through a tangle of vines. They followed around an imposing boulder and over a mass of fallen timber. The path disappeared but Leviticus moved without pause. Before long, a glint appeared in distance. The dense brush gave way and the lake appeared like an oasis.

They emerged into the clearing and a gust swept over them. Alex stripped his shirt off. He wrapped the fabric around the dagger and untied the Manrikigusari. He tied the weapon around the package. At the edge of the water, he set the bundle aside and jumped in. Liquid splashed in the air and cascaded down his torso. Goosebumps shot up his arm. He fell back and submerged his entire body.

Leviticus went to the shack and disappeared inside. Alex surfaced and scrubbed his face. A layer of dirt and grime floated away. He cleaned under his arms. He managed to get his pants off and washed his lower half. After a thorough soak, he put his trousers back on. He climbed onto the bank and laid in the grass.

"Sloth!" Leviticus hollered. He had changed from the dark layers he'd been wearing. A white tunic hung past his knees. "I would like to catch you on your feet for a change."

Alex sat up. "Man, you are cranky today," he said. "It's just hot out is all."

"I am sorry," Leviticus immediately relented. "It is hot, isn't it?" He sat down and stuck his feet in the water. "I tend to get emotional when I visit my," he hesitated, "history."

"That place was cool." Alex leaned over and grabbed the Manrikigusari. "I've never seen anything like this before." He pulled the bundle over and the dagger fell free. "I'll practice. I really will."

"I think it is time for lunch." Leviticus looked over his shoulder. "Maybe dinner. I had not realized how late it had gotten."

Alex grabbed the dagger. He got up and thrust the tip towards nothing. "This is so cool," he said absently.

"Fish, maybe potatoes." Leviticus stood. He stepped from the shallows and onto the bank. "I am quite hungry. I have a catch from this morning that should serve nicely."

Alex clutched the dagger. He pierced the air again and again. "I mean this is so cool."

Leviticus glanced towards Alex. "Do not be long. I will have food ready shortly." The sun reflected off his skin. He caught sight of something and paused. "What is that?" he blurted.

"What?" Alex swiped the blade to the side. "What is what?"

Leviticus moved in. "On your shoulder. What is that marking?"

"I don't know." The blade slashed from side to side. "It's just a scar."

"Stop moving," Leviticus insisted. "I need to see something."

"You're acting so weird today." Alex moved the dagger about. "It's just a scar."

Leviticus reached out. His fingers curled around Alex's wrist and he stopped moving. "No. I have seen this before." He traced the outline of the blemish with his finger.

"What are you doing," Alex giggled. He pulled his arm free but didn't move. "Seriously, it's just a scar."

"No," Leviticus repeated himself. "It can not be," his voice drifted.

Alex clenched his teeth. "Come on," he urged, "aren't we having lunch."

Leviticus closed his eyes. He shook his head from side to side.

"Yes," he suddenly said, "lunch." He stopped moving. "I will head in now. Shouldn't be long before it is ready. You stay out here if you would like. Practice. I will make sure we have plenty to eat." He turned towards the shack. "Never mind me. I am just getting old. I will make us something good. One of my specialties." Leviticus stumbled off.

"Man," Alex said to himself, "he's crazy. A nice guy, sure, but boy is he crazy."

3

The next morning Leviticus left before the sunrise. Alex stayed in bed for a bit but got restless. He tossed from side to side and pulled a sheet over his head. Outside, the birds began to sing. A gust of wind pushed the door ajar. The sun turned the room into an oven. It wasn't long before the heat overwhelmed the space.

Alex threw the covers off and got out of bed. He left his clothes behind and strolled out into daylight. At the water's edge, he stretched his arms and yawned. A few feet down, a furry little critter jumped. It caught sight of Alex it took off. The grass hid its movements before it disappeared in the scrub.

A light breeze picked up. The water rippled from shore. Alex stepped down. The sun warmed the lagoon into a tepid pool. White sand slid between his toes. A group of guppies darted away in every direction. He trudged his way out until the water was waist deep. He took a deep breath and submerged his head. The sound of the world faded away. Long locks of hair floated on the surface. The current carried him out until his toes just brushed the bottom. His chest started to pound.

Alex broke the surface and gulped down air. Hair clung to his face. Split ends sucked into his throat and he choked. His feet kicked around but he couldn't find the bottom. He tried to yell for help. Liquid filled his lungs.

"What are you doing?" Leviticus splashed into the water. He grabbed Alex by the wrist and hauled him to the shallows. "I thought you knew how to swim."

"I," Alex coughed out, "I know how to swim." He got to shore and the coughing subsided.

Leviticus climbed out of the water. "I don't know. Didn't really look that way to me." He sat on the bank with his legs crossed.

"I was just thinking is all." Alex straightened his boxer shorts. He gave himself a once over and laid in the grass. "Would you cut my hair?" he asked absently.

"I suppose that is something I could manage." Leviticus picked a rock from the soil. He brushed the dirt away and tossed it to the side. "If you would indulge me. I have something I would like to show you."

Alex sat up. His brow furrowed. "Can I get dressed first?"

Leviticus chuckled. "Of course. I will meet you inside. Best we talk in private."

Alex looked around the lagoon. "More private than this?" He swept his hand out over the water.

"Just meet me inside." Leviticus extended his legs. "We can have something to eat. And afterwards I can take a shot at your hair."

"Hey wait a second," Alex blurted. He got to his feet and brushed the dirt from his backside. "You had better take more than a shot at it. I want it to look good."

Leviticus stood. He reached down and grabbed at something under his shirt. "I will get some kindling. You should cut something up that we can roast."

"Like what?" Alex walked towards the shack. "Leaves? Sticks? You know I can't cook to save my life." He got to the door and stopped.

"Just find something." Leviticus walked behind the shack. His voice drifted until he was out of sight.

Inside, Alex dressed. The sheath and dagger were tethered to his pants. Ragged holes were cut into the waist. A leather cord was threaded through. He pulled the belt taught and cinched it tight. He wrapped the Manrikigusari over the top. He shifted the weighted stones so they were at his side and he could walk.

The fire was out. Alex turned his attention to a basket of purple carrots and white stalks. He grabbed a handful of the vegetables and tossed them on the table. He sat, pulled the dagger out, and put his fingers around the hilt. The ruby gems glowed in the subdued lighting. The silver was warm. A pulse throbbed deep within the weapon.

"Good. That knife needs to cut up vegetables for a change," Leviticus said. Branches were stacked to his chin. He turned to the side and slid through the doorway.

"What does that mean?" Alex hacked at the end of a white stalk.

"Weapons are like people." Leviticus dropped the bindle and broke the wood into smaller pieces. "They have memories. They remember what they have done."

Alex snorted. "That's just stupid," he said. "It doesn't have a brain."

Leviticus picked up the pile of kindling. He arranged it in the basin and blew on the cinders. They burst into flames. "I don't know," he said. A few logs were off to the side. He got them on the fire and sat down. "The world is an interesting place. An unpredictable place. Hence your arrival here."

Alex kept his head down. "An object remembering what it's done?" He finished cutting the white shoots and moved on to the carrots. "It's an object. An object."

"An object," Leviticus contemplated. He held his hand out. "Stop. I want to show you something."

The fire popped. Alex stopped chopping. The dagger trembled in his hand. "Show me what?" he asked. "Does it have anything to do with whatever is on your waist?"

"A very astute observation." Leviticus tossed a large black satchel on the table. A thin thread wrapped the top. "Do you feel anything?"

Alex sheathed the dagger. He rubbed the fabric between his index finger and thumb. "It's soft. It feels soft."

"Ha," Leviticus laughed, "no. The power. Can you feel the power?"

"I guess." Alex shrugged. "I'm not sure."

Leviticus pulled the satchel across the table. He worked at the thread until it came undone. When it was open, he tipped the contents onto the table. A pile of gems sparkled in the firelight. Various shades of green, yellow, red, orange, blue and pink were visible. They were amorphous rocks that looked pulled directly from the ground. Three gold rings were studded with translucent stones. A silver necklace was covered in crystals.

"What is all this?" Alex asked. He pushed one of the rings with his finger. "I definitely feel something."

"Yes," Leviticus said. He sifted

through the contents until he found what he was looking for. "These are Vitality Stones. Exceedingly rare. Very precious."

Alex leaned on his elbows. "Vitality Stones?"

"Not many of these exist anymore." Leviticus held out a dark red stone set in a gold ring. "Most people have never even seen one. The jewelry itself is incidental. It is the Vitality Stone that is the real prize."

"But you have so many," Alex said. "They can't be that rare." He took the ring and flipped it in his hand. "I do feel something."

"There are generations of stones here. Accumulated over many lifetimes." Leviticus spread everything out. He picked up one stone after another.

"What are they for?" Alex slid the ring on his middle finger. It hung loose so he put it on his thumb. "What do they do?"

Leviticus clenched a stone in his grip. "They are power," he whispered. "They are passion. They are calm. They are cleansing. They are anything and everything. The trick is to figure out what is at the heart of each."

"I don't get it," Alex scoffed.

"These stones, these crystals, they are the source of our magic."

Alex took the ring from his finger and set it on the table. "I'm lost," he sighed.

"Okay, I will explain it as I would to a child," Leviticus said sarcastically. He took the ring. "Each stone does something different. The stone in the ring here, the red stone, is one of power."

"So, I could lift a boulder over my head or something?" Alex interrupted.

Leviticus shook his head. "No. You could not lift a boulder. Someone else, perhaps, but not you." He took the satchel and picked up the jewelry.

"Whatever," Alex snorted. He rolled his eyes. "So how do they work?"

"I told you." Leviticus gathered up all the stones. He looked over the table and tucked the satchel away. "They are magic."

The fire cracked. Smoke hovered in the room and left through the ventilation pipe. Heat baked the table. Leviticus got up and retrieved a thick iron pan. He stuck the fat side into the coals and added the diced vegetables. The food started to sizzle. Before long, it was tender.

"What about my dagger?" Alex suddenly asked. "It has those same red stones. Is it magic?" He pulled at the hilt and exposed a small bit of the blade.

Leviticus speared lunch onto skewers. He set one before Alex. A smile was just visible under his whiskers.

"Another astute observation," he said. "We can get to that later. First lunch. Then I want to chop all that hair off your head."

Chapter 4

1

The world was dark. A deafening boom shook the ground. Light crossed the sky in a web of electricity. Fat drops began to fall. Wind ripped through the trees. Roots peeled away from the soil. Thick trunks toppled over like weeds. Branches became arrows. The rain turned into a downpour. A thunderous crack illuminated the sky like fireworks.

Alex looked around bewildered. In the distance something drew near. He started to run. Water saturated his clothing and filled his shoes. The added burden made his movements cumbersome. He worked one foot in front of the other. The ground sunk with every step. The trail vanished and the foliage encroached on all sides. Skeletal wooden fingers clawed at his face.

To his right, a stone slab rose from nowhere. Alex skid to a halt. Earth and mud gave way at the sudden change of direction. His eyes followed the circumference of the boulder. A small outcrop appeared just large enough to fit his frame. He dove for cover and his body fell limp. Every muscle froze in place. Pain pierced his abdomen. There was absolute darkness.

2

Alex awoke in a cold

sweat. The room was in a tailspin. He rolled to his side and heaved. Yellow liquid spewed to the floor. His fingers clenched the side of the bed. He heaved again. Fluid showered the books scattered about. A third heave caused his stomach to knot. There was pain but nothing came out. There was the taste of sour acid in his mouth and he gagged. His throat burned. After a few minutes the room began to stabilize. He eased to his back. The mattress was soaked through.

A light patter echoed off the roof. Across the room a fire crackled with life. Two terracotta bowls were worked down into the embers. Steam mixed with smoke and hung heavy in the air. Bulbs of garlic covered the table. A large butcher's knife was hacked into the wood. One of the chairs was moved to the side. A black duster hung over the back. Clothes had been neatly folded and stacked on the seat.

The covers were bunched up at the foot of the bed. Alex kicked his feet and they fell to the floor. He propped up on his elbow and looked around. Leviticus was gone. *The fire was fresh, so he knew it hadn't been long.* Tracks crisscrossed the floor. Bits of mud and grass went to the hearth and then back to the door.

"Man," Alex yawned, "that was some dream."

"What?" The door eased open. Leviticus backed in. "Were you talking to me?" A thin mist blew through his hair. He nudged the door closed with his hip. "Could not have been talking to me. I just got here."

"What have you got there?" Alex asked. "Let me help you." He swung his feet over the edge of the bed and stumbled. When he regained his balance, he hurried over.

"It is nothing, really." Leviticus

labored. "Quite heavy though." He clutched the bottom of a large wooden box.

Alex reached out. The crate slipped through his hands. It hit the ground with a thud. "Sorry," he said. "What is it?" He poked the side.

Leviticus shoved the box until it was near the bed. "Just some things I wanted you to have," he sighed. "I have no use for it anymore."

"You've already given me so much." Alex grabbed his blankets and tossed them back on the bed. He found a sheet and started to clean. "I threw up," he mumbled.

"Are you feeling alright?" Leviticus bent down. He pushed the box until it was out of sight. "Are you hungry?"

Alex put his hand to his stomach. "No," he gagged. "I think I need some air." He finished cleaning and hid the saturated linen under the bed.

The fire died off. Light reduced to a minimum. Rain fell on the tin roof above.

Leviticus crossed the room. He took the jacket from the chair and tossed it to Alex. "A messy one out there today." He picked up the clothes and set them on the bed. "I found these for you. Should fit fine."

"This is awesome," Alex said breathless. He ran his hand down the leather. The black shell had faded to a dark grey. The inner lining was a thin corrugated linen. Bronze striations ran vertically from seam to collar.

"I have had that since I was about your age." Leviticus took the silver dagger off the ottoman. "Take your weapons with you today," he said absently. He put the dagger back and picked up the Manrikigusari. "Just one of those days, I suppose."

Alex set the duster on the bed. He picked up the stack of clothes. Ivory buttons studded the center of a dark cobalt shirt. One sleeve billowed out and cinched with elastic at the wrist. The other was torn off at the elbow. The pants were a deep mahogany. A patchwork of leather strips scarred the knees. The legs were narrow and tapered off at the cuff. The same bronze striations as on the jacket lined both items.

"The shirt is ruined," Alex scoffed. "Why would you want me to have this?" He held the clothing up to see it better. "I mean did someone have their arm chopped off in this thing?"

Leviticus turned to the table. He grabbed a handful of garlic and tossed it in one of the pots on the fire. "No," he chuckled, "I do not believe so."

"I don't know." Alex set the shirt to the side. He sat on the edge of bed and pulled off his pajamas. "The pants you gave me have seen better days."

The fire roared with life. Orange flames lit the room. Leviticus worked the embers with a long iron rod. "Just put them on," he said sharply. "You will thank me later. They may not look like much but in this weather, they will save your life."

"Doubtful," Alex snorted. The pants slipped on. One leg was much longer than the other. The waist a few sizes too big. "What is with these clothes? They're absurd."

Laughter filled the room. "You will get used to them," Leviticus chuckled. "Trust me, Alex, you will need them."

Garlic started to roast. A sweet aroma burned his nose. Alex threw his hand over his mouth. Liquid filled his throat. He struggled to keep from throwing up. The wave of nausea passed, and he finished getting dressed.

The shirt was long. Even buttoned to the top it hung low on his neck. The pants were awkward as well. Alex rolled the cuff and tucked it in his sock. He did the same with the other leg. When he was ready, he wrapped the Marikigusari like a belt, slipped the dagger in his waist, and put the duster on.

"Well the rest of the outfit is weird, but this coat is something else," Alex exclaimed. The hem of the duster fell to the floor. The sleeves covered his hands entirely. "Maybe a bit big, but I'll grow into it. How do I look?"

Leviticus looked Alex over. He dropped his head. "Like you have lived here your entire life," he said. "Just be careful out there. This weather is bound to make things messy." He smiled. Wrinkles creased his brow. For the first time he looked tired.

"I will." Alex hitched up his pants. "I just have to get some air. I'm feeling

better but that smell is getting to me."
He walked to the door. A pair of black
boots were tucked behind a wooden
stand.

"Be careful," Leviticus repeated.

Alex tied a double knot. "I know," he
said firmly. "But are you okay?" He
secured the other boot. "You seem off
today."

The garlic started to burn. Leviticus
jimmied the pot from the fire. He
stomped an errant ember that rolled from
the basin. "Just one of those days," he
repeated. His eyes glossed over.

"Seriously," Alex asked after a
minute, "are you okay?"

"Oh." Leviticus shook his head.
"Yeah. Don't worry about me. I will be
here when you get back."

Alex cracked the door. The sound of
rain flooded in. "Are you sure," he
asked. Water came in on a slant. "I can
stay if you want."

"Go," Leviticus insisted. "This is your home now. You never need to ask for my permission. Not for anything. Live the life you want."

Alex shook his head from side to side. "Man, you are so awesome," he said. "I can't believe I got so lucky. See you later." He bound outside and slammed the door shut.

"Luck?" Leviticus lifted his head to the sky. "Oh, dear boy," he snorted. Tears fell down his cheek. "I believe this one is on the Fates."

3

The forest was reduced to a snarled mess. Branches as thick as trees snapped like twigs. Leaves tore from the canopy. Shrubs flew about like tumbleweeds. The detritus was a black muck. Years of decomposition churned to the surface. Thick clumps of dirt dissolved into a porridge of grass and sludge.

Alex ran headlong into the wind. Water spattered his face. His feet sunk into the earth. The onslaught of debris and rain slowed him to a near standstill. He dropped his head and dug in. When the trail veered, he continued straight. He broke through the edge of the trees. The overgrowth tugged at his jacket. A splintered trunk caught the hem and the heavy cloth tore the wood away like paper. Dense foliage shielded the forest floor from the worst of the storm.

In the distance something shrieked. Alex ignored the cry. A tangle of vines clawed at his ankles. Mud pulled at his boots like quicksand. He ducked under a fallen log and charged forward. Farther along a stone slab arose from the ground. He leapt and landed hard on the rock. Moss slid out from under his feet. His body flipped in the air. He threw his arms out and crashed to his back. Air escaped his lungs. A thick gash split the center of his left hand. Blood mixed with water. The viscous red fluid thinned and washed away.

Fat drops poured through a slit in the trees. Alex closed his eyes tight. His chest rose and fell in rapid succession. Pain throbbed up his arm, then down to his toes. Water saturated his new clothes. He laid still until his wound was reduced to a dull ache. He sat up. His hands groped around for his weapons. The dagger was tucked away under his shirt. The Manrikigusari had come loose. He cinched the chain tight.

He shifted and his knuckles brushed the inner lining of the jacket. Alex cocked his head to the side. The bronze striations glowed with life. Brilliant glitter sparkled in the dreary surroundings. He brushed the fabric with the back of his hand. Despite the storm, the corrugated lining was bone dry. The rain landed and instantly vanished. Alex reached down and felt the inside of his shirt. Water soaked the outer layer, but the inner shell was warm to the touch.

"Ha," Alex laughed. He pulled a small swatch of cloth from his pants. He wrapped his hand to stem the flow of blood. "I really do need to thank Leviticus."

A sharp crack rattled the ground. A brilliant flash of light lit up the sky. Wind swirled and the heavens opened. Far off, a tree fell. A second gust swept through the forest. Rain penetrated the canopy. A pair of trees snapped in uniform. The sound moved closer. More trees snapped in a rhythmic cadence.

Alex transitioned to his side. He planted his good hand on stone and pushed up. His eyes scanned the surroundings. He struggled to see through the trees. After a moment he jumped from the boulder. The ground swallowed his feet. Mud and water filled his shoes. He struggled and the commotion drew near. Trees snapped; animals cried out in terror. Alex managed to get one foot free. He propped it up on a rotted stump and grabbed his submerged ankle. He tugged and his foot popped from the muck. He lost his balance and fell back onto the rock.

Behind him something drew near. Branches crunched in rapid succession. Heavy panting was suddenly louder than the storm. Alex turned around. A streak of red glowed in the muted colors of the forest. An outline of a petite figure grew larger as it drew closer. Alex leaned forward. Rain obstructed his vision.

A girl charged towards him. Dark red hair bounced over her shoulders. She was on him in an instant. She leapt to the rock. Her eyes grew wide when she caught sight of Alex. She tried to pivot but her momentum carried her forward. Bone connected with bone. Pain shot through Alex. His nose crushed under the contact. Blood flowed down into his mouth. His body tumbled backwards off the rock.

"What the," the girl cried out. She fell forward into the mud.

Alex struggled to get up. His clothes were caked in filth. "Who are you?" he yelled. He fumbled for his dagger. "I said who are you?" he repeated.

The girl looked over her shoulder. She leaned to the side and stared beyond Alex. "We do not have time for that." Her eyes darted back and forth. "We have got to go."

"I'm not going anywhere," Alex shouted. Thunder cracked. Lightning lit the girl's face. "I mean why," his voice fell soft, "why do we have to go?"

"Don't you hear that?" the girl asked. "They are coming."

Alex glanced over his shoulder. "Who's coming? All I hear is the storm."

"We do not have time for this," the girl barked. "Follow me or not, it is your choice." She turned on her heels and sprinted off.

Alex hesitated. He watched where the girl had emerged. Something was coming. "Wait up," he yelled.

Alex dropped his head against the spray of rain. The girl was already gone. He scanned for tracks but there was nothing to follow. He saw a gap in the trees. Felled branches spread out like a bridge. He sprinted ahead and bound from one log to the other. The rain made the wood slick. His feet slipped but he maintained his balance. When the forest thinned, and he hit the trail.

In the open the storm raged. Wind swept through the narrow channel that cut towards the lake. Alex stopped. He looked for prints. The ground swallowed up any signs of the girl's presence. She had vanished. Whatever was chasing her was getting close. Alex turned and took off down the path. The onslaught of weather made his movements stunted. His boots were nearly sucked off his feet again. It wasn't long before his thighs began to burn.

Alex doubled over. He propped his hands on his knees and coughed in a fit. Water sucked into his lungs. He gagged. Stomach acid went up his esophagus. The world started to spin. His body shuddered, his knees wobble. He tipped forward.

"What are you doing?" The girl grabbed Alex by the shoulder. "They are coming." She tugged him and they fell into the brush.

"I'm," Alex swallowed. "I'm."

The girl inched them away from the

path. "Keep quiet," she hissed. She moved until they were completely covered. "Just keep quiet. And keep still."

"I'm," Alex mumbled.

"Shut up." The girl cupped her hand and threw it over his mouth. "They are coming," she whispered in his ear.

4

The ground trembled. An army of boots the size of cinderblocks hurled down the path. A stone mallet ripped through the air. The weapon connected with timber and splinters showered down with the water. A steel blade sliced through the foliage. Laughter echoed out like a hyena's call. The hideous cackle muted the fury of the storms rage.

The girl pulled her hand from Alex.

"Hush," she hissed. She clenched her fist and bit down on her knuckle.

Alex stared straight ahead. He pulled his knees to his chest and curled into a ball. Something moved close to his position. It came to a halt and sniffed the air. A hand swept out. The brush folded back. Alex clenched his eyes tight and stopped breathing. There was a loud grunt. Whatever it was moved on.

"Wait," the girl uttered. The group was gone but their laughter was still audible. "Let's give it another second."

They waited and the storm began to subside. The clouds overhead lightened. The life of the forest returned. A bird chirped with delight. An animal with a coarse coat and long tail crept from cover. It sniffed at the new company and moved on. Miniscule bugs buzzed around with fervor.

"What are you doing here?" the girl asked. She rotated to her knees and crouched.

"I could ask you the same question." Alex mimicked her movements. "I live here. And I've never seen you before."

The girl peered down the path. "Live here? No wonder you got in my way," she huffed.

"What's that supposed to mean?" Alex stood. His head popped up over the brush.

"Be careful," the girl insisted. She reached up and yanked Alex back to cover. "You are such an idiot."

Alex wrenched his arm free. "What's that supposed to mean," he spat.

"It means," the girl said, "you are acting like an idiot." She pulled him down. "Those things could have killed you."

"I would have been fine," Alex snarled. "I mean who do you think you are anyway?"

The girl shook her head. "I am the person who just saved your life." She looked back out. "I think we are okay now."

Deep treads ran in grooves through the mud. Trees along the edge of the path were devastated. Thick trunks were toppled into lines. Splintered wood covered the ground like sawdust. High above a crack in the clouds opened. The sun beamed down, and the forest glistened. The group moved farther on and the sound of their commotion diminished. Ambient sounds of nature floated in on the breeze. In the distance, a loud crash was followed by silence.

"They are gone." The girl walked from the brush. She picked up a piece of timber and tossed it aside. "I cannot believe they did all of this."

Alex stepped into the sun. He ran his fingers along the Manrikigusari. His hand bumped the dagger. "What were those things?" he asked. He pulled his coat closed and buttoned it halfway. "Why were they chasing you?"

"That," the girl hesitated, "is complicated." She brushed her backside and a clump of mud fell to the ground.

"How about we start with something easy." Alex looked up. His heart skipped. For the first time he could see the girl. "Like your name," he said softly.

The girl bent over. She brushed her knees and pulled at her boot. An arrow quiver was slung low on her back. A wooden bow was strapped to the side with leather. Her long brown coat hung over her shoulders and covered her clothes. On her head, a mop of brilliant auburn hair draped down to her waist.

"That is not an easy question to answer around here." The girl frowned. She stood up and wiped the sweat from her brow. "But, seeing as you are one of the wood folks, I suppose it would not hurt to tell you."

Alex scoffed. "What does that mean?" he demanded.

"I am Lasaria," the girl said. She hitched her pants and went to a fallen log. She scraped the heel of her boot on the bark. "What about you? What is your name?"

"I'm Alex." He gazed at Lasaria. Her skin was pale. She had soft features. Her eyes were wide and set high on her head. Her nose was slender with a slight point at the tip. "You're a jerk you know?" Alex said.

Lasaria shook her head.

"I do not know what that means."

"You ran into me," Alex spat. "I was just messing around and the next thing I know, I'm running for my life." He stiffened his spine. His hand groped for his dagger.

"Calm down. You are fine." Lasaria waved her hand. She brushed the collar of her jacket. "Maybe need to clean up a bit," she added. "I know I am filthy."

Alex turned and stomped down the path. He threw his arms in the air and laughed. "Calm down," he yelled. "I almost died."

"That was your own fault," Lasaria interrupted. "Besides, you are fine."

"Okay." Alex took a deep breath. He slowly exhaled. "You're right, you're right. I'm okay."

"Hey," Lasaria perked up, "didn't you say you live around

here."

Alex glanced over his shoulder. "Yeah," he said sarcastically, "so."

"Well maybe you can let me clean up." Lasaria marched ahead. "Get some rest before I am on my way."

"I don't know." Alex looked away. "I don't live alone. I doubt Leviti…" he trailed off. "No," he gasped.

"What?" Lasaria asked. "What is wrong?"

"No," Alex repeated, "they couldn't have."

"What?" Lasaria grabbed Alex by the arm.

"I've got to go." Alex stumbled back. "They were headed towards the lake." He turned and sunk into the mud. "I've got to go." He took off.

"What?" Lasaria asked.

She watched Alex curl around a bend and out of sight. "What," she hollered. Her feet sunk into earth. "Come on, wait up."

5

"Stop," Lasaria shouted. "Just stop."

The path opened into the clearing. Deep tracks tore around the near side of the lagoon. Ruts churned up the earth. Trees were tossed about like garbage. Something flat drifted on the surface of the water. The sun gleamed off the object as it bobbed in the current. On the far bank, the shack was reduced to rubble. A mound of debris stood in its place.

The ground was torn to bits. Large swaths of grass were thrown around in chunks. A tangle of roots snaked about the open wounds. Alex sprinted ahead.

He hopped from one track to the other. His ankle rolled under his weight, but he ignored it. The tail of the jacket caught under his feet. He stumbled but maintained his balance.

"Wait," Lasaria hollered. She got to the water's edge and checked the clearing. She saw the pile across the way. All the air escaped her lungs. "Please just stop," she pleaded.

Alex peeled off his jacket. "Leviticus," he shouted. "Leviticus say something." He got to the pile of rubble and dropped to his knees. "Say something," he choked.

The shack was in ruins. Pieces of the outer wall were torn apart like paper. Books and clothing were scattered about. The roof was ripped from the structure. One piece floated in the lagoon. Another was crumbled into a heap at the center of the toppled structure. Bricks from the fire pit were crushed into dust.

"Leviticus," Alex cried. He crawled forward. A piece of steel shifted under his weight. Someone moaned in agony. "Leviticus!" he choked.

Alex wrapped his hands around a jagged piece of metal. He wrenched it to the side. A naked toe appeared through the carnage. He worked the debris away from the foot. He followed the leg up to the torso. Blood covered exposed flesh. Alex started to hyperventilate. He found the outer edge of the roof. His fingers trembled. He lifted the corner and tipped it to the side.

Leviticus lay motionless amongst the debris. His top had been torn away. A large gash cleaved his chest in two. A square of punctures pierced his belly. Black and purple bruises circled his throat. His nose was crushed. Blood saturated his beard. His front teeth were broken into shards. His chin was perverted into a hideous grin.

"No." Alex reached out. Tears rolled down his cheek. "Please," he barely managed.

Leviticus shuddered. His chest rose and fell. "Alex," he moaned. His eyes open. "I knew you would come." He was barely audible. "I knew you would come."

"Don't," Alex cried. "Don't move. I'll get you some help."

"Oh," Leviticus chuckled, "that isn't necessary." His arm shifted. "I need to tell you something." He coughed. Blood trickled down the corner of his mouth. "Something important."

"It can wait. Whatever it is can wait."

"No." Leviticus turned his head but hardly moved. "Not much

time left I am afraid."

"Don't say that," Alex heaved.

"First the Vitality Stones," Leviticus coughed. A red mist spit from his lips. "They took my satchel, those are gone. But there are more. The box under the bed. They missed it. Take them. But be careful. Keep them to yourself."

"Please," Alex begged. "I don't want the Vitality Stones. I want you."

"Second." Leviticus ignored the plea. "Your shoulder. The marking on your shoulder."

Alex shook his head from side to side. "My scar? Why are you taking about my scar?"

"Not a scar," Leviticus choked. His voice fell low. Air escaped from his lungs. "A brand. It is a brand. It shows who you belong to."

"What?" Alex leaned in. Tears filled his vision. "What are you talking about?"

"Who," Leviticus choked. Blood spit from his mouth. "Who you belong to."

"I," Alex stumbled, "I don't belong to anyone."

"Yes," Leviticus shivered, "you do." His eyes rolled back in his head. His body went rigid.

"Leviticus," Alex shrieked. "Leviticus no."

A bird with long skinny legs watched from the shallows. It lifted its head to the sky and let out a mournful caw. The sound cut off and it lifted into the air. It swept up and circled the clearing. A second bird joined it in flight. They flew in tandem. There wings beat together in harmony. Before long they disappeared over the horizon. Silence descended on the lagoon like a burden. Alex choked.

He keeled over and hurled. When the convulsions relented, he wept.

Chapter 5

1

The sun was low on the horizon. Brilliant rays of orange and pink brushed the sky like a watercolor painting. Fresh dew sparkled off individual blades of grass. A breeze came in over the top of the trees. Leaves swayed about in time. Birds took flight from the cover of the forest. They circled the clearing and disappeared above. Water rippled out from the center of the lagoon. Whitecaps broke and lapped against the bank.

Along the boundary of the forest a small pit was dug into the compact soil. Roots and rocks were piled with mud at the head of the plot. An iron pick was spiked off to the side. Its cylindrical wooden handle was snapped halfway up the length. The box that had been under the bed sat open. Its contents were cleared out. At the edge of the pit, a long flat stone was worked into the earth. A circle was etched into the face. Two daggers were crossed at the center.

Alex wiped his nose with the back of his hand. Dirt smeared over his skin. Tears fell from his eyes. His lip shuddered. He inhaled sharply and let out a high-pitched squeal. When the crying subsided, he looked up to the sky. He took a deep breath. He held the air in until his body throbbed with agony. A hiss escaped his lips. In his peripheral vision the world faded to black. He tried to speak but his voice faltered.

"I don't mean to be insensitive," Lasaria said softly. She walked up behind Alex and put her arm out. "But I have got to go."

Alex coughed the air from his lungs. He planted on the ball of his foot and turned. "What did you just say?" He gritted his teeth and started to shake.

Lasaria took a step back. "I have got to go," she repeated. "You can come with me, if you want, but I have to go."

"Go." Alex screamed. "You got Leviticus killed and you want to just go. I have no one." He turned towards the hole. "I'll just stay here. All alone once again."

"Listen," Lasaria started. She faltered. Her brow scrunched up. "Wait a minute. Did you say Leviticus?"

Alex shook his head. He went to the pile at the back side of the grave. "What do you care?" he snarled. He got on his knees and clenched a handful of earth. "He's dead." He tossed dirt down into the opening. "He's dead and there isn't anything I can do about it."

"I," Lasaria said. She looked in the grave. A burlap sack was placed at the center. Weapons were laid on either side. Various trinkets encircled the body. "I have to go. Please," she pleaded, "come with me."

"Why?" Alex looked up. His eyes were bright white under a layer of grime. "You don't know me. You don't know anything about me. Why would you want me to go with you?"

Lasaria took a step. "You can stay here. Rebuild. Go on." She went to Alex. "But you could also come with me. Things will be different for you, that is for certain. But you will not be alone. I can guarantee you that much."

"You think I'm an idiot," Alex said sharply. He used his forearm to fill the hole. "Why would you want to hang around with an idiot?"

Lasaria sunk to her knees. She took a handful of dirt and let it fall into the grave. "I was angry," she relented. "If you want to stay, I am not going to force you to leave. But the offer is there. I want you to know that." She scooped up another handful of dirt. "I will help you bury your friend. But you are going to have to decide what you want to do."

"I don't know," Alex mumbled. His head fell. He slumped forward. "I just want to say goodbye to my friend… alone."

"That is fair." Lasaria got to her feet. She touched Alex on the shoulder. "I will wait for you by the water. Whatever you decide, I will wait." She turned and walked off.

Alex stared into the grave. Leviticus was a diminutive hump. In death, his body appeared to have shrunk. The once lanky torso was squat. Legs that were long and slender were now contorted and misshapen. The weapons at his sides were absurdly oversized. The various items to be interred with his body took up most of the space.

"I'm so sorry," Alex said. He pawed at the soil and sprinkled it over Leviticus. "You took me in. You gave me a home. You gave me a family. Look what it got you." Progress was slow. The grave filled up one handful at a time. "And now what do I do? You're gone. Jackson is gone. I'm all alone."

An animal poked its head from the brush. A long sandy snout was set below two jet black eyes. One ear was perked up. The other was bit off at the tip. Alex lost his balance and fell to his back. He erupted in laughter. The outburst cut through the silence. The animal jumped. It bounced around and bound back into the forest.

"Oh man," Alex cried. He laughed until he couldn't breathe.

"Are you doing alright?" Lasaria hollered. She dipped her boot in the lagoon and scrubbed the side.

"Yeah," Alex managed. He got to his knees. Tears fell down his cheek. "I'll be okay."

Lasaria finished with one boot. She set it in the grass and started on the other. "So, what do you think?" she asked. She used her fingernail to pry a stone from the soul of the boot. "Are you coming with me?"

"I don't know." Alex stood. He looked down and kicked the dirt. "Yes," he said, "it's what Leviticus would have wanted. He said as much to me yesterday."

"Alright," Lasaria said. She set her boots in the sun. "Do you want my help? I don't mind, really."

Alex smiled. "Thank you," he said

weakly. "That is a kind offer."

"You did not answer my question." Lasaria stood. She slipped a boot on and pulled the lace taught. "Do you want my help?"

"No." Alex grabbed the pickaxe. He pushed the dirt with the blunt side of the head. "This is my job. I'm going to say goodbye, get my things, and then we can go."

Lasaria adjusted the quiver on her back. "Don't be long. I need –"

"– to go," Alex finished. "I won't." He dropped his shoulder. A large mound of earth fell into the hole. Leviticus was completely covered. "I'm ready to get the hell out of this place," he muttered.

2

They had been on the move for two days. Early in the trek,

Lasaria tried to make conversation but got nothing in return. She asked Alex how he felt. Encouraged him to share. Told him she was there for him. At times she tried to explain where they were headed. Once she simply stopped and waited for a spell. He slumped to the ground in silence. Nothing could penetrate his sorrow.

The forest was so dense they could hardly walk. Below the canopy the temperature rose. Lasaria pulled a blade from a scabbard attached to her belt. She wrapped her hand around the grip and hacked at a tangle of vines. The bright green creepers cut in two. A void in the trees opened onto a stream. Water trickled down the incline into the brush.

"We will stop here for a bit," Lasaria said. She sheathed the weapon and sunk to her knees. "Once it is dark, we can get on again. It is just too dangerous to travel during the day. Not to mention hot," she added.

Alex carried a sack over his shoulder.
He dropped the bag to the ground and
tucked it under a fallen log. He peeled
off his outer layer and bunched the
heavy fabric into a pillow. He set the
jacket next to his bag and kicked them
together. He formed the clothes into a
small mound and laid down. He rested
his head and shifted. His eye lids drifted
closed.

"Alright," Lasaria snorted. She
scooped a handful of water and sipped it
from her hand. "I suppose I will get us
hunkered down," she paused, "again."

Lasaria got to her feet. She surveyed
the landscape around their position.
After a moment she set off. Branches
snapped under the weight of her
footsteps. A sharp crack broke the
silence. She went from one spot to the
other. Her outline disappeared into the
woods. Her movements became muffled.

When she returned, she sat next to Alex.

"I got us something to eat," Lasaria said. She unfurled a small checkered handkerchief. A pile of grubs squirmed about the center. "It is not much, but at least it is some protein."

Alex opened one eye. He grunted and turned to the side.

"You have got to eat something," Lasaria insisted. She snatched a fat little bug and tossed it in her mouth. "We have already gone through all the food you managed to get from the house. And who knows how long it will be until we get a proper meal. If you do not eat, you will never make it out of here alive."

"I'm fine," Alex mumbled. He dug his head into his jacket.

Lasaria scoffed. "I suppose that is something." She grabbed another grub from the handkerchief. "Most I have gotten out of you since we met." She popped the bug in her mouth and had another.

"How can you eat that?" Alex asked. He looked at Lasaria. "That's just disgusting."

"It is practical." Lasaria shook her head. "You cannot always find fresh game. Or do not have the time for that matter. But these little guys." She squeezed a grub between her finger and thumb. "They are always around."

Alex clenched his fist. He brought it to his mouth. "No way," he gagged. "I'd rather die."

"Suit yourself," Lasaria chuckled. She finished everything on the handkerchief. She tucked the cloth away and stretched back. "I have got to ask you something," she said tentatively. She waited for a reply. A small animal ran by her foot. The brush rustled. "Did you hear me?" she asked when Alex didn't respond.

"What?" Alex snarled. He kept his

eyes shut tight.

"I'm just going to ask," Lasaria shot back. "Seeing as you are in a wonderful mood as it is. Who was that man to you? You called him Leviticus?"

"What of it?" Alex shifted the jacket under his head. "He was my friend."

Lasaria sat up. "Was his name Leviticus?" she asked. She put her hand on Alex. "Was his name Leviticus? It is important."

Alex jerked his arm away. "Why? Why do you even care?" he growled.

"Because," Lasaria faltered. She brushed her hair with her hand. Her head dropped. "That is just a name I have not heard in a long time."

"What do you mean?" Alex opened his eyes and glared at Lasaria. "He can't be the only Leviticus to ever exist. It's probably like Smith over here."

Lasaria trembled. "No," she said sternly. "I don't know what a

Smith is, but there was only one Leviticus."

"That's right," Alex agreed forcefully, "there was only one Leviticus."

"You do not get it." Lasaria shook her head from side to side. "There was only one Leviticus. In HISTORY," she emphasized.

Alex dug his hands into the soil and got onto his butt. "What do you mean?" he asked sharply.

Lasaria averted her eyes. "So, it was him," she said softly, "Leviticus."

"His name was Leviticus," Alex snapped. "So what?"

"I…" Lasaria huffed. "I cannot believe it." She pinched the bridge of her nose. "I cannot believe it," she repeated breathlessly. "And you know nothing about him? Nothing about the man you lived with?"

"What?" Alex shouted. "No." His voice echoed through the woods. A bird perched above them took flight. "What are you talking about? What is there to know?"

"You need to calm down," Lasaria insisted. She backed away. "We are strangers. You cannot just be screaming at strangers."

Alex inhaled. "Okay." His voice dropped an octave. "If there was only one Leviticus, you must have known him then. It sounds like you knew him."

"Not personally." Lasaria looked around. "You are not going to like what you hear. I am not even certain I should tell you. I just needed to know if that really was him."

"Please," Alex pleaded, "tell me."

"Your friend," Lasaria started. Her lips moved but nothing

came out.

"What?" Alex begged.

"Your friend was a bad guy," she blurted, "a really bad guy."

Alex scoffed. "You're wrong," he said without hesitation. "He was a good man. He was a good man to me."

"He may have been a good man to you," Lasaria said carefully, "but he was a bad man to everyone else who knew him. He was one of the worst twins the world has ever seen."

3

Alex sat motionless. He watched a knot in the tree opposite his position. Sweat dripped down his temple like a leaky faucet. Air hissed from his nose. His chest shuddered. A mosquito landed on his arm. It pierced his skin and filled up on blood. In the distance an animal growled in fury. Something screamed out in horror. Silence descended on the surroundings.

"Are you okay?" Lasaria asked. "I know you probably think I am a, what, a jerk you called it, but that was not my intention."

"I," Alex muttered. "He couldn't have been bad. He was so nice to me. Bad people don't take in a stray. He could have left me to fend for myself, but he didn't. He took me in. He gave me a home. He helped me."

"We should not talk about this," Lasaria insisted. "We do not even know one another. I do not want you to hate me any more than you already do."

Alex itched the back of his head. "I don't hate you. I'm just lost. I don't know what to do." He sniffled. Tears threatened to fall. "I need to know.

Please, tell me who my friend was."

"Alright," Lasaria relented, "but just listen. Do not get mad, just listen. When I am done, we need to get some rest. No questions. No discussion. We sleep and then move. If you can agree to that, I will tell you what I know."

"I think I can agree to that," Alex grumbled. "Or I'll try to anyway."

"Where do I begin," Lasaria asked herself. She rubbed the point of her chin. "This all happened a long time ago, before I was born. Maybe sixteen or seventeen years ago now. Probably longer really. I have not thought about this since I was a little girl." She paused to contemplate. "Do you know about The Law of Twos?"

Alex stayed silent.

"Do you?" Lasaria repeated.

"I thought you didn't want me to talk," Alex quipped. He crossed his arms over his chest. A smile spread from cheek to cheek.

"Talk about a jerk," Lasaria scoffed. "Do you want to hear this or not?"

"Yes," Alex relented, "I know about Twins. Leviticus told me about them."

"I am sure he did," Lasaria snarked. "I am sure you already know that Leviticus was a twin. The Law of Two's states that when twins are born, they would come to possess great powers. These powers were ambiguous. I have read of twins who could conjure fire. Others who could manipulate space. The tale of Phillia the Vanquisher talks of her ability to move people through dimensions. Whatever they may be, history documents these powers as facts. In reality, twins have now vanished.

Whether they no longer exist, or parents go to great lengths to hide them, I do not know. But they have become those of legend.

Regardless of the story, regardless of the generation, there was one thing they all had in common, twins would always change. One would turn bad: one would turn good. There is not any explanation I can remember. Magic is the only word I have ever heard used to describe these powers. But they would change. And they would fight. And many would die," Lasaria drifted off. Her voice cracked.

"Are you okay?" Alex tentatively asked. "What does any of this have to do with Leviticus?"

"Leviticus and his brother, Marier." Lasaria looked up to the sky. "Yes Marier, they broke the mold. They were not just bad, they were evil. There was a revolt. A terrible twin named Ulrich Flemming killed his brother. He hunted down every twin he could find. They either joined him or died. The evil twins, I think they are called, Necromancers, were easy to persuade. Only one good twin turned."

"Leviticus," Alex whispered.

"Or his brother," Lasaria stated. She leaned against a log and shut her eyes. "Nobody really knows who was good or bad. They worked together. They killed together. They traveled the land and pillaged good people for Ulrich Flemming together. And then one day they vanished. I was maybe two years old at the time. They have been gone for fifteen years now. No one had heard from, or seen, either of them since. Until now. Until you." Lasaria started to fade. Her voice fell soft. "I am sure you have many questions for me, but they will have to wait. If we do not get some rest, tonight is going to be rough. Plus, just thinking about all that makes my head hurt."

"I promised I would wait," Alex accepted. "But I don't know how much sleep I'm going to get. I really don't even know what to say."

Lasaria slid back and put her hands behind her head. "Just close your eyes. We can talk more tonight. If my calculations are correct, it should not be much farther now."

"Much farther to what?" Alex asked.

"Oh Alex," Lasaria sighed. "Even after all of that, I am not sure you would believe me if I told you."

4

"Get up," Lasaria said, "it is time to go." She nudged Alex with her foot. When he didn't move, she kicked him again.

Alex sat bolt upright. His

hand dropped to his dagger. He wrenched his head from side to side. Behind him something moved. His voice squeaked. Goosebumps crawled up his forearm. Crickets chirped out from the void beyond. It took a second before he remembered where he was. His eyes adjusted to the darkness. Lasaria gradually appeared. He could just make out her silhouette standing over him.

"What was that?" Alex grumbled. "Why did you kick me?"

Lasaria turned her attention to the gear. She secured the hilt of her sword. "I am thinking about half a night until we hit the foothills. The trees thin out so it will be easier to see." She reached over her shoulder. Her finger plucked the bow's string. "After that it should not be much longer."

"I can't believe you kicked me," Alex moaned. He got up and slipped on his jacket. The sack he carried was pressed into a space between a log and the ground. He got to one knee and worked it from side to side.

"By midday tomorrow we should be there," Lasaria said.

"Shouldn't be much longer to what?" Alex demanded. He pulled the sack free and tossed it over his shoulder. "Where will we be by midday tomorrow?"

Lasaria hopped the creak. She reached her arm under an impediment of thick green branches. Tiny thorns pricked her overcoat. She lifted the brambles with her forearm. "After you," she said.

Alex swept his hands over the front of his coat. "Fine." He ducked under Lasaria's arm. A dozen needles stabbed him on the back of the head as he went under. "Come on," he moaned.

"Get rid of the attitude," Lasaria asserted. She bent under the obstruction. Alex was already out of sight. "And hold on, you do not even know where you are going," she hollered.

In the distance a nocturnal predator howled. The somber cry stretched out into the abyss. A second call matched the melancholy of the first. Lasaria held her arms high. To her left, a line of fallen timber made a gap through the woods. She propped her hand against a log. Rays from the moon illuminated a slit that cut to the right like a scar. She locked her elbow in place and pushed the tangle of vegetation away from her face.

Lasaria jogged ahead. She jumped a stump and her forehead smacked a trunk above. A cut opened over the bridge of her nose. Blood trickled from the wound, but she hardly noticed. The path veered and she followed, careful to keep her feet from getting tangled in the undergrowth. She rounded the corner and the path faded into the unknown.

"Hey," Alex whispered. "I'm over here."

Lasaria spooked. Her feet got caught underneath her body. She stumbled and fell to her knees. "Do not do that," she said sternly. "You almost gave me a heart attack."

Alex chuckled. "Sorry," he said sheepishly. "I couldn't see anything, so I had to stop."

"I told you to wait." Lasaria got up. She straightened her pants at the waist. "We should stay together. You do not know where you are. If you get yourself lost, I am not going to stick around to look for you."

"Whatever," Alex huffed. He stepped out from behind a mass of shrubs and frowned. "Try to keep up then."

Lasaria took a round locket from her

pocket. She pushed it open with her thumb and held it to her face. "To dark," she said. The locket closed with a click. It disappeared just as quickly as it appeared. "We need to follow the moon. If we do that, we should be okay."

"What do you mean, follow the moon?" Alex looked up. "I can't see anything," he insisted.

"Just follow me," Lasaria snarled. "I have done this before."

"Oh," Alex said sarcastically, "okay."

"Just do it." Lasaria looked back. "And try to keep up," she said in jest.

They walked in silence. Progress was slow. The vegetation hindered their movements. A barrier of vines forced them to double back the way they had come. Freshly fallen timber was slick with a sheen of dew. Sticks poked out from the darkness like blades. Exposed skin was quickly covered in interwoven abrasions.

As the night wore on, the forest eased its stranglehold. The terrain began to rise. Slender white trees replaced thick trunks. The first bit of light turned the horizon an incandescent blue. Rocks littered the ground. Small stones got larger as they ascended. When they reached the apex of the incline, the ground dropped off at a sharp angle. A vast valley stretched out as far as the eye could see. At the other end of the basin, brilliant peeks reached into the sky.

"Wow," Alex mumbled. "It's amazing. I've never seen anything like it."

Lasaria took the locket from her pocket. She popped it open and checked the face. "Good," she stated, "we are headed in the right direction."

"That is good," Alex said absentmindedly. He gazed at the mountain range in the distance. "Good," he repeated.

"This way," Lasaria said. She grabbed Alex by the shoulder. "We are almost there."

Lasaria started down the ridge. Loose gravel slid out from under her. She rode the momentum like a wave. Her arms shot into the air. The ground leveled off at the base. She hit the dirt and rolled onto her feet.

"Come on," Lasaria hollered. "It is easy."

Alex took a deep breath. A vain throbbed in his neck. He counted; one, two, three and stepped out. His foot slipped. His arms flailed over his head. He crashed onto his backside. The tail of the jacket caught under his boot heel. The fabric curled around his body like a cocoon. He threw the sack over his chest and gripped it tight. Debris churned up in his wake. Dust billowed behind him in a grey cloud. At the bottom he came to an abrupt halt.

Lasaria stumbled to get out of the way. "Are you okay?" she asked. She reached down and took Alex by the hand.

"I'm…" Alex turned and looked at the back of his legs. "I'm fine. I think the jacket saved me."

"What do you mean," Lasaria asked. She snatched the hem of the jacket. "It cannot be." She turned the fabric in her hand.

"Yeah," Alex said. "I think it absorbed the brunt of the impact."

"It cannot be," Lasaria repeated. Her finger traced a bronze striation stitched into the inner lining.

Alex pulled away. "What?" he asked. "What's wrong?"

"Gold tempered with lead," Lasaria said breathlessly. Her eyes grew wide. "That is Athenian Armor. Sewn into the lining of a jacket. It cannot be."

"I don't know what any of that

means."

Lasaria shook her head. "It cannot be," she murmured.

"What can't it be?" Alex asked assertively. "What's Athenian Armor?"

"It is…" Lasaria voice trailed off.

"What?" Alex demanded.

"It is not supposed to exist," Lasaria said.

"Come on," Alex scoffed.

"Alex," Lasaria shouted. She grabbed him with both hands. "Athenian Armor is a tale of legend. Yet here it is. I see it plain as day. On the inside of your hideous coat. Where did you get this?"

A crooked grin spread over Alex's face. "If you think this is cool," he said enthusiastically, "just wait until you see what else I have on."

5

"What is your story," Lasaria asked bluntly. "You do not know anything about anything, as far as I can tell, so who are you?"

They moved along the edge of a small stream. Water meandered in a lazy flow. A shoal of minnows swam against the current. Tiny gnats buzzed them in swarms. A bird the size of a potato swept over the valley. It plunged into the grass. High pitched shrieks pierced the solitude. When it emerged, a long slender animal hung limp in its talons.

"That was a rude way to put that," Alex answered. He bent over and scooped a handful of water. "But you're right. I don't know anything about anything. That's probably why I'm in this situation." He poured the water down his neck.

"But you have that jacket," Lasaria said. "And you knew Leviticus. I mean thee Leviticus."

"So," Alex snapped.

"I'm just saying, it is weird. That is all."

Alex clenched his fists. "I don't want to talk about Leviticus," he demanded. "Let's just leave that alone for now."

Lasaria nodded. "That is good. You will want to get used to that. Leviticus is a sore subject where I am from. A very sore subject."

Alex hustled to catch up. The sun had just reached the middle of the sky. Animals congregated in the shade of a large oak tree. They caught wind of the newcomers and scampered out of sight. A slight breeze came in from the west. Pale silver seeds floated into the air. They swept across the valley and out of sight.

"What about you?" Alex sneezed. "What were you doing running all alone in the woods?" He sneezed again.

Lasaria kept her head on a swivel. "I told you," she said, "it is complicated." Her eyes were fixed on a rocky ledge to the right.

"Tell me something," Alex said, "anything. You know about me. I don't know a single thing about you."

"What do you want to know?" Lasaria relented.

Alex thought for a moment. "Who was chasing you? Or why were they chasing you?"

"That is two questions. But I suppose the answer is one and the same." Lasaria stopped. She squinted against the glare of the sun. "I am part of an envoy for a small country. We were traveling to a province not far from where we met. Our mission was to deliver a message. Easy. Simple. Done. On the way home we ran into trouble. Those things came out of nowhere. They must have been waiting. Things that massive are not known for their stealth. Yet somehow, they were invisible. I am not sure who sent them, but I can take a guess. A guy named Ulrich Flemming, most likely. Anyway, we scattered. Those things followed me. I ran into you. End of story."

"No," Alex said bluntly, "not end of story. Beginning of story. You didn't give me a whole lot of information."

"That is all you need to know." Lasaria hopped over the stream. "Or all we have time for," she added.

"I don't think so," Alex demanded. "I need to know more. You're going to tell me what I want to know or I'm not going anywhere."

"Wait a minute," Lasaria interrupted. She put her hand up. "We are here." She trotted a few paces. A dozen rocks were formed into an upside-down V.

"What is it?" Alex asked. He jumped the water. "Looks like an arrow."

Lasaria smiled. "That is exactly what it is. Come on, follow me." She bounced up and jogged in a straight line. "It should be around here somewhere." A small rise in the soil shielded a stone slab. "This is it."

"This is what?" Alex asked. "It doesn't look like anything."

"That is the point," Lasaria insisted. She brushed a layer of dirt away. "It is not supposed to look like anything. But under here is our hideout."

Chapter 6

1

The sun sunk over a snow-capped peak and shadows cast the valley in a penumbra. Wind blew down from the mountains and brought a chill. The dark of night pushed away an azure sky. Stars twinkled to life on the distant horizon. A crescent moon cast a sliver of silver light onto the wave of grass. From the underbrush, a cricket chirped to life. Two more followed. In an instant a cacophony of music filled the air.

"What is taking you so long?" Alex asked. He laid back in the soil. "I thought you said we would be here by the middle of the day."

Lasaria planted herself at the far edge of the stone slab. "We were here at midday. Besides, we have not even been here that long, you are just being impatient." She stepped heel to toe. When she got to five, she halted. "It is supposed to be here. I cannot find it." Her eyes scanned the area.

Alex sat up. He pulled his coat closed and tucked the lapel under his chin. "What are you looking for?" he asked.

"There is a key around here somewhere." Lasaria dropped to her knees. She poked the ground with a stick. "Five paces north from the center of the slab. I just do not see it anywhere."

Alex got to his feet. He fastened the

middle two clasps of his coat. "It didn't look like you were taking paces," he said. "Plus, who took the paces to begin with? If they were taller than you the key would be further out."

Lasaria dropped her head. "You are right," she admitted. "The carpenter, Darien, he would have built this. He is huge. And if Diego paced it…" she trailed off. Her fingers searched through the dirt. "I am so stupid."

"What?" Alex asked. He made his way around the stone slab. "Did you find something?"

"Tracks," Lasaria laughed. "They were right here the entire time. I must be tired." She crawled forward. Her hands combed the ground. The distance from the stone slab nearly doubled. "Oh, come on," she laughed again, "it is right here."

A diminutive mound was indistinguishable from the others around it. Beyond the hump, a circular depression was covered with loose grass and dirt. A granite tablet was visible through the hastily assembled camouflage. The outer edge was raised in a ring around a shallow center basin. Dark lines of soil snaked out like a branch from a singular spot at the center of the stone. A trace of moisture stood out against the arid earth.

"Someone was just here," Lasaria said. She traced the circumference of the tablet. "I figured they would be," she added.

Alex got down on one knee. "Are they friendly?"

"Anyone who knows about this place is friendly to us." Lasaria looked up at Alex. Her eyes narrowed. "But I am going to warn you again, do not mention Leviticus. That is one name that is not welcome around here."

"But," Alex protested,

"he was my friend."

Lasaria put her hand on Alex's knee. "I get that, I really do. But if people know how close the two of you were, they will not trust you. They will probably think something is wrong with me for bringing you here. So just keep it to yourself."

"Fine," Alex relented.

Lasaria turned her attention back to the tablet. She swept the vegetation away with the back of her hand. Thin ridges emerged in the surface of the stone. At the center of the bowl, a hole plunged deep into the earth. When the bulk of the cover was clear, Lasaria bent over and blew the last of debris from the tablet.

A maze of pathways diverged from a single line like spokes on a wheel. At the first junction the line split into three. Each path split into three again. After a T junction, the right path split in two.

The center path cut both left and right. It crossed over the paths on either side. On the far side of the stone tablet, a single line emerged from the chaos. The groove ended at a small, flat ridge.

"Well that's cool," Alex said. He stuck a finger in one of the grooves. "It's wet," he exclaimed.

Lasaria smiled. "If you think this is cool, just wait. And watch. The path changes every time." She crept back inch by inch. When she was clear of the tablet, she jammed her knee down on the small rise in the soil.

The ground rumbled. A high-pitched whine pierced the evening. Behind them the stone slab slid beneath itself. At the same moment water bubbled up from the hole of the stone. Liquid filled the initial groove. It hit the first junction and followed the bend to the right. At the second junction it turned left. It defied all logic and crossed over the center path. It turned right and then immediately left.

"Watch," Lasaria barked. "We get one shot at this. If we don't remember this correctly, we are liable to get stuck down there forever."

"Oh crap." Alex knelt beside Lasaria. He did his best to ignore the sound of rocks crushing beneath him. "Why is it so complicated," he asked.

"Hush. Pay attention."

Alex focused on the early stages of the route. The trail of water was barely visible in the receding light. He committed what he could to memory and followed the route through the jumble of lines. There was a left turn, a right bend, another left turn. At the final ridge, the water flowed off the stone and into the brush.

"Okay…" Alex said. "Why was that so complicated?" The noise below abruptly cut off. It echoed through the valley and was silent.

Lasaria got up. She clapped her hands together. "Alright," she said, "let's get going." She turned towards the chasm where the stone slab used to be. "Do you remember the way?"

"I don't know," Alex scoffed. He picked up his sack and tossed it over his shoulder. He checked the weapons at his belt. "I guess we will see when we get down there, won't we."

The stone slab was gone. A black void was identical to the ground around it. Lasaria went to the outer lip and peered into the depths below. She walked the perimeter. Her eyes focused on the opposite wall of the pit. Something solid took shape. A ladder formed out of the ether. Thick wooden rungs floated without support.

"There," Lasaria shouted. She hurried around. "Best if we just go. I hate hanging steps. I always feel like I am going to fall." She dropped down and sat. Her feet dangled in the open space. "Here goes nothing."

Lasaria planted her hands in the dirt. Her arms trembled. Her elbows nearly gave way against the weight of her body. She kicked around with her heel. An echo reverberated down into the darkness. She secured the arches of her feet on the center of the third rung. She took a deep breath, stood, and rotated until her back was to the cavity.

"Follow me," Lasaria exhaled. Her fingers cut into the ground. When her head was just visible, she smiled and descended out of sight.

Alex plopped onto his butt. He set the sack to his side and felt for the ladder. When he felt assured there was something of substance to stand on, he looked to the sky. The stars shined bright. A line of clouds sliced the luminous moon in half. A light streaked across the open expanse and burned away.

"Here we go again," Alex said. He flipped to his stomach and dropped into the unknown.

2

The bottom of the descent opened into a small rotunda. A damp chill permeated the stale confines of the space. An unbridled silence penetrated the atmosphere. Smooth stone walls were chiseled out of the bedrock. Loose dirt and gravel encircled the base of the ladder. Footsteps led out of the rubble toward the entrance of a dark passage.

Lasaria stood at the threshold of the tunnel. A small lantern was clutched in her right hand. Dim yellow light radiated out in a ring. The glow cast a steady shadow at the back of the chamber. Her left arm was outstretched. Her hand hovered over an indentation in the stone wall. Beyond her, the darkness was impenetrable.

"You down?" Lasaria boomed.

Alex covered his ears. "Yeah," he whispered, "I'm down."

"Just wanted to check. You never know with these things." Lasaria put her hand against the indentation.

A deafening whine came out of the ground. The slab lurched into motion. The earth shook under the sudden force. Alex stumbled toward Lasaria. He lost his balance and his sack popped out of his arms. It hit the ground and something crunched. The sound was indistinguishable from the racket above. It crumpled into a heap.

The rumbling eased. Alex waited until he was certain the worst was over and dropped to check the pack. He touched the side. A shard pricked him through the fabric. Pain resonated out from the puncture. Blood formed in a tiny dot at the tip of his finger. He stuck the wound in his mouth and sucked.

"So, what now?" Alex asked. He got to his feet and held the sack to the side.

Lasaria looked over her shoulder. "Now we go," she puffed. She turned towards the unknown. "Let's just hope we remember this right."

"Seriously," Alex mumbled.

They moved forward in tandem. Stone walls curved over them. The lantern lit the path with an incandescent glow. The silence was replaced by the repetitive patter of movement. It wasn't long before the entrance to the passage was out of sight. Their world reduced to the circumference of a few feet. They continued and the pathway stretched into a loop.

"I feel like that map up there was deceptive," Alex finally said. He slunk behind Lasaria's shoulder. "It looked like this tunnel was super short. But it feels like we've been walking forever."

Lasaria shook her head. "It just feels that way. Have patience," she said, "and you will prosper."

"I don't know about that," Alex countered. "Patience hasn't gotten me anywhere."

"The problem with saying something like that is you can never truly know if anything would have been different. Patience. No patience. Life is linear. The decisions we make cannot be changed. For better and for worse, everything we do, takes us to our present moment in time. For you and me, those decisions have put us here." Lasaria stopped. She held her hand up and cocked her head. After a second, she continued. "For me, I say go forward with patience."

Alex laughed. "I'll try," he said, "but they have been telling me that at the orphanage for years and it never stuck. Maybe this time." He crossed his fingers and held them over his head.

"Whoever said that knew what they were talking about," Lasaria quipped.

"You don't even know me," Alex blurted. "Who do you think you are?"

Lasaria thrust her hand out. "Look," she exclaimed, "the first junction."

The path ended at a stone wall. It split to the left and right. "Well this one is easy," Alex said. "I know we have to take a right here."

"Agreed," Lasaria added. She rounded the bend and continued. "I feel like I remember we go left at the next junction. After that, though, I am really going to have to focus. Straight through the one after that, I think."

"Let's just keep going," Alex urged, "and take it one step at a time."

Lasaria smiled. "Look at that," she said, "you are already learning patience."

Alex chuckled. "Purely a coincidence, I assure you."

They kept on until a path branched off to the left. Lasaria looked at Alex. He nodded and they followed. The route was identical to the one before it. Sleek stone walls repeated themselves in dimly lit increments. Up close, the radiance of the lantern burned bright. A few feet out the light was consumed by the pitch-black beyond.

A stone arch marked the entrance to a squat, square chamber. The path split into four. Lasaria passed through and continued straight. At the next T junction, she paused. Alex stayed on the move. He passed her by and followed to the right. The route quickly split to the left and he followed. When it split again, he took a right.

"Not bad," Lasaria said. They hit another junction. Alex took a left and she followed. "I am going to hang back.

You have got this apparently."

"I can see it in my mind." The path swept to the right. Alex continued along. "Nothing has ever been so clear to me," he said excitedly. They took another left, a right, then another right. "I know we are going the correct way. Not like I kind of remember, I know it."

"Hey," Lasaria huffed, "why don't I remember?" She held the lantern up. "Whatever. If we get stuck down here, I will have you to blame. I can go to my death knowing that much," she snickered.

Alex followed to the left. "This is it," he said. "That was the last turn on the map. End of the line."

Lasaria pushed ahead. She took a few strides and stopped. The lantern lit the end of the path. A boulder was wedged between the walls. The face cut up to the ceiling at a steep angle. It sliced through the stone and out of sight.

"Oh man," Alex muttered, "I got it wrong." He dropped his head.

"No," Lasaria exclaimed, "you got it right." She stepped to the wall. "Watch this." She pressed a flaw in the stone. Something beneath them slid. The boulder plunged away. It crashed to the floor below. "We are here."

Behind the boulder, long wooden slats were twined together horizontally. At the center, a single piece of oak was secured on iron hinges. A gold lionhead was attached to the right side. Bright red stones were set deep in sockets. Light reflected from the predator's gaze.

Lasaria knocked. "It is me," she hollered. She hit it again when no one answered.

A loud metallic scrape pierced the silence. Two heavy thuds along the edge of the door shook the wooden frame. Someone grunted. The hinges creaked to life. The barrier cracked opened and a slit of light reflected off the wall. Dark pupils peered through the opening in the door. They studied Alex over and shifted to Lasaria.

Candles inside the room bathed the passage in warmth. A man moved through the entrance. He ducked under the doorframe and stood erect. The light was obstructed by his hulking torso. His muscles bulged underneath a white tunic. Dark stains covered the chest and arms. The fabric was tight against his body. A growth of chestnut hair covered his chin. His head was shaved bald. A scar cut from his eye down to the corner of his cheek. His boots were polished leather. He took a step, frowned, and scowled.

3

"Look at what we have here," the man said. His voice was a deep baritone. "I did not think you would show." He put his hands on his hips. "Looks like I lost a bet."

"I knew you were here," Lasaria cried out. She leapt into his arms. "So glad you made it."

The man held her by the shoulders. He set her down and smiled. "Me?" he asked sheepishly. A crooked grin revealed a missing tooth. "We were worried about you. When we got separated, I had thought for certain you would head home."

"Oh, no," Lasaria said. "This was the only place I was going to go." She pushed the man to the side. "Let us in, I am starving. And I stink something fierce."

The man let Lasaria by. Alex went to follow. The man pivoted into the doorway. He held his hand out and blocked the way. "I do not know you," he said. "I cannot just let you come in here without checking you for weapons first."

"That's not happening," Alex scoffed. "These are my things and you aren't going to touch them. Period."

"Interesting," the man said. He stiffened his spine. His head nearly hit the top of the passage. "I do not recall asking for your permission."

Alex stayed planted. He slid his hand to the dagger at his side. "You're not going to touch me, or my weapons," he growled.

"Really?" the man asked. His smile grew wide. "Are you going to stop me with that little thing?"

"Diego enough," Lasaria shouted. She grabbed the man by the back of his pants. "Get in here. And let Alex in."

"Alex," the man

repeated. He hunched over and backed through the door.

Alex walked into the room. A wave of heat swept over him. The stink of funk overpowered his senses. He put his hand to his face and surveyed the surroundings. A small chamber was chiseled into the earth. Lanterns hung along the wall in increments. A brass cauldron dangled from a bolt hammered into the middle of the ceiling. Flames danced above the surface of a clear viscous liquid. At the center of the space a long wooden board was propped on stumps. Trees were cleaved in half and laid laterally along either side. In the back right corner, a passage snaked out of sight.

A man and woman sat at the far end of the table. They saw Lasaria enter the room and beamed. They got up in unison, their movements a mirror image of one another. She hurried over and threw her arms out. They hugged as a group. The embrace lasted barely a second. When they separated, they whispered in earnest.

Alex approached from the side. "Lasaria," he interrupted, "care to introduce me. I've already got one person staring me down. I don't need another one. Or two."

The door shut behind him. Diego secured the lock and walked over to the table. "Yes, Lasaria," he said deliberately, "why don't you introduce us."

Lasaria put her hand on the man at her side. "Oh," she laughed, "probably not a bad idea. Introductions all around. Everyone, this is Alex. I ran into him in the woods a few days back. We have been together ever since." She put her other hand on Alex. "And Alex, this is everyone."

Alex shook his head. "I'm going to

need a bit more than that," he said. "How about names."

Diego held his arm in the air. "You all know me," he drawled. "And I have already had the pleasure to meet Alex here. And you both look hungry. We have already eaten, but I am going to go and get you two some food."

"Yes," Lasaria said, "excellent idea. I am starving. Alex here would not even eat a tiny little grub, so he must be hungry."

Diego turned and walk off.

"Hey," Alex called, "thanks. I really am hungry."

"I get it." Diego looked back. "I would never eat those bugs either. I will get you something good." He turned and set off down the passage.

"Thanks," Alex repeated. He watched Diego go.

Lasaria smacked Alex on

the shoulder. "Hey," she implored. "I am trying to introduce you guys here."

Alex rubbed his arm. "That hurt," he chuckled. "Okay, introductions then."

"What is up," the guy yawned. "Sorry about that. I am Deuce." He patted the woman on the back. "And this here is my older sister Danice."

"Come on." Danice shrugged away. "You always have to mention that I am the older one, don't you?"

The brother and sister shared a variety of similar features. The two were nearly the same height. She stood just a fraction of an inch taller. They both had sandy blonde hair. His was chopped short. The top looked wet and was flattened down against his head. Hers was pulled into a braid behind her ears. They had the same thin nose, upturned at the tip. His chin cut in at an angle. He looked gaunt. Her face was filled out a bit. Her skin was luminescent.

"Good to meet you Alex," Danice said. She stretched her arms over her head. "I really do want to know everything that has happened, but we have been up since dawn. Plus, we have a long day ahead of us tomorrow. I have got to go rest."

Alex nodded. "I totally get that," he agreed. He stepped over the log and sat. He set his sack at his side. "As soon as I eat, I need to sleep. Is there a place for me to sleep?" he asked tentatively.

"Oh yeah," Lasaria answered. She sat across from Alex. "There are chambers down the corridor there. You will have your own."

"The last chamber on the right is mine," Danice chimed in. "The last on the left is where Deuce will be. I think Diego is first on the left, but you will have to ask him when he gets back."

Deuce reached over the table. He clapped Lasaria on the shoulder. "I am out for the night, but good to see you here. You made me a gold piece just for showing up."

"Come on," Danice groaned. She pulled Deuce around. "You stop thinking when you are tired. Best to leave now before you make an ass of yourself." She put her arm around his shoulder. "Nice to meet you, Alex. May Morpheus bless you with a restful slumber." They left down the corridor.

Diego returned to the room. He held a loaf of dark brown bread in one hand. Thin white seeds were pressed into the crust. A jug dangled from two fingers on his other hand. He got to the table and sat beside Lasaria. He handed her the jug and she took a long, slow pull. Diego tore the bread in two. He set one half in front of Lasaria and handed the other to Alex.

"I hope that will do for tonight," Diego said. He took the jug and passed it to Alex. "I am going to go hunting in the morning. I should have something prepped for travel by midday."

Alex put his lips to the jug. He tipped it back and took a sip. "Oh man that water is ice cold." He tilted his head and gulped a mouthful. "It is so good."

"Drink up," Diego encouraged. "That is the one thing we have plenty of down this deep."

Lasaria pinched a piece from the end of the bread. "How long have you been here?" she asked. She stared at the food.

"Not long," Diego replied. "We got in last night. Been resting up, waiting for you since."

"Good." Lasaria took the jug back. "I was worried you would have left by now."

Diego snickered. "Your father would have my head if I returned without you," he said. "Besides, I knew you would be here."

"Didn't really sound like it," Alex interrupted.

Lasaria choked on a drink of water. "He has got you there," she laughed.

Diego went red. "I am curious about you." He pointed at Alex. "How did you find yourself in the company of my prin…" he stumbled on the word. "Of Lasaria here?"

Alex chomped on a piece of bread. He swallowed and took the water. "It was just one of those things that happens. I was hanging out in the woods. She was running from something. Our paths crossed. Then we were both running."

"Ulrich Flemming?" Diego asked. He looked at Lasaria. His eyes narrowed. "It had to be him."

"He was waiting for us. I barely escaped. Without Alex who knows what would have happened." Lasaria scraped out the center of the bread. She formed the dough into a ball and stuck it in her mouth. "The timing could not be a coincidence."

"How do we know Alex, here, was not waiting for you too. For all we know, Flemming sent him in because he knew you would not see him as any sort of threat."

Alex scoffed. "I had my own life," he snapped. "My best friend was killed because of those things chasing her. So don't insult me on top of everything else that has happened."

"Who was killed," Diego inquired. "If they killed some kid just to

214

find you, that means this has gotten even worse than we know."

"He wasn't some kid." Alex pushed the food aside. He jammed his finger into the table. "Leviticus was more of a father to me than anyone has ever been. He died a broken man. He died –"

"What did you just say?" Diego growled. He slid the bench back and lumbered to his feet.

Lasaria shot up. "Diego," she begged, "calm down."

"Did you hear what he said?" Diego demanded. "He said Leviticus. I knew he was a spy.

Alex twirled around. "Back off big man," he said. His hand fell to his side.

"Again, with that dagger," Diego barked. "I will take it off you and kill you where you stand. Do you hear me? Just try something."

Alex backed away. He snatched his sack and retreated towards the door. "I'm not going to do anything," his voice trembled. "So back off. Okay. Just back off."

"Come on Alex," Lasaria sighed. She held her arm out and kept Diego in place. He stayed where he was. "I told you not to mention him."

Diego's eyes blazed. "Are you saying you knew about this?" He looked to Lasaria. "Like a father to him," he scoffed. "He said he was like a father to him. The adopted son of Leviticus Cole."

"I – told – you – to – calm – down." Lasaria articulated each word.

"But," Diego started. "Fine." His shoulders slumped.

"Clearly there is a story here," Lasaria insisted. She dropped her arm and looked between the adversaries. "Both of you sit down. Nothing good is going to come from killing each other."

Diego threw his head back and laughed. "Not really a fair fight."

"Be quiet," Lasaria demanded. "Sit down and listen."

Alex slunk towards the table. "He needs to settle down. I'm not going to argue with someone who is all charged up like that."

Lasaria spun to the side. She placed her hand on Diego's chest. "He is right," she said softly. She rubbed his bicep. "Please, sit down and listen."

Diego stood entranced. He didn't blink. "No," he said decisively. "I am not going to listen to anything he has to say." He marched off without another word.

"Diego," Lasaria called. He was quickly gone. "Fine."

"Sorry about that," Alex said awkwardly. He moved over to the side of the table and set his sack down.

"If you want me to leave, I get it. I was just tagging along anyway. I knew it had to end sometime. Better now than when I'm invested in our relationship."

Lasaria rubbed her temple. "You are not going anywhere," she insisted. "Well not until we all leave together tomorrow. Diego will calm down. And it would have slipped out at some point." She shook her head. "I know he was your friend and all but man, Leviticus Cole, back from the dead. Just to die again." She chuckled.

"Come on," Alex groaned, "he just died." Tears welled up in the corner of his eyes. He sniffled and held the flow at bay. "I just want to go to bed."

"Sorry." Lasaria looked at her boots. "Death is kind of a regular thing around here. I see it every week. I forget it is not that way for everyone." She turned. "Let me find you a chamber."

Alex hurried after Lasaria. "I can't wait to get some sleep," he said enthusiastically. "And I should get plenty of it," he added, "provided there is a lock on the chamber door."

4

Alex awoke with a start. A dim flicker of candlelight allowed just enough light for him to see. The heat that had baked the common area the night before faded. A damp chill settled in the stale confines of the room. The linen blanket Lasaria had given him was wadded into a ball under his head. A layer of hay needled the exposed skin on the back of his neck.

Alex sat up and crossed his legs. He felt around for his things. His weapons were secured to his belt. The hilt of the dagger was cool to the touch. He grazed his fingers over the deep ruby gems inlaid in the handle and they pulsed. The Manrikigusari hung loose around his waist. The sack he stitched together by the lagoon was tucked snug against his side. His jacket was still in the corner where he had dropped it.

"I'm afraid to even look," Alex said aloud. He set the sack between his feet. Something inside crunched. "Oh man," he groaned.

The fabric was twisted together into a pair of overhand knots. Alex dug his nail between two loops. When he created slack, he stuck his finger through and untied the first. The second knot was bound tight. He worked it back and forth until a gap appeared. He slid the tip of his pinkie through the center of the two pieces and used his teeth to pull them apart.

Alex laid the edges back.

A hodgepodge mix of items spread out before him. Large chunks of rough-cut rocks were mixed with a rainbow of loose gemstones. Silver rings were embossed with tiny symbols. A gold strand necklace was set with half a dozen turquois stones. The palette of colors picked up what little light was in the room and sparkled. On the bottom of the cloth, a dull peach crystal was splintered into pieces. Sharp shards were set around a single broken chunk.

Alex took the lump and held it to his face. A wave of calm washed over him. He blew the dust away and watched the particles waft into the air. He studied the stone. One side was sheered into a point. The other three were strafed with deep striations. Lines of muted white gypsum were embedded within the core.

"Knock, knock," a woman said. The door swung open and

Lasaria strolled in. "We are going to get going soon. I wanted you to have time to get some food before we…" her voice broke off. "What is all that?"

"It's nothing." Alex dropped the stone onto the cloth. He snatched a corner and tried to cover the contents.

Lasaria shut the door behind her. "That is not nothing," she scoffed. "But there is no way." She moved closer. "Is there?"

"I have no idea what you are talking about." Alex leaned over and blocked the bulk of the lot from Lasaria.

"Come on," Lasaria begged, "tell me." She slunk to her knees.

"Tell you what? I really have no idea what you're talking about."

Lasaria crept closer. "I knew they could not be. It is just not possible."

Alex sneered. "I wasn't supposed to tell anyone about them."

"Nope," Lasaria said, "can't be."

"I don't know what you think these are," Alex insisted, "but these are something called Vitality Stones. Leviticus," he choked. His voice gave out. "Leviticus gave them to me before he died," he finished.

"No way." Lasaria jumped up. She paced the room. "No way, no way, no way," she repeated over and over.

"What's wrong with you?" Alex asked calmly. He took one side of the cloth and tied it with the opposite end. "I know they're supposed to be valuable, but you need to settle down."

"You do not understand," Lasaria stammered. She continued to pace the room. "They are not just valuable. I have seen two in all my life. Just two. What you have there is." She paused to think of a word. "Is unbelievable."

Alex got the cloth tied closed. He rolled over and got up.

"Wait," Lasaria said. She put her hand out. "Don't say anything about these to anyone. Stones like that are bound to cause problems. No," she insisted, "this stays between you and I."

"That is fine by me," Alex assured her. He got his jacket. "If you wouldn't have walked in on me, I never would have told you about them."

"Never?" Lasaria questioned. A smile crept onto her face. She opened the chamber door.

A blast of heat swept into the room. Alex walked into the passage. "Nope," he snickered, "never." He stopped and waited for Lasaria.

"I am sure you would have told me eventually." Lasaria smiled. She walked toward the common space. "But seriously." Her voice got soft. "Do not mention them to anyone. It is bad enough you have an entire outfit of Athenian Armor."

Danice sat at the end of the table. Her head was tipped back. A scowl was locked on her face. Deuce stood behind her; a large broadsword was in his hands. The two were deep in conversation. He gestured wildly. The sheath of the sword hit a ceramic jug. It crashed to the ground and smashed into bits.

Alex entered the room and it went quiet. "Something I said?" he asked. He picked the handle of the jug off the ground and set it on the table.

Deuce leaned down. His face scrunched into a frown. He whispered in Danice's ear. Her head shook. He whispered a second time. She turned and glared at him. They locked eyes. She shook her head again. For a moment nothing happened. Time stood still. Tension built to a breaking point.

Deuce huffed. He lowered his head and stomped towards the exit.

"Clearly I did something," Alex said. He slid onto the bench seat and grabbed a heel of bread.

"It is not you," Danice sighed. "He can be a bit… emotional."

Lasaria retrieved a jug from halfway down the table. "Diego filled them in on everything that happened last night," she said. She took a drink and handed it to Alex. "Deuce is just being overprotective. Give him some time, he will calm down."

"It sure doesn't seem like he wants me around." Alex sipped the water.

"He is more shocked than anything. Leviticus. That is just a name we have not heard in quite some time." Danice smiled weakly. "Made him act a little bonkers is all."

Alex choked on a piece

of bread. He swallowed a gulp of water and coughed. "I don't get," he said when the fit subsided. "I know he was supposed to be some bad guy and all, but what does everyone have against Leviticus? From what I gather, all of this happened over fifteen years ago. Time has passed. People should have let it go by now."

"Most people have," Lasaria said.

Danice nodded. "Most people," she agreed, "but not Diego."

"Why not?" Alex asked. He finished eating and brushed the crumbs from his lap.

"Well…" Lasaria hesitated, "um…" Her voice trailed off.

"Well," Danice said sternly. She looked at Lasaria and frowned. "We all know Leviticus. Or at the very least know of him. Diego especially so. It was Leviticus." She stumbled over how to finish her thought. Her voice was low. "It was Leviticus who murdered his father."

Chapter 7

1

The air was crisp. The first tinge of daylight appeared over a distant ridge. At the opposite end of the valley, a splattering of stars lingered in the sky. Snowcapped peaks lined the path north. A dense field of trees covered the base of the mountainside. A river snaked its way from the forest through the center of the basin.

Alex appeared from a crevasse slashed between the top of two boulders.

He pulled himself up to the surface and popped his head out. He surveyed the vicinity. The area was void of any activity. A flat piece of granite sloped away from the opening at a steep angle. A braided rope was secured to the stone with steel hooks.

"I don't see them anywhere," Alex hollered. He stepped up a rung and searched around. "Nothing," he added.

A hand pushed on the heel of his boot. "Move," Lasaria growled. "I want to get out of here."

Alex kicked his foot. "Hold on a second. I'm not really sure how to get down." He grabbed the rope. "It's an awfully long drop." He tested the anchor point. "But everything seems secure."

Lasaria pushed again. "Of course it is secure," she puffed. "Just swing your feet over and lower yourself down to the ground. It is not that far."

"I don't know," Alex said, "it looks

far." He got on the top rung of the ladder. "It looks really far." He pulled the rope.

"I knew I should have gone first." Lasaria shook her head. "Do you want me to climb over?" she asked. "If you are not going to go, I will climb over you."

"No," Alex insisted, "I can do this." He took a series of deep breaths. "I can do this," he said.

Alex set his sack on top of the stone and clambered from the ladder. He climbed on top of the rock and slipped. His feet launched into the air and he landed on his backside. His fingers tore free from the rope. He started down the descent. His hands clawed at the rock face. He managed to find the rope and squeezed. Skin ripped from his palm. He screamed in agony. His speed increased. At the bottom, the slope tapered off. Alex slid into the threshold where the stone hit the dirt. His momentum came to an abrupt halt. He flipped up and rolled into the grass.

"Are you alright?" Lasaria was already to the ground. She rushed over and dropped to her knees.

Danice slid down the incline. At the bottom, she popped to her feet. "Alex," she hollered, "do not move."

"Oh man," Alex moaned. He shook his right hand. "I'm fine, I'm fine."

Lasaria smiled. "Are you sure?" she snickered. "Because I probably should not be laughing if you are really hurt."

"Stop that." Danice smacked Lasaria on the back of the head.

"Sure," Lasaria giggled. "Sure." She threw her hand over her mouth to suppress a fit of glee.

Alex sat up. He felt the back of his head and winced. "Come on," he said to Lasaria, "it isn't funny."

Lasaria burst. "If you say so." She

fell to her side and laughed. "If you say so," she said between gasps.

Danice reached down. She clasped Alex by the hand and helped him up. His sack had tumbled a few yards out. She trotted over and retrieved it. When he had it back, she turned her attention to Lasaria. She flopped about in a fit of hysteria. Danice snatched her by the wrist. She yanked her to her feet and secured her around the shoulders.

"It is not funny," Danice said firmly. She dropped her head and scowled. "What has gotten into you?" she demanded.

"Nothing," Lasaria said. She tried to suppress her laughter. "No. I am alright. I am alright." She straightened her lapel. "I am alright," she insisted.

"Good," Danice said. She released her grip. "We have a lot of ground to cover today. Deuce and Diego are already gone."

Alex looked into the distance. "Why didn't they wait for us?" he asked. He lifted his hand to his brow. "And what's with the exit. Why didn't we just come in this way last night." He turned back to where they had emerged.

"They went north," Danice said. "Can't be more than an hour or so ahead of us. We should get moving." She set off at a jog.

"Wait a second," Alex huffed. "Just wait a second."

Lasaria checked her gear. "Don't bother," she said. "We won't catch them until they stop to eat. Danice is going to catch Diego to smooth things over."

Alex squeezed the knot at the top of his sack. Pain flowed through his hand. "Is that why they left?" he asked. "Because they don't want me around?"

"They will deal with it,"

Lasaria insisted. She smoothed the arms of her jacket. "We will all be together for a few more days. That will give them enough time to get to know you. Right now, they think you are some sort of spy." She shook her head. "I don't think it will take them very long to see that cannot be true."

"Hey," Alex whined, "I'd be an awesome spy."

"No, that is a good thing," Lasaria interjected. She patted Alex on the back. "You wear your emotions like a hat. They are easy to see. Once they get to know you, they will see you are no spy."

"I don't know. Diego has a really good reason to hate me." Alex stepped ahead. Danice was almost out of sight. "Should we go?" he asked.

Lasaria nodded. "That is true," she agreed. "But, then again, you would have a really good reason to hate me. And you don't hate me? Do you?"

"I don't have the capacity to hate anyone right now. I'm too tired." Alex rubbed his eyes. "Maybe when I have a chance to process everything, who knows."

Lasaria frowned. "That is a nasty thing to say. I hope you don't mean that."

"I was joking," Alex tittered. "But I am tired. And I could really use a bath. The sooner we get to civilization the better, I say."

"That is something we agree on," Lasaria said. She shook her hair out. Looping curls fell over her shoulders. "And yes, we should go."

"I'm ready." Alex spun around. "But seriously," he said sternly, "you really do need to take a bath. You stink."

2

Thick gray clouds drifted in over the valley. A slight breeze brought the smell of moisture to the atmosphere. Despite the cover, the temperature had risen significantly since the start of the day. An insufferable heat enveloped the surroundings. The air was heavy. A dense humidity covered everything in a haze.

The path north followed along the bank of the river. It neared the tree line and it narrowed to a point. Thin ruts disappeared completely in the overgrowth. Boot prints marched down the center of the cart path. They entered the woods where branches were sheared off in an arc. The trail was hacked large enough for a person to get through.

"Diego was not subtle, that is for sure," Lasaria said. She stopped at the opening of the route into the forest. She stooped and looked ahead. "But they left us an easy way to follow."

Alex caught up. "Oh man," he panted. "What's going on?"

"Diego was kind enough to clear the way." Lasaria stood. "We should go." She took off.

"Come on," Alex groaned. He quickly followed.

The woods were thick. Towering trunks were set amongst a tangle of bright green flora. A shag of dark vegetation covered one side of all the trees. The way forward was trampled down. Broken sticks and shrubs were squashed into malleable soil. Visibility was reduced to the singular scope of the route ahead.

"I need to know something," Alex finally spoke up. They'd been walking in silence for over an hour. "I mean I really need to know. Not just a little bit, but everything."

Lasaria kept moving. "Okay…" she drawled, "everything about what?"

Alex hesitated. "I need to know," he finally said. His voice went flat. "What happened to Diego? You said his father was killed. You said Leviticus and his brother murdered him. But what happened? I just can't believe the man I knew would be capable of something so terrible."

"I don't know, Alex, it is sad." Lasaria reduced her pace. "Diego has only ever told me what happened one time. And even then, he was drunk on Potsit Wine. That stuff is strong. It will melt the hair off a dog's tail if you dip it in a glass."

"What did you just say?" Alex asked confused.

"Who knows if what he said was true," Lasaria continued. She slowed to a crawl. "The rest of the story I know from the history books. And they were not fun texts. In fact, I already knew Diego at that point so I could hardly get through reading all of it without weeping. Are you sure you want to hear this?"

Alex pulled alongside Lasaria. "It isn't that I really want to hear it," he said, "I need to hear it. If I'm ever going to understand this place, I need to know who Leviticus really was. In the short time I knew him I came to love him as my father. But you all hate him so much. Tell me why. Tell me and I won't ask for anything else. I promise."

"Alright," Lasaria relented. Her voice dropped an octave. "I am going to tell you what I know. But I am only doing this so you can understand why Diego was so upset. He is a good man. If you tell him I told you any of this, I will have to kill you."

"Okay," Alex snarked. "Like if you tell me you'll have to kill me type thing." He rolled his eyes.

Lasaria put her hand out. "No," she said sternly. "Like Diego will kill me so I will have to kill you first type thing. If I tell you this, it is in our sole confidence that I do so. These are not stories we just talk about. We are at war. Everybody has lost someone important to them. The event I am about to tell you about is just an example of the atrocities that have been committed throughout the years."

"Wait a minute," Alex interrupted, "did you say war?"

"Yes," Lasaria said sternly, "war. But we can talk about that later. This story will not take long." She started walking. "It happened fifteen years ago now," she began, "yeah fifteen years I would say. Man, time is a funny thing," she faded off. "Anyway, I was just a baby. Maybe two at best. Diego was already fifteen by then. He lived with his father in a remote farming village here in Sparham. His mother had passed away a few years prior. A natural death. Caught a bad fever in the coldest part of the winter. Was gone by the summer.

There were twenty of them that lived in the village. Whether it was that small or not, I have no idea, but, either way, it really does not matter. What matters is what happened to them. Leviticus and his brother, Marier, the two of them, just the two of them, descended like animals. They killed all the elders in the village. Men, women, they killed them all. When they were dead, they tortured the young ones for their valuables. Diego wasn't young, but he was young enough. He was tortured for information. Even after he gave them everything, they tortured him still. For gold, for jewels.

When it was over, they finished what they started. Somehow Diego escaped. The texts don't mention him by name. He is referenced as the lone survivor.

When I asked him how he managed to get away, he shut down. Later that night I heard him crying. He was drunk, remember. Four bottles of Potsit wine will do that to you. But that was the end of the story. When I asked him about it the next morning, he simply said he took up arms and vowed to avenge his father's death. Yet, not a year after the slaughter in the village, Leviticus and his brother were gone. Vanished. Diego was robbed of his vengeance. The brothers were resigned to the history books. Most people thought them dead. Until you showed up."

Alex put his hand over his mouth and gasped. "It can't be him," he mumbled. "It can't be. The man I knew was gentle. He was kind. He took me in and gave me a home. He saved me. I'm a kid Diego's age, he didn't hurt me. He didn't hurt Jackson either."

Lasaria stopped. "Hold on," she

insisted. She cocked her head and listened. She sniffed the air. "I think we are getting close. There is a fire going not far along."

"But what if it wasn't him?" Alex implored. "It couldn't be him. Maybe another pair of twins. Another pair of twins with the same names…"

"If we get moving, we should be there shortly," Lasaria said. She looked at Alex. "And remember," she insisted, "not a word of this to anyone."

Alex bowed his head. "I guess I can understand why Diego hates me so much," he conceded. "But there has to be more. If they just disappeared like that, there has to be more."

"I am sure there is more." Lasaria set off. "There is always more. But I told you what I know. And with that you promised you would not ask for anything else."

"But," Alex protested. He struggled

to keep pace.

"No," Lasaria said sternly. "You are going to keep your promise. A person is only as honorable as their word. Don't make me regret thinking the best of you." She pulled ahead.

Alex slowed to a trot. Sweat poured off his forehead. "Slow down," he hollered.

"No," Lasaria yelled back. Her voice dissolved into the trees. "You need to hurry up. I am ravenous. I am not going to slow down for anything."

3

High above the sky had lightened. The clouds parted and the sun came out. Deuce, Diego, and Danice sat on the outskirts of a small clearing. A pile of kindling burned at the center of a stone ring. The aroma of roasting flesh hovered with the smoke. Three wooden skewers were whittled down and spiked into the ash. Hunks of charred meat were stuck on the top. Juices dripped into the embers. The fire flared and the food sizzled.

"What took you so long?" Danice hollered. She gnawed on a chunk of dark gray flesh. "I thought you were right behind me."

Lasaria jogged from the cover of the trees. She joined her companions and peeled her coat off. The chatter amongst the group was lively. Everyone was in high spirits. Deuce started to laugh. He grabbed his gut and doubled over. A smile spread over Danice's face. She said something and everyone hooted.

Alex stayed back. He slunk around the perimeter of the field. He drew near, paused, and waited at a distance. When no one said anything, he set his sack to the side. He slid his duster off and let it fall to the ground. When there were still no objections, he sat down and tucked his legs under his body.

"Hey," Alex said softly. He looked around the circle. "Smells really good."

Danice wiped her chin. "That is Diego for you," she said. Flecks of food flew from her mouth. "He is one of the best cooks around. Snare him some game and he will make you think you are at a royal feast." She tossed a piece of gristle on the fire. "And look at him. You would never think that with the way he looks. With all those muscles and such."

"You said that already," Diego snorted. He tore a chunk of meat from one of the skewers. He let it cool and handed it to Lasaria. "I cook as a practical matter. If you happen to enjoy what I have prepared, that is just a bonus."

Deuce chuckled. "A pretty nice

bonus if I do say so myself," he said. "I have eaten some interesting things in my time. Not all of them pleasant. Give me something like this every day and I could die a happy man."

"That is kind of you to say," Diego flushed. "But we should finish here and get back on the move." He grabbed another piece of meat and tossed it to Deuce. "We should stick together this time. We will be more conspicuous, but there is safety in numbers."

"How much longer?" Lasaria asked. She stopped eating and rubbed her hands on her tunic. "Can't be more than a day or two."

Diego nodded. "Just a half day once we are out of the forest. If we push, we should be back by midday tomorrow."

"What if we don't push?" Deuce moaned. He flopped to his back. "I am sick of pushing. I want to relax a little bit."

"Knock it off," Danice said sternly. She swatted Deuce on the foot.

"Yeah," Lasaria agreed, "knock it off." She chuckled. "But Diego is right, we should get going. I have cost us enough time already."

Deuce grinned. He smacked the dirt. "I don't want to," he whined.

Danice snatched Deuce by the ankle. "Stop it," she insisted. "We are going."

"That hurts." Deuce smacked her hand away. "I was joking. You know I was only joking."

"This really is not the time," Danice insisted. "Stop being a baby and let's go."

The mood suddenly shifted. Everyone began to move at once. Deuce sat up. He sighed, laughed, and hopped to his feet. Lasaria leaned back. She grabbed her jacket and threw it over her shoulder. Danice checked the area around her. Satisfied she had left nothing behind, she stood. Diego shoveled at the dirt. He buried the glowing cinders as best he could. When the smoke faded, he stomped out the remnants of the fire.

Alex stayed planted. "Do you mind if I have that?" he asked. "It smells really, really good." He motioned to the piece of food that remained.

Everyone stopped.

"You didn't eat?" Lasaria asked. She glanced around the group. "Why didn't you eat?"

Alex shrugged. "I didn't want to take something that wasn't mine," he said.

Diego pulled the spike from the ground. He held it out to Alex. "There might be some ash on it," he grumbled, "but otherwise it should be fine."

"Thanks," Alex mumbled. He pulled the meat from the skewer.

"And don't ask to eat," Lasaria said, "just eat. I mean don't steal food from the market or anything. But when there is food to be shared, share. We are not going to remind you of every meal. We are not your parents." She grimaced.

Alex bit a burnt end of meat. "It is really good," he said. He swallowed it down and chomped off another piece. "Really good."

Diego nodded. "Can you eat and walk at the same time?" he asked caustically.

"Come on," Lasaria implored, "play nice."

Alex waved his hand. "No," he said, "it's okay. I can totally eat and walk. I'm the idiot who forgot to ask for something earlier." He stuck the meat in his mouth and gathered his things. "I'm ready when you are."

"Good." Diego looked around. He drew a steel broadsword from his side. "Let's go."

4

They settled down for the night at the bottom of a shallow basin. A growth of peat covered the forest floor. Thick oaks towered over the backside of their camp. Dense greenery filled in the void between trunks. Thorn studded brambles wove through the heart of the shrubbery. A scorched log was wedged between the bifurcation of the two closest trees. It tilted at an angle and threatened to drop.

"No fire," Diego insisted. He slumped under the protection of a small rock outcrop. "We are already far too exposed. I had hoped to be out of the forest before nightfall. Clearly that did not happen. Now we will have to be more vigilant in our security."

The heat of the day dissipated. A frosty chill swept over the area.

"Man, I would really love to warm up," Deuce said. He shivered wildly.

"Are you sure we can't have a little fire," he joked.

Danice rolled her eyes. "Quiet down," she hissed, "or I'll smack you so hard." She took Deuce by the arm and pulled him close. "You will be fine. You are such a baby." They sat back and closed their eyes.

"I will take the first watch," Diego said forcefully. He laid his sword over his knees. "Try and get some rest. I want to be gone with the first bit of daylight."

Alex held his hand in the air. No one saw him so he waved it back and forth. "I'll take a turn," he said.

Diego shook his head. "No need. I will take the first shift and Danice the second. We will be gone before anyone else has to keep watch."

Lasaria shuffled over to Alex. "Thanks for the offer. Diego can be overprotective. He will probably just stay up until we go. It is kind of what he does when we are out in the open. Don't pay him any attention." She sat down and tucked up to his shoulder.

"I just want to help," Alex said softly. "To do my part." He glanced at Lasaria. His cheeks flushed pink.

"You do not need to worry about that right now." Lasaria leaned back. She tugged Alex on the collar of his jacket. "Get some sleep. Tomorrow is a big day for you. First time in proper civilization in how long?" she chuckled.

Alex huffed. "Whatever," he said. "If anybody should be worried, it's you. You stink worse than I do." He pinched his nose and wafted the air.

"Not bad," Lasaria giggled. Her lids drifted closed. "I think you will fit in fine around here. Only my closest companions can get away with talking to me like that."

Danice opened one eye. "Quiet," she asserted.

"Quiet," Diego agreed.

"Okay," Deuce snickered. Danice punched him in the arm and he fell quiet.

Silence descended. A breeze blew in and the trees rustled. Diego shifted positions. Leaves crunched under his movements. A branch snapped. The crack reverberated into the darkness. He stopped in place until the sound faded away. The silence returned and he went to the opposite side of the basin. He thrust his broadsword in the dirt and knelt beside it.

The rhythm of gentle breathing filled the air. The wind picked up. In the distance, a crow called out in distress. It screeched and took flight into the foliage. The uproar died off and everything was quiet. High above the clouds passed by. They cut the moon in two and obstructed what little light it had allowed. The stars disappeared from the sky. Something moved in the underbrush. The blackberry brambles at the rear of the camp stirred. Taciturn shadows scaled the trees in every direction.

"Come on," Diego whispered. He grabbed the hilt of his weapon and held it to the side. "Get up," he said frantically.

Lasaria rolled to her back. "What is going on?" she asked. "It cannot be time to go yet, can it?"

"No." Diego rapped Danice on the side. He did the same to Deuce. "Get your weapons out. I think we are surrounded."

"Weapons?" Alex murmured.

Diego grabbed Alex by the arm. "Time to finally put that dagger to use," he spat.

Alex jumped to his feet. He snatched

his sack with his left hand. He reached across his body and yanked the silver dagger from its scabbard with his right. The guard of the weapon caught the chain of the Manrikigusari. The links curled around the pommel. He tugged again and it tore free.

The group backed into a circle. Lasaria threw her bow up, an arrow notched, the string pulled tight. Diego clutched his broadsword with both hands. His left leg was positioned in front of his body. He stood on his toes with the blade perfectly vertical. Deuce and Danice melded into one. They rotated in harmony; matching curved blades held at the ready.

"Stop," a high-pitched voice pierced the silence from above. "Put your weapons down."

"We have you surrounded," someone screeched from the opposite side of the basin.

Diego bent back and forth. He searched for the source of the threat. "Who are you?" he bellowed. "What do you want?"

"I said put your weapons down," the voice above repeated the command.

"We won't put anything down until you tell us who you are." Diego took a step. He raised his weapon. "Show yourself."

A ridged spear launched into the air. It arced through the center of the group and planted in the ground at Diego's feet. The voice in the trees hooted. A second spear ripped in at a lower angle. The granite tip sliced Diego's arm. His shoulder dropped. He lost his grip and the broadsword wobbled to the side.

"Wait," Lasaria pleaded. "Just wait." She lowered her bow. She stuck the arrow in the quiver and put her hand up. "Get your weapons down. Diego, weapons down."

Diego hesitated. He grunted and lowered the sword. In short order, Deuce and Danice followed suit. Alex mimicked their movements. He dropped his hand to his side. He cinched his fingers around the grip of the dagger and positioned it behind his back. Lasaria glanced over. She locked her stare and winked.

"Smart," the man on the ground said.

"Very," the voice in the trees chirped.

Bright white sclera's blinked from all around. A single pair of eyes was wider than the others. They floated towards them through the darkness. A man slowly materialized. His skin was coated in a thick layer of mud. His hair was plastered to his head. A rectangular burlap cloth hung loose around his belly.

Deuce gasped. "Oh man," he muttered, "it is Lady Carol's Mudmen."

"What do you want with us?" Lasaria asked. She repeated herself when he said nothing.

"Answer her," Diego roared. Blood flowed down his arm.

The man smiled. "You," he said. He stuck his finger at Lasaria. "You come with us and nobody else has to get hurt."

Diego stepped in front of Lasaria. "That is not happening," he growled. He kept the tip of his blade pointed at the ground.

"You are outnumbered four to one," the man said. He took a step. "We will gladly kill all of you, but that was not the order. We just want her."

Deuce swung around. He stood arm to arm with Diego. "Yeah, that is not going to happen," he quipped.

"So be it." The man scowled. He took another step and held his hand into the air. "We need her alive," he yelled. "Kill everyone else."

Alex swung his arm to

the side. The point of his dagger tore into flesh. He twisted his wrist and shoved out as hard as he could. A piercing shriek escaped the man's lips. He stumbled backwards. His heel caught on an exposed root. He tripped, overcorrected, and fell forward. The blade sliced along the side of his sternum. It wedged into his ribs and got stuck. Blood poured from the gaping wound. Alex pulled back. His feet slipped out from under him as he scrambled to make his escape.

Diego wrapped his arm around Lasaria. He pushed her low to the ground and took off at a sprint. They crashed ahead. A spear ripped through the air. It sliced off a chunk of Diego's ear and buried in a tree behind them. He ignored the pain. Behind them, Deuce lifted his sword above his head. He danced backwards. A grin spread over his face. He shot forward and swiped at the closest set of eyes. Someone cried out in agony. He twirled and lunged for another target.

"Move it," Danice hollered. She reached back for Deuce. She tried again but couldn't break his attention. "Deuce, come on!" She took off running.

"I'll be right behind you," Deuce laughed.

The group charged into the protection of the forest. They weaved through a maze of branches. Behind them, someone shouted. A volley of arrows cut through the leaves. Someone screamed louder than the rest. The energy intensified. Dozens of voices barked incoherent commands. A sudden spike in the commotion was followed by silence.

They ran until the first bit of light illuminated their surroundings.

"Stop," Alex panted. "Wait." He dropped his hands to his knees and struggled to breath.

Lasaria slowed to a halt. "Are you okay?" she asked. She took a few deep breaths but was otherwise fine.

Diego was farther along. "We need to keep moving," he hollered. He turned back and then looked ahead. "We are almost out of here."

"It's just that," Alex said. He panted.

"Where is Deuce?" Danice interrupted. Her head shot around. He was nowhere to be seen. "Where is Deuce?" she shouted.

Alex dropped his sack. "Those things," he labored, "I think they got him."

"No," Lasaria gasped. "No, they couldn't have."

Diego trotted over. "What is wrong?" he asked. He looked about. "Where is Deuce?"

"They got him," Danice mumbled. "The Mudmen got him."

"Oh man," Diego groaned. "That is not good."

Danice went catatonic. "We have got to go and get him. We have got to go and get him," she repeated over and over.

"We can't." Diego put his hand out. "Not yet."

Danice shrugged him away. "We have to go get him," she said again. "We have to."

"Yeah," Alex agreed, "let's go."

Lasaria shook her head. "We will," she chimed in, "soon. But if we go now, we are as good as dead."

Alex stirred. "Those things," he huffed, "they weren't so tough."

"The Mudmen are just the start," Diego said. "They live in the woods around Lady Carol's plantation. But they were on us for a reason. They want Lasaria. That means they will use Deuce as bait. If we go charging in there, they will be ready. Best we regroup and formulate a plan."

"They won't kill him?" Alex asked. He looked at Danice. "I want to get him back."

Lasaria shook her head. "They will not kill him," she said, "they will use him."

"As bait," Alex confirmed.

"Not just bait," Danice murmured. Her eyes closed. She tilted her head to the sky. "Lady Carol needs someone to work her land. Whispers say she takes people in and never lets them leave. The same whispers say more. They say she turns them into something terrible. They say she turns them into monsters."

Alex gasped. "What? That can't be true."

"They say," Danice continued solemnly, "she turns them into zombies."

Chapter 8

1

The new day dawned and Diego, Danice, Lasaria and Alex left the forest behind. The impenetrable tangle of vegetation gave way to a field of squat pines. Long, tan grass filled the spaces between the trees. Bright purple flowers sat perched atop translucent stems. Tiny yellow bugs buzzed from one to the next. They disappeared in haste when their early morning breakfast was disturbed by the sudden appearance of intruders.

"We have got to go," Danice barked as they got into the open. She jogged ahead of the group. At the crest of a small rise, she paused and waited for them to catch up.

It wasn't long before they joined her. When they were all together, they paused to assess their surroundings. Before them, the ground tapered off at an incline. Thick roots and jagged chunks of stone protruded from arid soil. At the bottom, a vast grassland swept out as far as the eye could see. Rolling plains disappeared into a sea of blue sky. In the distance, a dark speck was just visible to the naked eye. A cloud of white smoke blanketed the horizon like a fog.

"That has to be Atina," Danice said. She analyzed the slope for a way to proceed. "If we can secure transportation we should be to the castle by nightfall.

With a little bit of luck, we might even be back on the road tomorrow."

"I know someone that can help," Diego asserted. "She will get us whatever we need. I will just have to find her first."

Lasaria snorted. "Do not tell me you're talking about Rosa," she said. She smacked Diego with the back of her hand. "Is it Rosa?" she demanded.

Diego looked away. "What would you have me do?" he asked. He said something to Danice and she nodded. "We need help. If you know of anyone else, please tell me."

"After everything she did," Lasaria snorted. "After everything she put you through. Even her own family will not have anything to do with her. They exiled her to the middle of nowhere for a reason."

Danice got down. She lowered herself over the drop and tested her weight on a corner of stone. "Stop this," she said coldly. "We have more pressing matters to attend to. If Rosa can help, then we will let her help. Diego and I can go ahead and find her. Lasaria, you and Alex meet us on the north side of the village when you arrive. That way you will never even have to see her. But please," she added, "hurry." She turned her head and dropped. A trail of dust drifted up behind her as she disappeared.

"What did she just do?" Alex stammered. He peered over the ledge. Danice was already on her feet at the bottom. "I'm not doing that."

Diego seethed. "Then go around," he said vilely. He pivoted and disappeared.

"Oh come on," Alex moaned. "No way."

"We will find a different way," Lasaria said. She looked down the ridgeline. "Follow me."

The ridge curved around in a

sweeping arc. It climbed higher before falling away at a gradual slope. Along the lip, trees and brush ripped from the earth. Chunks of sod were upturned and completely dried out. Centipedes scuttled about. Rocks broke free from the soil and littered the base of the decline.

They walked along the edge of the drop. When he couldn't take it anymore, Alex turned to Lasaria. "So that woman Danice was talking about," he said, "Lady Carol she called her. She's going to turn Deuce into a zombie. Like walking dead, brain eating, flesh falling off zombie?"

Lasaria furrowed her brow. "I don't know what any of that means," she stated.

"Where I'm from we have all sorts of stories about zombies," Alex said. "Movies too. Sometimes people die and come back as zombies. They walk around with their arms held out looking for brains to eat."

"What?" Lasaria coughed. "They actually eat people's brains. So, they are cannibals?"

Alex laughed. "Well no, I don't think so," he said. "They're already dead so I don't know what they would be called."

"The dead come back to life?" Lasaria asked loudly. "When the people we know die, they stay dead."

"Well it isn't real," Alex acknowledged. "The stories are fiction."

"They are what?" Lasaria came to a halt. She crossed her arms over her chest.

Alex faltered. "They're fake," he said.

"Our zombies are not fake." Lasaria turned and continued. "They are not the walking dead or brain eaters either," she asserted. "And they are very much alive."

"What are they?" Alex asked. He hustled so he could walk next to Lasaria. "There are so many things I don't know about," he exclaimed. "Zombies. Mudmen. War. It's just all so much."

Lasaria hastened her pace. "You already know about the Mudmen," she started, "or as much as any of us know, really. They were nomads who settled the woods back there. They chose a side in this war and now they take their orders from Lady Carol. The zombies are something different. Something much more terrifying. Our stories say Lady Carol turns people into slaves, that she gains control over their mind and wipes it clean. She takes away their humanity. And then she implants a single purpose, to serve her."

"Deuce," Alex whispered.

"Yes," Lasaria agreed, "Deuce. You see why Danice is so worried. If the stories are true, it may already be too late to save him. Our only hope is if Lady Carol keeps him as bait. If she does that, we might still have a chance."

"Then why didn't we go after him?" Alex interrupted. "We could have chased those Mudmen down and gotten him back."

Lasaria slumped her head. "It is not that simple," she said. "If we could have just gone after him, I would have, believe me. But we were outnumbered. The Mudmen know those woods better than we ever could. And Lady Carol's plantation is impenetrable. No," she insisted, "better we formulate a plan, gear up, and then go and get Deuce back."

"Okay," Alex said. "But what about Lady Carol? Why would she want you in the first place? Plus, those things were chasing you when we met. Why were they after you? Who are you exactly?"

"Me?" Lasaria said absently. "I am

nobody." She peered over the edge. "I think we can make a go of it. It is still a long way, but the landing looks like it will be softer."

Alex looked down. His head got woozy and he stumbled back. "Come on," he gasped. "That's still so far."

Lasaria turned. "Everything I told you and you still won't slide down this little hill. Well good luck then." She stepped over the edge and vanished.

"What?" Alex gaped. He glanced over the edge. "Come on," he said again.

Dust flittered in the air. The wind blew and a track materialized through the haze. The intimidating drop was gone. A slight gradient started vertical but promptly transitioned into an oblique decent. It plunged straight down to the bottom of the cliff. Lasaria stood at the base of the slope. She waved her arm over her head and hollered. Her words floated away on the breeze. She yelled again and walked off.

"Wait," Alex shouted frantically. Lasaria tilted her head. She slowed but didn't stop. "Come on, just wait a minute," he shouted again. "I'm coming." Lasaria continued to get farther away.

Alex clapped his hands. He sat on the lip of the ridge and kicked his legs out. Gravel rolled down the slope. A large stone slid out from under him and tumbled away. When the dust settled, he lowered himself as far down as he could. He held in place until his biceps began to burn. His elbows trembled.

"Here I go," Alex sighed. He clenched his jaw and fell away from the edge.

The ground came up fast. Alex landed on his backside. His arms flew up over his head and he started to slide. He pulled his sack to his chest and hugged it tight. His free hand clawed at the ground. He dug his heels in and a cloud of dust engulfed him. After a second, the drop leveled off and he came to a rest.

"See," Lasaria laughed, "that wasn't so bad." She put her hand out and helped Alex to his feet. "Although for a minute, there, I thought you were going to kill yourself."

Alex got up and dusted himself off. "Thanks for coming back for me," he scoffed. He straightened the lapel of his trench coat. "I figured you were just going to leave me here like everyone else," he added.

Lasaria starred into the distance. "Knock it off," she demanded. She put her hand over her eyes to deflect the glare of the sun. "We should hurry. Diego and Danice are probably already to Atina. I doubt they will wait for us if we take too long."

"Give me a second," Alex said. "I

almost died getting down here."

"Give you a second?" Lasaria snapped. "Give me a break. If that is your idea of some sort of ordeal you should probably stay back while we rescue Deuce. Things are bound to get a lot more dangerous from here on out."

"I was only joking," Alex assured her. He flipped his sack. It hit the center of his back and he winced. "Well," he said, "let's go then."

Lasaria put her hand out. "Remember what I just told you," she urged. "Things are going to get a lot more dangerous. You have already watched one friend die. If you continue with us, chances are you will see many more cross the River Styx."

Alex stiffened his spine. "I'll do whatever I can to get Deuce back," he said confidently. "I'll do whatever I can or die trying."

2

The village of Atina was a small hamlet settled atop a sweeping knoll. A hodgepodge of wooden huts and stone structures lined a central thoroughfare. Broken cobblestones were covered in a thick layer of soot. The pungent stench of burning oil overwhelmed the senses. Smoke poured from an edifice at the end of the street. A crowd of men stood single file at the door. When one person left, another entered in turn.

"Let's go around," Lasaria said. She tugged Alex by the arm. They slipped between a row of houses. "It is not a big town. Someone is bound to recognize me if we spend too much time here."

Alex followed Lasaria into the shadows. "Why do all these people care about you?" he asked. He stayed close behind as they dashed from one point of cover to the next. "The Mudmen want you. That Lady Carol wants you. Now you're worried about people in the village recognizing you. What's going on here? Are you famous or something?"

Lasaria crept up to the corner of a toppled hovel. She poked her head out and surveyed the way ahead. "I'm nobody," she insisted. "I want to keep a low profile is all." She shuffled over a gravel road and waved for Alex to follow.

"They have to be after you for some reason," Alex continued. "You're special or something. I know it."

"You talk too much," Lasaria interrupted. Her head swiveled. "We should be close. The barn behind the slaughterhouse, we can wait there until twilight. If they have not arrived by then we will set off on our own."

"The barn behind the what?" Alex scoffed. "It sounded like you said slaughterhouse."

They crossed a robust intersection. A passing pedestrian eyed them as they went by. An older woman watched from her front porch. She yawned and went back inside. On the far side of the street a group of men engaged in a heated conversation. One of them gestured manically. Someone slugged him in the face. His eyes rolled back into his head and he dropped to the ground. The commotion suddenly erupted into a fit of violence.

"Let's go," Lasaria said. She passed the uproar. When they were out of sight she started to jog.

"Seriously," Alex huffed, "did you say slaughterhouse?"

An open pasture buttressed against the town boundary. A sunken stone culvert ran the length of the field. It veered around in an arc and disappeared beneath the side of a slatted wooden barn. A dark, gelatinous sludge inched its way along the bottom of the ditch. Solid chunks of pliable material stuck to the stone walls.

"Disgusting," Alex gagged. He pinched his nose. "What is all this stuff? It looks, and smells, terrible."

Lasaria jumped the gap. "Don't touch that stuff," she insisted. She offered a helping hand, but Alex refused. "It is a slurry runoff from the factory. They use it as feed for all the animals in the castle. It is horrible stuff, but they eat it right up."

Alex hopped over and they jogged behind the barn. "I don't even know what to say," he scoffed. He sat down and leaned against the building. "And Diego knows someone who lives here? Who could stand this place for more than an hour?"

"Atina may not look pretty," Lasaria said, "but it serves an important function. Without it our animals would starve and so too, would we." She got to her knees. "But Rosa is another story all together. She is here because there is nowhere left for her to go. If I had it my way, I would have her banished away to The Barrens."

"What did she do that was so bad?" Alex asked. He tilted his head back and closed his eyes.

"She's really not that bad," Lasaria relented. "But she hurt someone I care for. That is not something I can easily forgive."

"Diego," Alex mumbled. "She hurt Diego?"

Lasaria smacked Alex on the leg. "A story for another day I am afraid," she said. "I see Danice. And Diego. He's riding a… Oh, come on," she moaned.

"What?" Alex followed Lasaria's eyes. "At least we don't have to walk for a while," he said. They got to their feet and hustled into the pasture.

Diego sat atop a single seat at the head of a wooden wagon. Deep mahogany timber was cut into a rectangular body. Thick planks formed a box at the rear of the cart. A pair of iron axels were secured to the undercarriage with steel spikes. Large black wheels were connected to the center of the axels by a series of spokes. At the front, a single thoroughbred was tethered to the yoke. Its head was held high on a long, muscular neck. White mesh fabric covered its eyes and ears. It trotted along the path at a leisurely pace.

Danice walked ahead of the conveyance. She saw Lasaria and Alex and held her hand in the air. They were still a bit off. She turned towards Diego and said something. He shook his head.

She motioned towards the back of the cart. He shook his head and looked away. Danice kicked at the dirt. She grunted and gave up.

"I thought we would have enough horses to go around," Lasaria quipped. She stripped her jacket off and tossed it behind Diego. "Not bad though. Did Rosa help you find this? Or maybe it was hers and she gave it to you," she snickered dryly.

Diego rolled his eyes. "It is Rosa's cart, but she did not give me anything, she borrowed it to me. I promised to drop it off on my way back through town."

Lasaria laughed. "Looks like she made a nice little life for herself out here," she said. "With your gold no doubt."

"That is not fair," Diego retorted. "She did not have many options and you know that."

"Enough," Danice roared. "You will have time for this argument later. Right now, all I want to do is get to Sparham. The longer we stand around, the longer it takes to get home."

Alex nodded. "I'm glad we don't have to walk for a bit," he said awkwardly. He set his sack in the back and clambered in after it. "Plus, it is kind of cozy in here. There's a lantern in case it gets dark. Some hay to stretch out on."

"It could be filled with thorns," Danice snapped, "and we would still be getting in." She climbed onto the side of the cart and put her hand out. Lasaria clasped her by the forearm. Danice dragged her up and they both hopped in. "Let's go," she yelled.

Diego cracked the reigns. The horse neighed and they jerked into motion. Far above the sun tracked their movements through the sky. They followed a heavily trodden path that stretched into the valley. People went by in both directions. Hard men on horseback galloped up behind them and passed without incident. A convoy of empty wagons rolled towards Atina. Half a dozen armed guards' road in columns at the front and rear. Three women went by in a covered carriage. They looked out on the passerby's and quickly spun away.

"I am going crazy." Danice broke the silence. She grabbed her hair and yanked a handful from her head. "I cannot stop thinking about Deuce. We should have gone back for him. We did not even look to see if the Mudmen left him behind. What kind of sister am I to just leave him like that? I would not have done that to any of you. But my brother, my own brother."

Lasaria curled her fingers around Danice's hand. "Stop," she said. "Hurting yourself is not going to help anyone. And I am fairly certain Deuce would freak out if he came back and you were bald."

"I just," Danice mumbled, "I just don't know what to do. I cannot stop thinking of him. All the horrible things Lady Carol could be doing to him right now. It is too much. My head feels like it is going to explode." She smacked her forehead with her free hand.

"I said stop it," Lasaria demanded.

"Tell me about him," Alex chimed in. He sat up and pulled his knees to his chest. "I mean tell me about you guys, about your family."

Lasaria shot Alex a cold stare. "It is not your place to meddle," she said. "Who do you think you are?"

Alex shrugged. "It might help," he insisted.

"And it might not," Lasaria responded. "The last thing she wants to do is –"

"No," Danice interjected, "I think Alex is right. Everything just keeps spinning over and over in my mind. The things we have gone through together. The things we have seen. I cannot believe," she faltered, "I cannot believe it could all be done. That I might never see my little brother again."

"Don't say that. You will see him again," Lasaria's voice cracked. "We will all see him again."

A smile played at the corner of Danice's lip. "I remember when he was born. I was a few years old and I told our mother that I did – not – want – another – brother," she said emphatically. "Then he came along and that was it, we were thick as thieves. And when we got older actual thieves."

Lasaria smiled. "I think that is how my father came to know you," she said. "The Great Bandits of Braha Market they called you."

Danice threw her head back and laughed. "And all we did was take a little food," she heaved. "Those merchants were ready for blood. It did not help that we eventually tried to sell it back to them at a discount. I guess we were not very bright back then."

Lasaria started to laugh. "Oh, they wanted you dead alright. I was Deuce's age. I told my father if he was going to punish the two of you, he'd have to punish me too."

"That night was the first time we slept in doors in ages." Danice put her hand to her chest and took a deep breath. "And the first time we had bathed in even longer."

"Oh, I remember that," Lasaria barely managed to get out. "The stink was unbearable," she teased.

Alex raised his hand in the air. Danice pointed to him. "I don't get it," he chortled. "Why were you stealing in the first place? Were you just having fun or something? Because I get that. At the orphanage I didn't take extra food because I had too, I did it because I knew it would drive the nuns crazy."

The laughter died away. "By then we had to take the food," Danice said. "There wasn't much of a choice. After our village was destroyed, we did what we had to do. We were just kids and we were on our own."

"What," Alex started to say. He trailed off and looked around. "What happened?" he asked.

Lasaria smacked Alex on the leg. "Don't ask her that," she snarled. "What is wrong with you?"

"It is okay," Danice said dryly. She shifted. "We lived in a little logging village not far from here. There were six of us in all. Deuce and I were the youngest. We had two older brothers, Dutch, and Darry. It was mostly peaceful. A few animal attacks here and there, some sibling squabbles, but nothing our elders couldn't handle.

But then everything changed. People came to our village. Terrible people that couldn't be reasoned with. Our parents made us take cover in the woods. When they didn't return, our brothers went looking for them. Night came. We heard screaming. A fire sparked to life and destroyed everything we knew. After that we just huddled together under the cover of a large pine."

"Oh no," Alex gasped. He put his hand over his mouth.

"When morning came," Danice continued, "we heard someone crying out for us. Our father and our brothers were gone. Our mother had survived, but barely. I remember she used to wear these little yellow flowers in her hair. She would give them to Deuce and I and we would take them down to the river. Most of the time we would set them in the current and watch them float away. When we found her, she still had one of those flowers. After everything she had gone through, after everything she had seen, she still had one of those flowers."

"You don't have to talk about this anymore," Lasaria assured Danice. "It is alright to stop."

Danice dropped her head. "Anyway," she said, "after that we had no where to go. We found ourselves in Sparham stealing to stay alive. That is when we met Lasaria, here, and never had to steal again."

Alex stroked his chin. He looked at Lasaria cockeyed. "What is it about you?" he asked. "I have some ideas, but they seem foolish."

Lasaria sighed. "I am nobody," she assured him again. "But what about you? Don't you think these two deserve to know how you got here, how you came to know Leviticus."

Up front Diego squirmed. "I sure as hell would like to know," he derided.

"Me too," Danice agreed.

Alex was silent for a moment. "Alright," he relented, "but you'd better let me tell the whole story. Don't cut me off or stop listening because I talk about Leviticus."

Diego shuddered. "Just talk," he said snidely, "and I will not say a word."

"Alright." Alex took a deep breath. "Let me tell you about my life."

3

Diego drove the cart at a hastened pace. In the distance, an imposing stone barrier had been visible for much of the day. They drew near and foot traffic increased with some consistency. Men and women scuttled about. They caught site of the wagon and hurried to get out of the way. A farmer trudged from the surrounding fields. An emaciated ox followed behind. As the sun set, brass braziers along the length of the wall came to life. Bright orange orbs lit up the sky like beacons in the night.

They arrived at the capital city of Sparham at dusk. The path narrowed and came to an end at the bottom of a pair of arched doors. Deep gouges and tiny punctures scarred the surface of the wood. The right side of the entrance was black with scorch marks. A wrought iron portcullis had been lowered halfway down. Soldiers in dark silver breastplates and matching helms stood on either side. They waited at attention.

"How is it going boys?" Diego asked. He pulled on the reigns and the horse came to a halt.

One of the soldiers hurried forward. "Diego," he said eagerly, "King Wasagowi has had us stationed out here for days. He would have sent a search party if you were not back by morning."

"We are almost all here," Diego conceded. "One extra in fact. Hurry up and open the gate. We need to get to the castle right away."

The second soldier motioned to someone on top of the wall. A piercing whine came from overhead. There was a thud and the doors crept open. "Of course, sir," the soldier said. "But what do you mean by 'almost' all here? And who is this extra companion you speak of? He will not be allowed an audience with the King. Not at this hour anyway."

Alex lifted his head. He went to say something and Lasaria pushed him down. "He will not be meeting with the King," she snarled. "Diego and I will be doing that alone. Now hurry up and get those doors open. Every minute you keep us here is a minute you have wasted."

Both soldiers snapped erect. "Princess," they said in unison.

"We did not see you there," one of the soldiers included.

Lasaria curled her lip. "Yes," she scoffed, "I can see that. Now step aside. I have an urgent matter I need to discuss with my father."

"Of course," the soldier on the left said.

"Your father will be waiting for you in the throne room," the other finished. They both ducked to the side and bowed.

Diego snapped his wrists. The horse snorted and lifted its hoof in the air. "Yeah, yeah," he said to the animal, "you are almost done for the night." He looked over at the two men. "Carry on," he told them. "You know your job better than I do." He cracked the lead and the horse jump into motion.

"Princess," Alex muttered, "were they serious?" He glared at the back of Lasaria's head. "Were they serious?" he demanded an answer from her.

Danice touched Alex on the arm. "Come on," she said to him, "you and I are going to The Blood and Dagger." She scuttled over to Diego and tapped him on the shoulder. "It is just a fancy name for the Knight's Guild," she added to avert any confusion. "We get off here."

"Diego and I will take the wagon over to the stables," Lasaria told them. "After that we will go and see my father. When we are done, we will meet you at The Blood and Dagger.

With any luck, we can be on our way by morning."

"Please hurry," Danice pleaded. She hopped over the side. "And do not take no for an answer. Either way I am leaving tomorrow. With or without your father's approval."

Lasaria nodded. "He will not say no," she promised. "He will probably want to save Deuce himself."

Danice took Alex by the arm. "I know." She helped him down. "But the idea of sitting there all night doing nothing is killing me."

"As soon as we can," Lasaria said firmly.

"As soon as you can," Danice urged.

Diego pulled the reigns. "Go," he bellowed. The horse put its snout in the air. It tossed its head back and the cart lurched forward.

The natural light died away. The sun set and the moon was absent from the sky. A woman in a dark blue blouse with long white hair stepped from a building. She ignited the wick on a brass lantern and hung it next to her door. Her neighbors followed in kind. The city was suddenly awash in firelight.

"What do we do now?" Alex asked. He looked around and shivered. "Without you helping me out, I'd be lost," he readily admitted. "But I sure would love to meet a real-life knight."

Danice pivoted towards a side street. "You have already met more than one," she said. "Now follow me." She took off without another word.

They disappeared into a back alley. Away from the main thoroughfare the light quickly vanished. A compact scattering of stone buildings was set a few feet apart. Behind a two-story structure, a man sat slumped over. His head was rolled to the side and his eyes were barely open. The aroma of barley engulfed the tight space. An array of cracked wooden crates and broken clay vases littered the ground. The debris was stacked into piles and clogged the way ahead.

"Where are we going?" Alex asked. He maneuvered around a pair of feet that stuck from a pile of boards. "Who are all these people."

Danice kept on the move. She left one alley and turned down another. "Most of them drink in the tavern up the road. They do not have anywhere else to go so they sleep it off back here."

"So, they're not dead?" Alex inquired. "Because they sure looked dead to me."

"Some of them are probably dead," Danice said bluntly. "But we have other things to worry about right now. We always have other things to worry about," she trailed off.

They traversed a series of back alleys

and their pace slowed to a steady crawl. The litter and filth of the outer districts were replaced by cloth nets and squat cylindrical barrels farther in. They went deeper and the smaller stone buildings gave way to more imposing structures. In one alley, a large flat chest was tucked behind a reinforced steel door. In another, cloth tunics dangled from a long wooden I beam. Near the center of the city, every two buildings shared a single alleyway to themselves.

"We are here," Danice announced. She went to a nondescript door and rapped her knuckles.

"Wait a second," Alex said. He shifted and looked at the ground. "I've got to ask you something before we go in."

Danice took her hand off the door. "Okay," she said, "what is it?"

Alex bit his lower lip. "Is Lasaria really a princess?" he finally asked. He kicked the ground and looked away. "I mean like a real-life princess?"

"Oh, she's a princess alright," Danice said.

"Wow," Alex marveled. "She seems so tough. I always figured a princess would be in a pink dress and maybe braids or something. I didn't expect her to be..." he thought for a second.

"To be what?" Danice put her hands on her hips.

Alex shook his head. "No, no, nothing bad," he insisted. "But she is so..." he thought again. "Tough," he repeated.

"Not only is she tough," Danice said, "but I have seen her kill more people than you can count on both your hands. And if you do not behave yourself," she teased, "she just might kill you too."

The back door to the building slowly opened. A petite young lady with a tan dress and tight white shirt smiled.

"Danice," the girl said gleefully. "I am so glad you're back." She looked at Alex and frowned. "You are not Deuce." She peered over his shoulder and shifted her focus back to Danice. "Where is my sweetheart?" she asked. "Where is Deuce?"

Chapter 9

1

The room was on the third level of The Blood and Dagger. It was nearly empty say for a single leather pad supported by a wooden frame. Uneven stone bricks were mortared together and into a lopsided addition. The floor was beveled from one wall to the next. A long tapestry was secured to a steel rod above a concealed doorway. The ceiling leaned in at an obstructive angle. Heat radiated up from the floors below. In the corner, a crooked window was thrown open. A brilliance of moonlight suffused the space in a temperate blue glow.

Alex laid with his tunic wrapped around his head. He remained perfectly still until his nose started to itch. When he couldn't take it any longer, he reached up and scratched. He made a second attempt to sleep. He tossed over and huffed. After a few minutes he gave up. He rolled to his back and sat up.

"Well that's that," Alex said. "Can't say I didn't try." He untied the shirt around his head. He stretched his arms in the air and yawned.

His vision returned and Alex jerked his legs over the side of the bed. He reached down and felt for the ground. His fingers brushed over the Manrikigusari. The steel links were cool to the touch. The stones weighted at either end felt lighter. The sack was where he had left it the night before. The silver dagger was still hidden away underneath.

Alex got up and dressed. He secured the Manrikigusari around his waist and did the same with his dagger. He finished getting ready, picked up the sack, and sat on the bed. The knot was tied tight. He worked his fingernail under a loop. After a brief struggle, he managed to get a bit of slack. He loosened the knot and unfurled the bundle.

The pink shards that lined the bottom of the sack had been crushed into a fine powder. A silver ring was mangled, the inset gem broken from its setting. The necklace with six turquoise stones was the only other item that appeared to be damaged. The clasp at the back was bent at a ninety-degree angle. The two ends barely held together. All the remaining jewelry was still intact.

The loose stones and faceted crystals looked no different than they had before. A rainbow of colors coalesced into a single heap.

Alex pushed the jewelry to the side. He grabbed the cloth and dumped the contents onto the bed. With one quick motion he tore the sack down the center. He gathered up the rings, the necklace, and most of the stones and put them in one half. He took the remaining stones and put them in the other. After both sacks were secure, Alex put his boots on. He got to his knees and slid the sack with the jewelry under the bed. He pushed it until it jammed against the wall. Confident it was out of sight, he stood. He put the second sack into his trousers, checked to be certain he hadn't left anything out in the open, and dipped through the tapestry.

Outside the room, the floor suddenly fell away. A series of pegs were hammered into the vertical decent. Each stuck out just enough for a person to get a toe and a hand on to navigate. At the base of the wall, a long corridor ended at a set of steep stairs. Thick wooden doors were spaced along either side in even intervals. Brass sconces flickered with dim white light.

Alex lowered himself onto the pegs. He climbed down and made his way through the hall. At the top of the stairs he paused. A low, inaudible drawl came from the chamber below. A woman spoke in a monotone repetition. She talked but her words seemed heavy. When she was done, a high, female voice responded. It elevated in pitch and the person sobbed.

The crying became muffled. Alex took two deep breaths and went down. Danice stood near the center of the room. A petite young lady with dark brown hair stood before her. Her arms were draped around Danice's waist. Danice clenched her in a bearhug. Her chin was propped on top of her head. She caught site of Alex and nodded.

Danice held the girl out. She smiled and kissed her on the forehead. "This is him," she said to the girl. She turned her attention to Alex. "Could not sleep?" she asked. She didn't wait for an answer. "That is good. I know you want to help us save Deuce. This, this right here, it shows me where your head is at." She nodded.

Alex walked to the far wall. "I really wanted to get some rest," he said, "but I just can't stop thinking of Deuce. It is making it impossible to sleep." He pulled a stool from under a small table and sat.

The young girl yelped.

"We did not have time for a proper introduction last night," Danice interposed. She touched the girl on the shoulder. "This is Alex. I was just telling you about him." She led her over and they sat. "And Alex, this is Sai Lee," she said. "As you have probably already guessed, she and Deuce are close."

The girl yelped again. "I am," she hiccupped, "so sorry about last night. When Danice told me what happened to Deuce, I kind of lost it."

Alex shook his head. "No, no, it's fine," he assured her. He reached his hand out but pulled back. "This can't be easy, but I'll do whatever I can to get Deuce back. I feel like this is all my fault anyway. If I hadn't attacked that guy in the forest, maybe we could have all gotten out of there. Instead I just acted without thinking. I used to do that all the time at the orphanage. Man, I can be so stupid sometimes."

"Come now," Danice said, "you did not do anything wrong. Without you, we could have all been captured. This way we have a chance. We still have a chance."

"I thought," Alex said tentatively, "I thought you hated me." He dropped his gaze. "I would hate me if I was you."

"If you think I hate you," Danice sighed, "then that is my fault. Deuce is gone and I took my anger out on the rest of you. Diego, Lasaria, they know me. They know I did not mean anything by it. You and I have only just met. You do not know me in the slightest. My actions were unacceptable. Please, Alex, forgive me."

Alex looked up. "There is nothing to forgive," he said flatly. "You didn't do anything wrong. Let's get Deuce back from Lady Carol and none of this will even matter."

Sai Lee sniffled. "I want to go," she said intently. "Deuce needs me, and I know I can help."

"Deuce will kill me if I

bring you with," Danice insisted. "Plant me in the ground, bury me, never to return, dead."

"But I need to go," Sai Lee persisted. "You cannot stop me. I want to go. I am going to go." She hit the table.

"No," Danice said directly. "I am not going to have this conversation with you again. Our forces are spread thin enough as it is. Your job is here at The Blood and Dagger. You need to prep the empty room upstairs for our return. If Deuce is under the influence of Lady Carol, or gravely injured, we will not have much time to act. You need to stay here."

Sai Lee croaked. She heaved and continued to cry. "Do not say that," she muttered, "please do not say that."

"This is why we need you here," Danice said. She got to one

knee and focused on Sai Lee. "You will get your chance to fight, I promise you, but not today. Not tomorrow. I know you are a skilled warrior. But all the training, all the strength in the world, does not matter a pinch when your mind is not in it. If you go out there, the chances you come back are slim. If you can trust us, and I know how difficult that is going to be, we will get Deuce back. We will all make it back ali –"

There was a bang in the next room and they jumped. Danice shot to her feet. Alex dropped his hand to his belt and yanked the dagger free. He spun around in his seat and nearly fell. Sai Lee sprung up. Her stool flew back and tumbled to the floor. She took two steps and froze.

"Just me," a deep voice droned. "I can hear you acting all crazy over there." Diego marched in. "Good," he said to Alex, "you are awake."

Alex glanced at Danice. She shrugged. "Me?" he asked. "Are you talking to me?" He put his dagger away.

"Yes, you," Diego assured. "There is a blacksmith you need to meet. He is prepping a weapon for you as we speak. He needs to know your height to properly weight the blade."

Danice moved to the side. "I guess nobody is getting any sleep tonight," she said. "Where is Lasaria," she suddenly asked.

Diego motioned for Alex to stand. "She will be here shortly," he said. "She is meeting with her father now. He is trying to convince her not to come with us. Said he wants Deuce back, but not at the expense of his daughter."

Danice scoffed. "Are you kidding me?"

"We tried to raise an army," Diego said, "we really did. But in the end, it will is just us going after Deuce. Me, you, Lasari." He paused and closed his eyes. "And Alex. The four of us are going to take on the whole of Lady Carol's plantation. I would say the odds are slim but honestly," he faltered, "I do not think we have any odds at all."

"See," Sai Lee shouted, "you need me."

"No," Danice said emphatically. "I have already told you no. You two." She gestured to Diego and Alex. "Go to the blacksmith, but hurry back. I want to be on the road at sunrise. I will not wait any longer than that. For me, today, I get Deuce back. I get Deuce back or I die trying."

2

Diego hustled from The Blood and Dagger and Alex followed. The streets were empty. The night sky was clear. The stars and moon were unobstructed and made it easy for them to see. They turned left and away from center of the city. The ornate stone buildings closest to the King's castle gave way to structures of more modest means. A series of small terraces were covered with straps of leather. The smell of chromium sulfate hung in the air. A lone man slept in a vacant lot. He coughed, choked, and started to snore.

Alex followed in silence. He tried to keep pace, fell behind, and jogged to match Diego. They approached the outer city wall and turned off the main road. Diego maneuvered passed a large chunk of limestone. He ducked under a line strung between two buildings. The alley narrowed and spit them out onto a gravel street. They crossed over an adjoining intersection and finally stopped on the front stoop of a diminutive building.

Repetitive bangs emanated from inside. A splintered wooden sign hung on an iron rod. An anvil was etched deep into the grain.

"A friend of mine is a blacksmith," Diego said. "He is not usually awake at this hour. Today he made an exception." He banged on the door. "I expect he will still be in a foul mood. Do not think anything of it."

The hammering ceased. A deep voice mumbled something, and the door creaked open. A short, thin man wrenched back. Thick wire glasses balanced on the end of his nose. A bushel of white, frizzy hair was tangled in a horseshoe around the side of his head. The exposed skin was covered in a thick layer of soot.

"Need some help with that Marvin?" Diego asked. He put his hand on the door and shoved it open.

Marvin ambled backwards.

"Careful," he growled. "That is why I keep it open during the day. It helps with the heat but mainly, I cannot open the stupid thing all alone." He pushed up on the rim of his glasses and did his best to flatten his hair.

Diego stepped through the doorway. "Come on in." He turned and swept his arm out. "This is Alex," he said to Marvin. "And Alex, this is Marvin." When Alex got inside, Diego went back out.

On the far side of the room, a large hearth barely contained a roaring fire. An anvil was bolted to the center of the floor. The face was chipped and dented. The horn was warped and unrecognizable. Near the apparatus, a large barrel was filled with ashen water. On the side wall, a wooden case was loaded with steel ingots.

"As you can see, I specialize in blades," Marvin said. He disappeared up a small set of stairs and returned with a piece of rope. "I am going to craft a weapon specifically for you." He measured the length of Alex's legs. "Diego tells me you are good with a dagger. Do you think you can handle something bigger?" He finished and measured his arms.

"I think so," Alex said softly. Marvin spun him around and he didn't resist. "My Manrikigusari is pretty heavy and I've learned to use that. I could adapt."

Marvin finished his measurements. "Yes, yes, yes," he agreed, "I am sure you can." He went to the cabinet and ran his finger over an iron ingot. "The perfect piece. Each blade needs the perfect piece," he uttered.

Diego came inside. "Do you have everything?" he asked Marvin. "Because we need to go. We have one more stop to make before we head back. And you need to make that weapon. We cannot wait around if you have not got it finished."

"I will get it done," Marvin said indifferently. He felt another ingot and went to the next. "Stop by on your way out of the city. You will not be disappointed in what I have for young Alex, here."

"I am never disappointed in your work." Diego wiped the sweat from his eyes. "But time is not our friend today. You either get it done, or we leave without it."

Marvin waved them away. "Now you are interrupting me," he snarked. "So leave. Come back at dawn and I will have your weapon."

"One more stop," Diego said. He put his hand on Alex's neck and led him out the door.

Alex shook away. "You told him I was good with my dagger?" He smirked.

"We need to get you some armor."

Diego said. He glanced up and down the street. "We cannot have you face Lady Carol in what you have on."

"I don't need anything else," Alex insisted eagerly. He pulled the collar of his duster with both of his hands. "This jacket, these clothes, they are special to me. Besides that, I think there is actually something special about them."

Diego looked at Alex cockeyed. "What do you mean by that?" he asked. He inspected the outer layer of the outfit. "The coat is impractical. It is far too large for you to wear. And it will only serve to get in the way when you need to flee again. I am surprised it did not cause you problems back there in the forest."

"Look." Alex ignored the bait. "Lasaria called it Athenian Armor. She said it was really rare." He opened his coat and stroked the lining. "So far all it has done is keep me dry. But that was cool enough as it is. With a name like

Athenian Armor, I figure it can do a whole lot more than that."

"Where did you get this?" Diego asked forcefully. "Athenian Armor does not exist. It is something we would jest about in the barracks. That whoever could get Athena's armor would be unstoppable. But we always imagined it to be a piece of wonderful magnificence. Not a simple ensemble of mismatched items."

Alex chuckled awkwardly. "I don't know about all that," he insisted. "Even if this is, somehow, Athenian Armor it can't be what you were thinking of. I just like it because it is comfortable. And it keeps me dry. I probably wouldn't be able to walk, let alone fight, in anything heavier than a thin fabric."

"The thing is," Diego said breathlessly, "I recall a man who wore something similar to what you have on. Minus the coat, but the tunic, the trousers." He didn't blink. "The colors are the same. Maybe faded a bit but they are the same. Plus, they are big on you. Quite big."

"I," Alex stuttered, "no." He ambled backwards.

"I did not notice it until this moment," Diego continued. "But now I see it. I had a good look at them all those years ago. Leviticus, he gave you those clothes?"

"Don't do this," Alex pleaded.

Diego smiled wildly. "Just tell me," he urged. "Did you get these clothes from Leviticus?" He snatched Alex by the lapel.

"You know I did. He told me he had saved these clothes. That they were clothes from when he was just a kid."

"How curious," Diego said. "Just a kid." He released his grip. "You are wearing the very same thing Leviticus and his brother were wearing when they murdered my entire village." He snorted. "And now I know why we never stood a chance against them. Why no one has ever stood a chance against them. They had the armor of the Gods."

3

Danice waited at The Blood and Dagger. She paced the main hall, stopped, and glared out the window. A hint of the sky was just visible over a chimney on the adjacent building. Smoke combined with mist and created an ethereal haze. The first pedestrians of the day made their way into the street. Two women in long black cloaks turned the corner. They saw Danice watching and jumped. When they recognized who it was, they giggled and waved. A stocky man in a tall, puffy hat and white apron pulled a cart through her view. Steaming loafs of dark brown bread were stacked in perfect piles at the rear.

Diego and Alex strode in through the back of the guild. A burst of air swept over a row of candles that lined the center of the closest table. Flames flittered but stayed alive until the door was closed. They chatted amicably. Alex said something and Diego laughed. They saw Danice and went silent.

"Are we ready?" Danice asked. She folded her arms over her chest. "You two are all chummy all of a sudden," she added bluntly.

"Alex and I had to work through a few things," Diego said. "But we figured it out."

Danice rolled her eyes. "Clearly," she snarked. She leaned back to the window and looked up at the sky. "The sun is out. Are we ready to go?"

"Is Lasaria here?" Alex asked. He looked into the other room. "I don't see her anywhere."

"That is because," Danice said slowly, "the princess is not here yet." She walked over to the table and put her hands down. "I am not going to wait much longer."

Diego went to Danice. He pulled on the back of a chair and motioned for her to sit. "Come on," he urged. "She will be here shortly. Let's relax until then."

Alex slunk to the end of the table. "I'll sit." He eased into a seat.

"Come on," Diego implored, "sit."

Danice huffed. "Fine," she relented, "you are right. I know you are right. We will not leave without her. I just do not know what to do. I feel like I am standing around, doing nothing. Deuce is out there, all alone, and I am just standing here." She collapsed into the chair.

"Shortly," Diego assured her. He sat beside Danice and took her hand. "We will get him back. All this will be done and over with. We will get him back."

They fell silent. Light crept across the floor in a seamless flow. Upstairs, someone stirred. Footsteps shuffled from one side of the ceiling to the other. A soft patter followed the movement. Outside, the street filled with people. Neighbors gathered in groups. A buzzing chatter elevated in earnest. The fervor intensified until it was directly on the other side of the front entrance.

"I wonder what is going on," Alex said. He pushed from his seat and tried to see what was happening.

Danice got to her feet. "I think I know," she said.

The door eased open and Lasaria backed in. "Thank you, thank you," she said. "I will tell my father you said that. Yes, I will remember your name. And yours. Okay that is all. I have important matters to attend to." She got inside and kicked the door shut.

"Everything alright?" Diego asked. He stayed in his seat.

Lasaria shook her hair. "These people," she gasped. "I mean I love them all but come on. I was clearly in a hurry, but did they care? No." She turned around. A rolled chart was in her right hand. She waved it in front of her. "We have a map," she announced, "and a plan to go with it. A simple plan, but a plan."

Diego took the map and laid it on the table. "Okay," he said. He unfurled the parchment. "This is it. This is how we get Deuce back."

Lasaria went to Danice. She put her arm around her shoulders and pulled her in for a hug. "And we will get Deuce back," she emphasized.

Alex shifted so he could hear. "What's the plan," he asked tentatively.

Danice nodded. "Yeah. What is the plan?"

Lasaria took her arm away. Diego gave her space and she leaned on the table. "The King sent people to the river," she started. "They took our transport, provisions, and armor. We will make our way on the water until we are here." She pointed to a dot on the map. The bottom of the parchment was colored a subdued tan. "After that we have to walk." She ran her finger in a line to a red X. "It should take us two days to get to the plantation in total, four days back because we have to go at it on foot. Maybe longer, depending on…" her voice faded away.

"Deuce," Danice interjected, "depending on Deuce."

"Yes," Lasaria continued cautiously, "depending on Deuce. If he is hurt, or otherwise incapacitated, we might need to carry him. If that is the case, it will take us longer. But we will manage."

Diego flattened the parchment. "It

will make us vulnerable on our return," he said absently. "But there is not much we can do about that."

"No," Lasaria agreed, "there is not."

Danice swept her hand out. "Forget the way back," she insisted. "What do we do when we get there? I know you are not going to let me run in sword first."

Lasaria grinned. "I did not say that." She pointed between Danice and Diego. "You two will cause a distraction. Kill a few guards. Set fire to a few fields. It does not matter. I doubt Lady Carol will have Deuce out in the open anyway. Alex and I will sneak in and confront her. We will make her tell us where Deuce is. One way or another, we will make her tell us."

"That's it." Alex interrupted. "You think that it will be that simple?"

The noise from the street was suddenly amplified. Someone mentioned

Lasaria by name. Another person said something and squealed. A head popped up on the opposite side of the window. They locked eyes on the group and vanished. In the other room, someone shuffled down the stairs. Their movement was just audible over the chatter from outside. After a moment, Sai Lee came into the room.

"I was not sure if you would still be here," Sai Lee said softly. She looked at her feet. "I was not sure I wanted you to still be here."

Danice patted the seat next to her. "We will be going in a moment. Sit with us until we do. Please," she added.

Sai Lee walked over. She sat and listened.

"That is the only plan we have," Diego spoke up. "But it will work. Danice and I will rain down hell on those in the field." He slammed his index finger on the table. "Lasaria and

Alex will get into the main house. They will find Lady Carol and get Deuce back. After that, we regroup north of the plantation. We get back to Sparham and then figure out what to do next."

"But what if," Sai Lee said softly, "what if he is already gone? What if Deuce is already," she choked, "dead?"

Diego balled his fist. "That is not an option," he said emphatically. "I am not going to entertain that possibility." He pulled his hand away and rolled up the map. "He is alive. We get him back. That is it. We are going to get him back."

A tear trickled down Danice's cheek. A second and third followed. "We are going to get him back," she reiterated. She put her hand on the table. Sai Lee reached over and set hers on top. "I do not care what the cost," Danice continued, "we are going to get him back."

The sounds from the outside world faded away. Movement from above went unnoticed. A person walked in through the rear door. They said something in a senseless babble. When they got no response, they gave up and went into the other room. Gentle sobbing gradually pulled Danice from the trance.

Sai Lee covered her mouth. "I am sorry," she said through tears. "I am so sorry," she repeated.

"It is okay," Danice insisted. She got to her feet and smiled weakly. "We are going to go. And when we get back, Deuce will be right here with us. That much I promise you. Deuce will be right here."

Lasaria blinked rapidly. "Yes," she agreed, "let's go." She turned her back to the table and sniffled. "It is about time we save Deuce from that horrible woman. I cannot even imagine what he is going through right now."

"Then don't," Diego demanded. He got up and went to the back door. "Imagining the worst will not help us achieve a thing. We have a plan. We stick to that plan. We focus on getting Deuce back in one piece and everything will work out fine."

Alex stayed planted in his seat. "Wait a second," he said. "Is that it, are we going?"

Diego looked to Lasaria. She nodded. "We are going," she answered.

"Well hang on," Alex was suddenly flustered. "Don't we still need to go to the blacksmith? And I have some of my things upstairs. I can't just leave them here. Can I?"

Sai Lee wiped her eyes. "I will watch your things," she said to Alex. "I will not let anyone up to the third level. That is your room now. It will be exactly how you left it. I hope that is okay."

"Um," Alex stammered, "of course that is okay. Are you sure I can just have the room?"

Danice took Sai Lee by the hand. "Sai runs this place," she insisted. "If she tells you your things will be fine, they will be fine." The two women embraced.

"Alex and I will stop by and see Marvin on the way out of town," Diego spoke up. "Lasaria, you and Danice go to the stables. Two horses should be fine to take us to the river. We will meet at the west gate when we are done. It will not be long."

"It is time we go and save Deuce," Lasaria chimed in. "I am ready."

Danice held Sai Lee tight. "I will go and get Deuce," she whispered. "You just get ready to put a beat on him. A few bruises at least.

Maybe a black eye to go with them."

Sai Lee dug into Danice's shoulder. "I will," she insisted. "I will beat him up good for you."

Danice squeezed Sai Lee tight. "I know you will," she said softly. "That is why I love you so much."

Chapter 10

1

Lasaria, Alex, Danice, and Diego left the city through the west gate just after sunup. A pair of mules had been brought from the stables for them to use. The animals were gaunt. The skin around their midsections pulled tight against skeletal ribs. Tufts of fur had come free from their bodies. Patches of cracked hide were faded to a pale grey. On their backs, dual leather saddles were tethered in place. Long wooden rods were balanced over their diminutive hindquarters. Dark cloth packs were secured to each end.

"This is all we could get," Danice sighed. "The rest of the cavalry is otherwise engaged." She held the end of a leather strap. "We will not need them long. The river is only a short way off. I figure Lasaria, you and Alex can ride, Diego and I can run alongside."

Alex looked around. "I don't need a ride," he insisted. "I'll run alongside. I need the exercise anyway. My cardio is just awful." He chuckled.

"Nonsense," Lasaria said. "These animals may look a little rough around the edges, but they will carry us."

Diego stroked one of the mules. Thin ridges of spine were visible beneath its mane. "You have to be kidding me," he laughed. "I would not even eat this thing."

Lasaria yanked his hand away. "We

are not going to eat them," she scowled, "we are going to ride them." She stroked the animal on the snout. It closed its eyes and tilted its head back. "You just have to treat them well. All the other animals get the glory, but I prefer my humbled little friends here."

"There is no way I can ride that thing," Diego announced. He walked over to the second mule. "This one appears to be healthier than the other." He ran his hand over its neck and head. "But no, no way. If I climb on either one of these things, I am bound to kill it."

"Too good to ride a mule?" Lasaria asked. She slipped her foot into a stirrup. She lifted her leg to the other side and secured her other foot. "That is fine by me. But I am going. You three work it out." She kicked her heels and trotted off.

Danice threw her arms in the air. "Oh, come on," she yelled. "Are you serious?" She took off after Lasaria.

Diego looked at Alex. "All yours," he said. "I am not riding him." He smiled and turned away.

"Wait," Alex hollered. "I've never ridden on…" he thought. "On anything before."

"It is easy." Diego waved his hand over his head. "Just get on and go," his voice faded.

Alex watched his companions shrink into the valley. He took a tentative step. The mule dipped its head and scraped at the dirt. Alex looked around. Nothing happened so he took another step. The animal bobbed his head up and down. It bent onto its front knees and snorted. Alex checked to see if anyone was around.

"You want me to get on?" Alex asked the animal.

The mule snorted. It shook its mane and bobbed its head.

Alex couldn't speak. "Will do," he managed to get out. "As long as you don't mind." He mimicked Lasaria. He put his foot in the stirrup and lifted his leg over. When he was secure, he planted in the saddle. "I'm ready whenever you are," he said. "If that's alright with you?"

The animal got to its feet. It shook its tail and set off. Alex gripped the reins. His hands trembled and his arms shook. He held tight. After a few minutes he relaxed. The animal sensed his comfort and lowered its head. It dug in and moved fast. It wasn't long before he overtook Diego, passed by Danice, and drew even with Lasaria.

"You were right," Alex shouted. "Just treat them well and they will respond in kind." He smiled and kicked his heels. The mule lurched and they pulled ahead.

Lasaria stood in the saddle. "A

race?" she yelled. "Not with these guys." She sat down and jeered.

At the river, two men waded in the shallows. A gentle current lapped at their knees. They pivoted in time as they passed bundles from the shore to the boat. A pile of items on the bank quickly diminished. When it was gone, one of the men shifted to the side. He lifted an oar in the air and held it to the sky. He laid it down and checked the second oar.

"Princess," the other man said. He climbed out of the water and bowed. "Your father had us get everything prepared for your journey. A bit much," he added, "but I do not believe he even wanted you to go at all."

Lasaria climbed down from her saddle. "He was not going to stop me," she said plainly. "Not when it is Deuce we are going to save."

The man nodded. "All of us want to go with you," he said. "We all want to help save Deuce. But your father, he would not even entertain the idea. He told me it was not my place to question his decisions. I fear reprisal for speaking up."

"I will talk with him when we return," Lasaria assured him. "Endure until then." They clasped hands.

Danice jogged upon them. She went straight into the river. "Alright," she barked, "move." She pushed the man in the water out of the way and jumped into the boat.

Water splashed over the man's torso. "That was not necessary," he grumbled. "It is all packed. You are all ready to go." He got out of the water and shook the bottom of his shirt. "You did not need to do that," he said again.

Diego stumbled in. He put his hands over his head and panted. "I am here," he moaned, "I am here. Are we all ready?"

"Danice is," Lasaria said bluntly. She went over to one of the men and put something in his hand. "I just need to have a word with these two before we go, otherwise I am ready."

"I know I'm ready to go," Alex chimed in. He got down and patted the mule. "You did a great job," he said to the animal. He hitched his pants and strode into the water. "Will this really carry all of us?" he asked.

"We will make it work." Diego said. He grasped hands with one of the men. They nodded and he marched away.

Alex pushed down on the rim of the boat. The conveyance was fashioned from one solid piece of wood. Timber planks lined the bottom. At the bow, a narrow bench seat was carved into the inside frame. In the middle, the center thwart was elevated. It stretched across the width and made a second bench. A set of thick wooden oars were secured to the rowlocks on each side. In the stern, half a dozen parcels were secured in place with cord.

"Good enough for me," Alex said. He rolled into the boat. His head knocked against the knob of an oar. "Come on," he chastised himself.

Diego was already in the water. He stepped into the boat after Alex. "This is it," he announced. "There is no turning back now." He sat beside Danice at the helm. "We come back with Deuce or not at all." He put his arm around her shoulder. "We come back with Deuce," he repeated to her softly, "or not at all."

2

The first day on the water was uneventful. Diego took command early. He maneuvered them to the middle of the river and pulled the oars in. He sat with Danice on the center bench. Together they kept watch on the route ahead. He scanned the bank on one side. She kept her focus on the other. Lasaria rested in the stern. She stretched against their gear at an angle. Her head was tilted back, her eyes closed. Dazzling golden rays showered her face in a radiant glow. Her ginger hair lit up like fire.

Alex watched Lasaria from the front of the boat. Her skin was a milky white. Light brown freckles started at her temples and went above her brow. They covered her cheekbones and the tip of her nose. Her upper lip was thin. It stuck out just a bit over her bottom lip. Her chin was sharp and rounded off at the tip.

"Hey," Diego said. He snapped his fingers in front of Alex's face. "Hey," he repeated louder.

Alex stared at him blankly. "What?"

he mumbled. He shook his head. "Wait, what?"

"It is not a good idea to stare at a princess," Diego said sternly. He smiled. "Especially around two people she considers a big brother." He stuck his thumb at Danice. "And a big sister."

Danice sneered. "I will have to tell Lasaria you were leering at her," she said softly. She lowered her voice. "I do not believe she will like that very much."

"I wasn't," Alex stuttered. "I didn't."

Diego let out a hardy laugh. "No, she would not like that at all."

"I am not sure what is happening," Lasaria cut in. Her eyes were shut. Her arms were folded over her chest. "But I do not want to catch anyone looking at me funny. We can start the fight early for all I care." She tried to keep a straight face but smiled.

Diego smacked Alex on the thigh. Danice tried to repress her delight. She turned her head to the side and snorted. The boat rocked against the current. They both burst into laughter. Alex looked away. His cheeks flushed. He focused all of his attention on the riverbed. He covered his mouth and counted the pebbles.

"Alright, alright," Lasaria said, "knock it off already." She sat up. She surveyed their surroundings and laid back. "Get some rest. I want to be ready for tonight. We will stay on the water, but that does not mean we are out of danger."

Danice turned around. "We are not going to stop?" she asked.

"No," Lasaria stated. "We stop when we get to the plantation. Then we will rest for the night and hit

Lady Carol at sunup."

"I am okay with that," Danice said. "I just wanted to make sure I heard you right."

Lasaria slipped her hands behind her head. "You heard me right."

"You do not have to tell me twice." Diego grabbed an oar. He looked at Danice and she handed him the other. "I will pick up the pace." He jammed the blade into the riverbed. He shoved and they veered towards the center.

It wasn't long before the sun started to set. A towering peak to the west cast the boat in a blanket of shadows. The river weaved out along the border of the sweeping valley. It looped back in a horseshoe and cut through a dark green pasture. Wooden shacks were clustered along the bank of the water. A trio of men in tan trousers pulled a large net to shore. One glanced up and jumped. He said something to the others. They looked over and paused.

Farther south, an imposing expanse of woodland encroached on all sides. Dense vegetation covered the bank. Branches jutted out over the water. Thick roots ate away at the soil. The trees closest to the edge on both sides tilted in on a slant. They came together over the water and blocked out the sky.

Lasaria pulled her bow over her shoulder. She grabbed an arrow and notched it. "It is darker than I thought it would be," she observed. "Stay sharp."

"We do not know what is out here." Danice turned and crammed onto the bench with Alex. "This way you have some room if we need to make a quick getaway," she told Diego.

"Preparation," Diego said. "I like it."

"Okay," Lasaria whispered, "everybody quiet down."

They floated through the

cover of night. In the darkness, their pace seemed to come to a standstill. Life abandoned the forest. Silence descended. Wind blew through the trees. Leaves rustled in the canopy above. Foliage crunched along the bank. Water lapped at the side of the boat. Time slowed to a crawl.

The river veered to the east and the boat resisted the current. It continued straight and plowed through the dirt. The keel dug into the sediment. A stone pierced the hull. Black liquid gurgled from the wound. Diego hollered in surprise. He slammed on one of the oars and overcorrected their position.

"Hang on," Diego said frantically. "I will get us out of this. Alex, take care of that breach."

Alex dropped forward. His knees hit the water and barely got wet. "It isn't that bad," he stated. He felt for a hole. "Sounds worse than it is. I think we will be okay." When he couldn't find anything, he got up. "It might be a crack. I don't think it is an actual puncture."

"Sit down," Diego ordered. "You are throwing the weight off." They sloshed into deeper water.

Alex scowled. "Come off it, Diego," he said jokingly. Something moved in his peripheral vision. He did a doubletake. "Wait a second." He tilted his head to the side and squinted. "I think I see something. I can't be sure but…"

"What is it?" Lasaria questioned. "I do not see anything." She leaned on the lip of the boat. "I do not know how you can see anything at all."

"It is hard to tell." Alex said. "It could be a person."

The air screamed to life. An instant later a thump punctuated the silence. Alex stumbled back. His eyes bulged from their sockets. He tried to move his left arm, but it hung limp. He tried to lift it a second time. His elbow twitched. His vision blurred. He put his right hand to his neck and traced around his windpipe. When he got to his clavicle, a searing pain ripped through his body. The bone was cracked in two. A cylindrical shaft protruded out. He patted the tunic around his shoulder. He pulled his hand away and it was wet.

"What happened?" Danice sprang to her feet. The boat tipped. The stern lifted into the air. "What happened?" she repeated.

Alex swayed. "I think," he stuttered, "I think I've been shot." He reached up and touched the arrow. "Yup, I've been shot." His eyes rolled in his head. His knees buckled and he collapsed.

"Diego, move." Lasaria popped to her feet. She drew her bow back and fired a shot into the darkness. "Move,

move, move," she shouted.

Diego wrenched on one of the oars. "I am trying," he grunted.

A second arrow cut the air. It caught the top of the oar and deflected away. A third and fourth shot followed in rapid succession. One pierced the inner shell of the boat just above the waterline. The other dropped towards them at a steep angle. It carved through the night and stuck into the outer frame.

"I think it is one person," Danice hollered. She crouched over Alex and blocked his head. "We have to get out of the line of fire. We cannot fight what we cannot see."

Arrows rained down around them in a steady succession. Diego rowed as hard as he could. He worked his arms in tandem. After every stroke he felt for the bottom. If one side made contact, he adjusted their course accordingly. A frantic volley streaked in their direction.

The barrage fell short and the assault came to an end.

"How did we let this happen again?" Diego gasped. He settled into an easy cadence. "I cannot believe this happened again."

Lasaria laid her bow at her feet. "Whomever it was," she said, "it was like they knew we were here." She looked to the front. "How is Alex? Is he going to be alright?"

"He is alive," Danice sighed, "but he needs to be patched up. This arrow is wedged in fairly good." She touched the projectile. "We cannot do anything about it right now. We will have to wait until it is light enough to see."

Diego looked back at Lasaria. "Mudmen again?" he asked.

"Watch over him until we can get him cleaned up," Lasaria instructed. "I am going to keep a look out for any more fun surprises." She climbed the center bench and plunked down next to Diego. "I do not think that was the Mudmen at all," she said in a hushed tone. "Whoever it was, I do not think they were after me this time. But I do think they knew exactly where we were. I am not really certain, and I have no idea how or why, but I think they were after Alex."

3

Alex moaned. He came to and opened his eyes. They pulled apart a bit but were stuck shut. A layer of crust formed between the delicate skin of his top and bottom lid. He rolled to his side. Pain shot through his stomach and down his legs. His head trembled. His entire body shuddered. He sank back and let out a muted grunt.

"Are you awake?" Lasaria asked.

She swiveled around on the center bench and put her elbows on her knees. "You lost a fair amount of blood." She leaned over and ran her index finger just above Alex's shoulder. "But it could have been worse."

"What happened?" Alex asked. His left arm was laid over his chest. He tried to move his hand. The muscles in his neck tensed. He clenched his teeth and groaned. "How long have I been out?" he asked softly.

Lasaria reached behind her seat. Danice handed her a thin leather pouch. "You don't remember?" she asked. She popped a cork from a small hole and held it out. "You are dehydrated. Here, have something to drink."

Alex forced his eyes open. A blinding glare radiated down from a crystal sky. He blinked repeatedly and his vision came into focus. He was spread over the rear seat of the boat. A swath of fabric was secured around his neck. It wrapped his elbow and forearm. His jacket was folded and placed under his head. The packaged gear that had been stacked in the rear was lined across the bottom boards.

"I remember getting shot," Alex winced. "After that, not so much." Sweat saturated his tunic and the front of his pants. "Was anyone else hurt?" He took the waterskin and put it to his lips.

"Just you," Danice chimed. "You were the only one hit."

"I do not even know how that happened," Diego interposed. He pulled on one of the oars. Gravel crunched under the tip of the paddle and the boat turned to the side. "The arrow missed your tunic and your jacket by this much." He held his finger and thumb close together. "Lucky shot I suppose. If it hit that armor you have on, it never would have gone through."

Alex snorted. "Lucky shot?" he scoffed. "I will call it unlucky in my case."

"Unlucky indeed," Danice agreed. She looked downriver. "We have to be getting close," she said, "everything is starting to die."

Alex propped against the bench. He pushed until he had a bit of leverage. When there was enough space, he arched his back and swung his legs around. For a moment he balanced on his backside. He leaned forward and his torso lifted. He planted his feet and used the momentum to sit up.

"Where are we?" Alex asked breathlessly. "What happened here?"

They left the forest behind. The steady flow of the current fell stagnant. The water level receded from the bank. A narrow strip of liquid ran down a trench that cut the center of the channel in two. Near the outer edge, the bed was dried solid. A vast sea of bleached sawgrass swept across the plains to the south. Peaks towered over their position. Giant granite boulders had transformed into brittle sheets of shale. Large slabs broke free from the face. They shattered into fragments on the way down. Jagged pieces of sedimentary rock piled up at the bottom. What trees remained were desolate. They poked from the ground like wooden spikes.

"This used to be part of Harwell," Danice said, "a Kingdom on the opposite side of the mountains."

Diego dropped the oars into the water. "Now it is the Barrens," he said somberly. He jerked and they started to drift.

"The Barrens?" Alex adjusted his feet. He pushed a parcel to the side. "What is that? If it was another Kingdom, how did it turn in to this?"

Lasaria watched the way ahead.

"Ulrich Flemming happened," she said absently. "He killed the entire Benton family. After that, every other living thing just faded away. It was like the family was connected to the land or something."

"He killed an entire family?" Alex cried. "Why would he do that?"

"It was their Kingdom" Lasaria said. "Ulrich wanted it. They were in the way." She stood and looked around.

The sun descended behind the top of a flat peak and cast the foothills in shadows. On the east side of the river, saplings were interspersed with shrubs. A gravel path was barely distinguishable from the pasture. Deep grooves emerged from a thicket and swung along the edge of the water. They followed a sweeping bend in the river and veered away. After a few feet, they disappeared between a hedgerow.

"We are here," Lasaria announced.

"This is Lady Carol's plantation."

The road turned and there was a direct line of site to the plantation. A line of living oaks shielded the path. Thick skirts of moss enveloped the bottom of the trees. Dark brown bark was latticed up the length of the trunks. At the end of the drive, yellow flowers graced a pair of matching pillars. A stone wall wrapped an inner courtyard. At the front of the house, the dwindling light reflected off a pane of glass. A set of double doors were open in the middle of an arch of windows.

Alex whistled. "That place is massive," he said. "Not just the house, but all of that land too. How are we ever going to find Deuce in there?"

Danice crouched. She curled her fingers around the rim of the boat and squeezed. "Lady Carol will have him close," she said quietly. "You and Lasaria will beat his location out of her if you have too."

"Let us hope it does not come to that." Lasaria sat down. She leaned over and shifted the packages around. "But if it does." She lifted one up and held it chest high. "We will be ready."

Diego pulled with all his might. Stones crunched under wood. "What about you, Alex?" he huffed. "You are hurt, your bone is broken, are you ready for this?" He worked the oars. They crept along.

"Marvin gave me my new karabela," Alex said. He reached across his body and patted his belt. "I just need one good arm to use it. Thankfully, the arrow got me on the left side. If I'd been hit anywhere on the right, I'd be useless."

"Worse than useless," Lasaria snarked.

Danice chuckled. "The two of you are working together on this," she said, "you might want to play nice."

"Yeah," Alex agreed, "play nice." He stuck his tongue out. He made a funny sound and they laughed.

They continued passed the plantation. What little water remained had gone stagnant. Diego labored against the added resistance from the riverbed. He got them dislodged and they jerked ahead. The bow lifted and they skimmed the surface of the river. They drifted perpendicular to the shore. The weight settled and the boat scraped along the bottom. The keel cut into the earth. Thick lumps of oxidized clay stuck to the bow and they ground to a halt.

"It is time we walk," Lasaria said. She turned towards the helm. "Diego, you and I will get the gear unloaded and the boat hidden away as best as we can. Danice, you already know what to do. We get a little rest tonight if we can, and then hit the plantation in the morning."

Alex raised his hand. "What about me?" he asked. "What do you want me to do?"

Lasaria reached into her jacket. She pulled out a small piece of flint. "Get us a fire started," she said. "Build it about ten feet from the largest tree you can find. Something tall, but strong too. And do not worry about trying to hide it."

"Won't people see it?" Alex asked. He took the stone and put it in his pants. "Plus, I don't even know if I will be able to get it started with one good hand.

"Well give it a try," Lasaria insisted. She stood and braced her hand on Diego's shoulder. She stepped over the side of the boat and hopped into the water. "If you do not get it going, I will help you when I am done here." She stacked their gear. "And like I said, if you do manage a fire, do not worry if anyone sees it. I am done stalking around. Let them come at us if they want."

"Um," Alex mumbled, "are you sure about that?" He got to his feet. "After everything we have been through, do we really want to call attention to the fact that we are out here?" He lifted his leg to exit and nearly fell over.

Diego caught Alex about the waist. "Careful," he said. He slid his arm around his stomach and lifted him out of the boat.

"Thanks," Alex mumbled. He saw something out of the corner of his eye. Danice stooped low in the bushes. "What is she doing?" He gestured with his chin.

Lasaria picked up the last bindle and gently set it on the center bench. "You do not need to worry about her," she said. "Do your job and find us somewhere to camp for the night. Get us away from the riverbed. I do not want to be funneled into the channel if we must flee." She looked up at Alex. "But you are right, someone at the plantation is bound to see we are out here. I doubt they would wake Lady Carol for that. And, besides, who would ever think it was us."

Alex trudged to the bank. "It just feels like we are tempting fate," he said. He stepped up and shook his pantleg. "But what about Danice?" he asked. "What is she doing?"

Diego moved to the front of the boat. He got out and faced the bow. "She is going to keep a look out for us," he said. He gripped a small nob at the bow of the boat with both of his hands. "That is her job. Your job, as Lasaria pointed out, is to find us somewhere to camp and, maybe, make a fire." He dug his heels into the dirt. He pulled back and the boat moved an inch. "My job is to get this out of here. So, if you do not mind, do your job, and let us do ours.""

"Just give me a second," Lasaria barked at Diego. "Let me get some of these things out of here and lighten the load."

Alex walked off. He got a short distance away and stopped to survey the land. The environment was sparse. A vast amount of acreage was covered in arid brush. Thick patches of tangled thorns were strung together along the boundary of a large field. A cluster of trees were set back from the edge. An empty patch of earth circled out from underneath the isolated grove.

"I found it," Alex said cheerfully. He marched ahead.

Alex fashioned a small pit in the ground. He used his free hand and pried as many rocks from the dirt as he could muster. After he'd amassed a sizeable pile, he pushed them into a tight circle. He gathered a handful of grass and tossed it in the center. He took the flint from his pants and held it as tight as he could. He brought it down onto one of the rocks. The stones struck together. Sparks showered the tinder. It started to smoke. Alex took a deep breath and blew on the cinders. The parched vegetation burst into flames.

"Not bad," Diego said, "not bad at all." He strolled into camp and flopped to the ground. "I am proud of you. Lasaria thought you would never get it started."

"I did not say that," Lasaria hollered. She walked in behind Diego. She tossed a chunk of bread at Alex. "I just said I would be surprised if he could get it started."

Alex picked his food out of the dirt. He set it in his lap and wiped away what he could. When it looked clean, he took a bite. "Is this it?" he asked. "Am I really just supposed to relax? I feel so exposed out here."

"Yes," Lasaria drawled, "relax." She tore the bread with her teeth. She got a mouthful and eased back to the ground. "Re – lax," she said slowly.

Alex shrugged. He laid on his side and nibbled at the food. The flames quickly dissipated. The dried grass burned to ash and was gone. His eyes started to get heavy. His shoulder started to throb. He flipped to his back and slid his hand under his head. Within a matter of minutes, he fell asleep.

"Wake up," Lasaria whispered. She smacked Alex with her knuckles. "Come on, get up."

"Ughh," Alex groaned. "What? I just got to sleep a second ago."

Lasaria shuffled around the firepit. "Someone is here." She knelt next to Diego. His eyes were wide open. He was motionless. "They are close."

"Is it Danice?" Alex asked. His voice boomed in the darkness.

Diego lifted his finger to his lip. "Quiet," he mouthed.

"What is it?" Alex uttered. "What is going on?"

"It would seem," a voice answered sharply, "that we have gotten the upper hand on you yet again. Not a smart move to have a fire. We thought better of all of you. I suppose we will have to rethink our stance on that."

Lasaria put her hands above her head. "What do you want with us?" she asked. "Are you Mudmen?"

"You do not know who we are." The voice moved. "Just give us the stones and we will be on our way."

Lasaria spun to her knees. She kept her hands elevated. "I have no idea what you are talking about," she answered. "Who are you? What stones are you talking about?"

"The one I shot before," the person responded. "Ask him about the stones.

He will know what I am talking about."

Alex tried to sit up. His feet lifted into the air and he tipped backwards. "Wait a second," he said, "just wait a second. I don't know what you are talking about." He couldn't see a thing

"Do not lie," the person shrieked. "Do not lie," his voice squeaked. "I shot you once, do not give me a reason to shoot you again."

"Well now," Danice spoke softly, "why don't we all settle down for a second." Her words drifted through the air. Everything went silent. "That is better. Let us talk about this, shall we."

Lasaria swiveled around. She tugged something from her pants and fumbled at the ground. She made a series of frantic movements. The firepit filled with a dozen black lumps of carbon. Her arm flew into the air. She brought it down and a spray of light erupted in the night. The tinder caught fire and exploded into flames.

"Stop," someone cried. A young boy in all black stumbled into the camp. Orange light lit him from below. "Come on, stop."

Danice followed behind him. She held her sword out. The point was buried in the boy's back. "You are lucky I did not kill you," she said sternly. "I think anyone else, including my friends here, would have killed you." She dug the tip in, and he jolted. "What were you thinking attacking us back on the river. Or now, for that matter, what was the end goal here?"

"I," the boy stammered. "I."

Diego got to his feet. He took a step and stood toe to toe with the intruder. He towered over him. "Well," he said. His eyes narrowed. He looked down. "Spit it out."

"I know he has Vitality Stones," he yelled. He pointed at Alex. "And I need them. I have to have them."

Alex squirmed. "What?" he said. "How did you? You're the one who shot me?"

"Vitality Stones?" Diego swiveled on his heels. He glared at Alex and looked back to the boy. "You are telling me he has Vitality Stones," he punctuated the S. "Plural? Stones?"

The boy shook his head. "It does not matter how many he has," he said flatly. "I need them. I need them all."

"You are just a kid." Lasaria stood and went over to the boy. "What is your name?" she asked. "And what could you possibly need Vitality Stones for? How did you even know about them in the first place?"

The boy averted his eyes. "I am Archer," he said softly. "And I can feel them, can't you? They are so powerful. I can almost see a haze around him. It is like he is glowing or something."

"Okay," Danice said, "but why would you need them. I did not think Vitality Stones even existed anymore."

"There are not many," Archer said, "but my mom taught my how to see them. And that is why I need them, for my mom."

Danice's face dropped. "Your mother," she said desperately. She took Archer by the arm and pulled him in. "Where is your mother? Why do you need the stones to help her?"

"Lady Carol has her," Archer said. He looked over and locked eyes with Alex. "She turned her into a zombie. Please," he pleaded, "the only way to save her is with those stones."

Chapter 11

1

They took Archer captive with little resistance. Danice used a length of braided rope to bind his hands behind his back. When they were secured, they uprooted camp and relocated to the far side of the riverbed. Diego remained behind. He smothered the fire and thick white smoke billowed into the air. As the embers cooled, he dismantled the pit. A dozen stones were carefully arranged into an oval. He took them away two at a time and scattered them in the field. Once finished, he crouched down and hurried away.

The group took an elevated position on the edge of the river. A thatch of brown vines studded with thick black thorns covered the bank. They weaved together into an impenetrable wall of vegetation. Behind them, the boat they used to traverse the waterway was tipped on its side. The equipment was piled under the forward thwart. A mass of twigs and grass had been gathered and used as an additional layer of camouflage.

"So," Diego said softly. He crept in and dropped to one knee. "What did we find out?"

Lasaria looked over at Archer. "Go ahead," she said. "Tell him what you just told us."

"Well," Archer started, "the first thing was an apology. I did not mean to attack you. I mean I did, but now that I know you are decent folks, I am terribly sorry. Especially to this one." He nodded at Alex. "That is a bad wound. But, like I told them already, the Vitality Stones can help him heal."

"I still want to know how, by the way" Alex interrupted. He rubbed his arm and winced. "What you've told us so far doesn't make much sense to me."

Lasaria put her hand in the air. "Let us catch Diego up," she said sternly. "Then we can work on your arm."

"Fine," Alex pouted.

Archer looked from Alex to Lasaria. "Anyway," he continued, "what I was telling them was that my mother and I were living in the woods. We had not been here long when we were attacked. There were dozens of them. Men covered in mud. They came for us while we slept. One of them had me. I thought he was going to kill me. Instead they captured us and took us up to the plantation. I was so scared. I…" He closed his eyes and dropped his head. Tears ran down the sides of his nose

"Go on," Danice urged. She put her hand on his shoulder.

"I started to cry," Archer went on. "Then I got really scared and, and," he stuttered, "and other things happened. When my mother saw me, when she saw what happened, she could not take it anymore. She erupted. It took most of the men to bring her down. As it happened, she told me to run. She did not say it out loud, and I know you probably will not believe it, but she told me in my head. We have always been so close, there were times when we did not need to speak. We would have entire conversations in my head."

Diego looked at Danice cockeyed. "And we believe this?" he asked.

"Let him finish," Lasaria said. "This

could help us."

It was quiet for a moment. "I got away," Archer said. "My mother did not. For a short time, I could still hear her in my head. She told me to run. She told me to keep running. But then she was gone. Her voice was just gone. I thought maybe she had been killed. I cried over that. But I stayed. I did not know what I was going to do, but I stayed. I started to watch the farm. There is this big tree that overlooks the entire thing. I would climb to the top and just watch for days at a time. And then I saw her. She was in one of the fields. She looked different, but I know my mother, it was her." He stopped talking.

"Okay," Diego huffed, "what happened after that?"

Archer looked up. "That is as far as I got with them," he confided. "But after that, I did not know what to do. I could not fight alone. I am good, but I am not that good," he snorted. "Instead I thought I would go and find help. Then a few nights ago I saw it. I saw what could help me get my mother back. I saw you." He lifted his head and locked eyes with Alex.

Alex shifted. "You say you saw me," he asked tentatively, "but you told us before you could see the Vitality Stones, which is it?"

"You," Archer said, "the Vitality Stones, when you have them you become one and the same. When I saw the Vitality Stones, I saw you."

"That doesn't make any sense," Alex growled. "How can you see them? They're in my jacket, you couldn't possibly have seen them."

Archer shook his head. "They radiate an aura," he said, "a kind of glow. I did not see the physical stones, no, but I saw them pulsing with life. And then, when they moved, I knew someone had them.

I followed you until it was impossible to see anything but the stones. I did not know how many of you were out there, I just fired my bow. You disappeared and I thought I missed my shot entirely. I came back to the farm in complete distress. When it was dark, I saw your fire. And the rest," he paused, "the rest you know."

Diego looked to Danice. Her face was void of all emotion. "Well that is one interesting story," he chuckled. "Maybe it is true. But how does any of that help us save our friend. These Vitality Stones are powerful. That much I know. But how," he asked, "how will they help him?"

"The stones affect the mind," Archer cut in. "If we can get one to my mother, anyone, any stone, the power should be enough to bring her back. If Alex, Lasaria and I go and find Lady Carol."

Danice pulled her hand from Archer. "That is not how this goes," she stated. "We save my brother first, and then your mother."

Alex got to his feet. "There is absolutely no way you are coming with us," he said loudly. "I don't trust you one bit."

"Quiet down," Lasaria insisted. She grabbed Alex by the sleeve and tugged him to the ground. "Everyone knows they are your Stones."

"I agree with Alex," Diego said. "Archer comes with me. You are leaving something out." He glanced between Archer and Lasaria. "What is it he has not told us. We are supposed to believe he was living all in piece out here with his mother. How does he know so much about Vitality Stones?" He looked to Archer. "He knows so much, in fact, that he can see them when they are not even visible." Diego turned red.

His arms shook. "We have been traveling with Alex for some time now, and none of us knew he had them. And then he runs around with that bow. He broke Alex's arm, for goodness sake. That was a good, no better than good, shot. In the dark, a moving target. You are not some helpless little kid, are you?"

Archer rubbed his hands together. "You want my entire life's story?" he snarked.

"Not your entire life's story," Diego rumbled, "but a little more would be nice."

"Alright." Archer rolled his eyes. "I was born in Everton in the dead of winter. Near the base of Mount Zeelee. My father left when I was just a boy. I never knew him properly," he said sarcastically.

Lasaria propped up. "Stop it right now," she hissed. She

made a fist and punched the dirt. "We do not have time for this. The sun is coming up."

The first signs of daylight broke over the horizon. Pallid pink and orange light pushed the stars across the sky. The faint slice of moon from the evening prior turned translucent. A choir of virile blackbirds swelled to life. The vast expanse of sagebrush that encompassed the plantation was immersed in a lively tune.

"This is it," Lasaria said in a hushed tone. "Is everybody ready?"

Diego nodded. "It is now or never," he replied.

"I am ready to get Deuce back," Danice said. "I have been ready?"

Alex looked at Archer. "Any stone?" he asked.

"Any stone," Archer replied.

The group fell silent. The enlightened melody of birdsong scored the moment. "Well," Danice wondered, "what are we waiting for? Let's get our family back."

2

Lasaria crouched at the end of a long hedgerow. Fat droplets of condensation clung to a mix of light green and brown leaves. The web of branches that weaved through the inside of the shrubbery poked out like needles. One pricked the back of her neck and she jumped. Blood trickled from the puncture. She put pressure on the wound and grimaced. When she pulled her hand away, a red smear covered her palm.

"You okay?" Alex asked. He peered out from cover. A dirt track led up to the front of the plantation. "I don't see anyone," he said. "Even the house is quiet." He looked down the path. It hit the edge of the river and curved away. "There's nobody."

Lasaria pointed toward the north side of the house. A red bead fell to the soil. "We can get a better look from over there." A tall tree was set behind a grove of dark conifers. The trunk was nearly bare. Thick branches studded up the entire length. An isolated patch near the top was covered in greenery. "That is the one Archer told us about," she said. "If we can get to the top, maybe we will have a better view of the plantation."

"I don't know," Alex groaned. "It looks awfully high up." He leaned out. "And I don't see anyone near the front of the house. Why don't we just make a break for it."

"Are you kidding me," Lasaria uttered. She yanked Alex back. "This is not some kind of game. We cannot just go running in there. One wrong decision, one brash move, and someone dies."

Alex took a deep breath. "I know," he admitted. "Can you take the lead. I've never done anything like this before."

"Now that is the first sensible thing you have said all morning," Lasaria said. She got up and scoped the landscape. "Stay low," she asserted, "and follow me."

Lasaria watched the house. She dipped to one side and altered her position. After a minute, she turned around. She locked eyes with Alex. They held a fixed stare until he dropped his head. A smirk played at the corner of Lasaria's mouth. She smiled. Her hand went to her chest. She held it there and took three deep breaths. When her lungs were empty, she took off. She dashed across the dirt drive and weaved between two living oaks. At the border of a small coppice, she dropped into the prone position. She threw her arms out and dug her fingers into the dirt. Her red locks crept across the top of the brush. After a few feet she paused. She dipped her head and pulled her hood up.

Alex knelt behind the hedge. He rocked forward and dug the heel of his boot into the earth. A vein in his neck throbbed. Everything faded away. He hiccupped and nearly toppled over. His hand curled into a fist. He sunk his knuckles into the dirt and closed his eyes. He inhaled as deep as he could.

"One," Alex said, "two." He took a breath and slowly exhaled. "Three."

Alex rushed from cover. Bits of gravel crunched under his boots. He pivoted and skid across the drive. A scar curled under his heel. He shifted and his body flipped. His legs flew into the air and he crashed onto his shoulder. His broken clavicle crumpled under the force of the fall. He hit the ground and a hideous noise escaped his lips. His vision blurred. He dared not move.

When his senses returned, Alex rolled to his stomach. He put his right arm out and clawed his way into the field.

"What took you so long," Lasaria whispered. She crouched at the base of a large tree. Her eyes watched the house. "I cannot reach that first branch." She glanced at Alex. "I need a…" her voice faded. "What happened to you?" she asked

Alex struggled onto his knees. "I slipped," he moaned. Sweat poured down his face. He tried to stand and fell. "My shoulder is done for." He swayed. "If I go with you, I'm just going to be in the way."

Lasaria took Alex by the wrist. "Come on," she said softly, "lean back against the tree." She put her hand in the small of his back and helped him up. "What about your Vitality Stones, there has to be something in there you can use."

"I don't know," Alex cringed. He let Lasaria guide him. "They're just stones. But right now, I will try anything. I've never been in so much pain." He pressed against the bark and slid down until he hit the ground. "The stones are tucked in my pants. I have them tied to my belt. You'll have to get them."

"Very," Lasaria wavered, "well." She reached down and pulled his trench open. "What side is it on?" she asked.

Alex motioned with his head. "The right," he said calmly. "You should be able to see the cord. Next to the dagger," he added.

Lasaria struggled to get the heavy fabric out of the way. "I don't," she started to say. "Wait, I think I see it." Her hands went to Alex's belt. She lifted his tunic and her fingers brushed his skin. She trembled. "It does not look like it is tied very well." She picked at the knot with her nail. "Almost have it," she drawled. "There." She leaned back. A small cloth sack dangled from her fist.

"Well," Alex groaned, "open it."

"It is just," Lasaria mumbled. "I have never," she stopped. She set the sack to the ground and untied the top. "Something in here will help you, I can feel it." She unfurled the corners. The Vitality Stones separated into a single layer.

Life around them slowed. "You're right." Alex opened his eyes. "I can actually feel them. I've had these stones on me for this entire time, but now I get it. I get what Archer was talking about."

"I know some of these," Lasaria interrupted. She moved the pile around. She found a stone and pinched it between two fingers. "This is Watermelon Tourmaline." She held it in the air. A phthalo green stone was set around a claret center. "Let's see if it can help."

Alex put his hand out. "I know what a watermelon is," he said, "but I have no idea at all what tourmaline is."

Lasaria placed the stone in Alex's palm. "When I was younger, we had a healer at the castle," she said. "She used Watermelon Tourmaline in her treatments. It is one of the only Vitality Stones I have ever seen."

"What does it do?" Alex asked. The tourmaline was cool to the touch. He placed the piece in his left hand and squeezed. Pain shot down his forearm. "It isn't an instant fix," he snarked.

"How many times have I told you to have patience," Lasaria snapped. She picked up a second stone. Blue and red streaks dotted a black bloodstone. She turned it over in her hand. "I can tell you what the one you have does," she said. "It removes the bodies resistance to healing, or something to that effect. That is really all I can remember. It must have helped, anyway. I was never hurt or sick for long."

Alex tried to curl his fingers. They bent slightly at the joint but went no further. He took the stone with his opposite hand. His heart skipped a beat. All his thoughts were sucked from his consciousness. A blank void flooded in his head. The plantation swirled into focus. Deuce stood in the doorway. A grin was plastered across his face. He threw his arm in the air and waved enthusiastically. Danice faded in from the darkness. She put her arm around her brother and pulled him in for a kiss. Diego walked over from the side. He looked at Alex and put his thumb in the air. He grabbed his friends and they laughed.

"It will all be okay," Alex

said softly. "If we stick together, it will all be okay."

Lasaria shot up. "Alex," she said enthusiastically, "your arm."

Alex pulled his hand from the sling. "What about my arm?" he asked. He put his hands in the air and stretched to the sky. "You'll need to give me a little more information…" His voice went mute. His mouth fell agape. "My," he muttered, "arm."

"Yes," Lasaria laughed, "your arm." She touched Alex's shoulder. "Does it still hurt?"

"I mean," Alex started. He grabbed his left wrist with his right hand and tugged it straight. "Barely," he scoffed. "It's like I was never even hurt."

Lasaria smirked. "Can I keep this?" she asked. She flipped the bloodstone over in her hand and secured her grip. "I feel something." Her pupils dilated. "All the obstacles in our way, I can feel them. I don't know if that makes any sense at all. But if I have this stone, nothing will stand in our way. Somehow, I know it. I just know it."

Alex nodded. "Keep it," he said. "It makes more sense than you realize. This stone, here, healed my broken bones." He set the Watermelon Tourmaline back into the pile and picked up the sack. "If one stone can do that, you better believe I know they can do anything." He put the stones away and secured them to his belt.

"We should go," Lasaria ordered. She pulled her bow from her back and braced against the tree. "The sun is already up. We don't know what is going on with Diego and Danice. The sooner we get in there, the sooner this is over with."

Alex stared at Lasaria. "Aren't you going to climb up there to get a better look at the plantation?" he asked. He rubbed his shoulder. The pain was nearly gone. "I know you wanted to get a better view of everything," he added. "To get a look at Lady Carol if you can."

Lasaria kept her eyes on the house. "I have seen enough from down here," she said calmly. "I want to get in there."

"Do you really think we are ready to go?" Alex slipped his dagger from its sheath. He turned his head to see around the tree. "Really?"

"Stay close to me." Lasaria hunched as low as she could. Her eyes were hollow. "It is high time we get in there and eliminate Lady Carol from the equation."

3

Lady Carol's plantation was a vast plot surrounded by a desert of scorched earth. A cacophony of dead and decaying flora hit her property line and transformed into a sea of life. Emerald grass covered nearly every inch of the grounds. Brilliant shades of red and pink flowers glistened in the morning light. A row of manicured oaks lined a gravel drive. It entered the front courtyard and circled around on itself. At the center, a white, two-story structure lorded over the estate like a tyrant. Large columns were spaced evenly around the outside. A veranda wrapped the entirety of the second level.

Behind the house, a line of cypress trees boxed in a pair of fields. Tall, thin plants were set in horizontal rows. Bright green florets dotted the outside of the matching shrubs. At the very back of the estate, a pair of rectangular buildings were set side by side. The first was a towering log structure. Thick trunks were stacked to make the outer walls. A pale grey adhesive was slathered between each beam. In the middle of the edifice, a small porch was elevated above bare earth. Just beyond, a wooden door was sealed tight. A single glass windowpane encompassed the entire right half of the house. The second building was an old barn. Its frame was slanted to the side. A gaping cavity on one end served as the structures lone exit.

Archer fell to his hands and knees. He crept forward and slid his head from cover. "I do not see anyone," he whispered. He looked over his shoulder at Diego. "If we keep low, we might be able to slip in undetected."

"Slip in where?" Diego asked. She shifted to his elbows and the bushes rustled. "We cannot stay here much longer," he said. "My gear will give me away before long."

Danice was face down on her belly. She wiggled towards Diego. "What is the plan?" she asked. She inched her way through the brush.

"The big one lives there." Archer pointed to the far side of the field. A muted tin roof was just visible from their position. "His name is Plient. He oversees the workers. If we take him out, the rest of his men should scatter."

Diego jammed his finger into Archer's side. "You seem to know an awful lot about this place," he growled. "Maybe you are leading us into a trap."

Archer shook his head. "I would be a piss poor spy if I told you everything I already have." He eased back until he was cloaked in vegetation. "I am just trying to help," he said defensively.

"Maybe you are not very bright," Diego retorted. "It would not be the first-time stupidity caught up with you, would it?"

"I really do not like you," Archer snapped. He swatted Diego's hand away.

"Keep speaking to me that way and I will teach you something about manners."

Diego grinned. "And how are you going to do that?" he queried.

"Enough." Danice clenched her jaw. Her body shook. "Trust is a luxury we do not have time for right now," she said. "He could be Lady Carol's son for all we know." She turned to her back.

Archers jaw dropped. "How dare you," he scoffed. "I am not."

Danice put her palms up. "I did not say you were," she insisted. "I said we do not know. And realistically, it is irrelevant. We are here together. There is no turning back now."

"I don't know," Diego said under his breath.

"Well I do know," Danice punctuated. "I am done with all this talking. It is time for us to fight." She put her hand on the small of Archer's back and pushed. "Get out there," she demanded. "We will be right behind you."

Archer was extricated from the trees. His body jerked and his chin hit the ground. Stars whirled through his vision. He regained his composure and got to his knees. He surveyed their way ahead, clambered to his feet, and perched on his tiptoes. A slight breeze sailed in. The crops swayed. A gap in the apical of the plants appeared and light reflected off something. He adjusted his head and focused in on same spot. Whatever was there before had vanished. He took a final look. When there was nothing, he beckoned the others to follow.

Danice crept from cover. She braced her hands in the dirt and pushed up. Her torso elevated. She pulled her legs under her body and popped up. Her head was on a swivel. She checked one direction and then the another. She took a tentative step and turned. Diego smiled. He slid the hem of his tunic back and exposed the hilt of his sword. His grin swelled. He bent his fingers around the end of the weapon and bobbed his head. Danice sucked air through her nose. She pulled her sword from its sheath and trotted off.

Diego crouched down. A pop radiated from inside his knee. He shook his head and scowled. The throbbing faded and he snuck into the open. He tracked Danice's footprints along the outer edge of the field. They turned down a row of crops and he followed. Deep into the field, he heard a commotion. A man's voice issued a command. A high-pitched retort cried out in defiance. Diego didn't wait. He yanked on his broadsword. He thrust the blade out and charged ahead.

"Stay where you are," someone screamed. "I said stay where you are."

There was a brief pause. "Get back here," they yelled even louder.

Sudden movement caught Diego's attention. "What the," he bumbled. Archer shot passed. "What is going on?" he hollered. "Where are you going?"

"They know we are here," Archer yelled. His voice faded as he moved farther away.

"Coward," Diego screamed. He thrust his sword into the air and let out a great roar. "Coward," he repeated even louder. He pivoted and took off towards the scuffle.

Diego charged through a row of crops. He continued along until he came upon a large gap between the two fields. A shallow culvert bisected the center of the opening. Water flowed down the gradient in a steady stream. He turned right and stayed parallel to the ditch. At the end of the field, he shot around the corner and stopped dead in his tracks.

Two armed guards held Danice at bay. They edged her backwards towards the residence. Her left leg was thrust out. Her sword was perpendicular to her chest.

"Tell me where my brother is," Danice yelled. A vain throbbed just above her eye. "I will kill you both if you do not tell me where my brother is." She swiped the sword across her body. The guards slowed but didn't stop. "Tell me what I want to know."

One of the guards lifted his arm towards Danice. A chrome gauntlet clanked against the connecting vambrace. "Drop the sword and we will take you to him," he said calmly. His voice was muffled by a slatted visor that protected his face. "Neither of you have to die here today. We just want the princess. You give her to us, and you get your brother."

"No," Danice said defiantly. "That is

not how this works. You tell me where my brother is. We go and get him. Then we leave. It is your choice who dies today, not mine."

The guards chuckled. "Your little friend has already abandoned you," one said.

"You are all alone," the other added.

Diego crept as close as he could get to the confrontation. He took his broadsword and turned it over. He gripped the pommel and twisted. There was a click and the grip came free of the blade. A serrated dagger took the place of the bulky weapon. Diego laid the blade to the ground and shifted the dagger between hands.

Danice saw Diego. "No," she yelled as loud as she could. She jabbed her blade out. "You think he was my friend? If that is true, then you have a pathetic idea of what a friend really is." She spit at their shoes.

"I am done playing around with you," a guard said. They both took a step. "This has gone on long enough."

The guards advanced and Diego made his move. He plowed into the closest enemy and they toppled over. As they fell, he found an opening in the armor plating. He slipped the blade through and punctured the guards lower back. They hit the ground and the combined weight of their bodies spiked the blade into the man's coccyx. He let lose a horrible shriek. His entire body trembled.

The second guard wrenched to the side. A small space opened between his breastplate and his helm. Danice flipped her saber into the hair. She caught the handle from underneath and brought the weapon above her head. She focused the tip of the blade on the junction between the two pieces of armor. With one graceful motion she plunged her arm straight down. The polished steel pierced the man's throat. A gasp escaped his lips. His eyes went hollow and his body slumped over.

"We will not be getting anything from them I suppose," Danice said. She put the sole of her boot on the guard's chest and kicked him from her sword. She looked up and faltered. "This is not over."

A second set of guards materialized behind Diego. They held their weapons out but didn't approach. More emerged from the field. They formed a wall around the front side of the house. Diego pivoted. He opened his stance and clenched the dagger. Danice wiped the broad side of her sword on her forehead. A flat streak of blood smeared over the skin.

"No," Diego agreed, "it is not over."

Danice stepped forward. "I want my brother back," she shouted. Her voice cracked. "Give me my brother."

A great howl shook the house. "Seriously?" a voice boomed. "I give them one job to do. But can they take care of it," the person moaned, "of course not. I have to take care of everything around here myself." Heavy feet stomped across the floorboards. "Who did we get today?" The front door swung open. Plient ducked his head under the frame and stepped through the doorway. "The young princess I hope."

Diego looked behind him. He shook his head and turned towards the line of guards. His mouth fell agape. He kept his feet planted and looked back over his shoulder. Plient was the size of three men. His head was shaved bald. His torso completely bare. Thick, muscular shoulders reinforced his massive frame. A large link chain was looped around his neck. It curled down his arm and into his hand.

"I know you," Plient declared, "the girl's caretaker. The one who plays dress up all day with the princess. Where is she?" he asked. "Where is your ward?"

There was silence.

"No matter," Plient continued, "we will find her. And she is the only one that really matters. The rest of you are…" He spun the end of the chain. "Expendable. I proved that when I killed your brother." His arm stopped.

Danice swiveled around. "What did you just say?" she asked forcefully.

"Your brother," Plient derided, "he is dead. I killed him. What are you going to do about it?" He put his hand on his hip. "Avenge him? Because that will be a tall order to fill."

"What did you do?" Danice growled. "What did you do?"

Plient laughed. "I told you what I did," he said. "You are as stupid as your brother was. My question to you was what are you going to do about it?"

Danice's hands shook violently. Tremors went up her arm then down her legs. "What am I going to do about it?" she asked. "What am I going to do about it?" Her body went perfectly still. She lifted her head and stared straight ahead. "I am going to kill every one of you on this farm. And when I am done, I will burn it all to the ground."

Chapter 12

1

The front sward of Lady Carol's plantation was a botanical garden. Vibrant blue and yellow blossoms were set amongst manicured topiaries. Red and pink roses lined the center loop of the drive. Deep green rye grass was trimmed and carefully shaped. It shimmered in dramatic contrast to the rainbow of flowers. A fortified stone barrier boxed in the facade of the house. A mix of granite and limestone boulders were arranged in perfect rows. Pale grey mortar was slathered between each layer. The excesses filling had spewed out and formed horizontal lines of plaster. A maze of, opaque, vines covered the barricade. Petite elliptical cones flourished across the liana. The top of each was split down the middle. Dark stigmas pushed from their pistils. At the height of the wall, the new buds blossomed into miniature palm fronds.

Lasaria crouched behind the far corner of the barricade. A lock of hair had come free and fell down her face. She swept her thumb up and tucked her bangs behind her ear. When her head was covered, she slid onto her toes and looked over the courtyard. There was nothing. The sentry positions at each end of the porch were vacant. The guards from the night before were gone. Those who watched over the grounds during day had yet to take up their position. All the activity from the evening prior had ceased.

A set of white wooden steps led up to the first-floor entry. At the top, a pair of vaulted double doors were covered by a sweeping verandah. The balcony overhead was a single seamless perch that wrapped the entire second level of the house. Narrow rectangular windows flanked the entrance on both sides. A curved brass handle was bolted along the inside edge of both doors. The plated finish was polished to a lustrous shine.

Lasaria watched for movement. When there was nothing, she eased out and looked towards the tree. A face was hunkered in the brush. She beckoned with her hand. The figure nodded. Alex tipped from cover. He checked to his left and his right and dashed into the open. Halfway across, he thrust his hands out. He leapt into the air. His body slammed to the earth. All the air left his lungs and he grunted.

"Something is wrong," Lasaria said. She popped up and checked the courtyard. "Where is everyone? I thought it would be quiet, but this does not seem right."

Alex crawled over. He got onto his knees and flipped into a sitting position. "What should we do?" he asked. He ran his fingers over his Manrikigusari. He touched the hilt of his dagger and then his karabela. "If it was a trap, wouldn't they have attacked us by now?"

"I am thinking," Lasararia mumbled. She put her hand to her face and rubbed her chin. "I say we get in there. Maybe we see if there is a side door before we charge in the front." She slipped her hand into her pocket and curled her fingers around the vitality stone. "Deuce is in there," she said. "I know he is. And I know we are going to save him." Her tone suddenly shifted. "We are going to do this right now."

"Right now?" Alex asked. He shuddered. "Right now," he said softly.

Lasaria nodded. "Follow me," she said sternly. "And try and keep up. I want to get in, get Deuce, and get out of there as quickly as possible. Once that is done, we can regroup with the others and figure out what to do next."

"You make it all sound so easy." Alex got to his feet. He stooped over and stayed low. "What do we do if it isn't..." He hesitated. "You know, easy."

"We improvise." Lasaria looked over the wall. "It is all going to be fine," she said. "Now come on." She crouched down and dipped her head.

Lasaria waddled along the base of the wall. Where the deck and courtyard converged, she paused. She leaned over the railing and swiveled her head. The entire property appeared deserted. She took a second look in every direction. She lifted her foot and positioned her heel between two posts. She gripped the top rail with both of her hands and vaulted onto the deck. Her feet hit the baseboards. A thud reverberated through the wood. She stopped in place. She tilted her ear towards the house and listened. When she heard nothing, she reached back and helped Alex onto the porch.

"This is all too easy," Alex whispered. He stayed low and crept to the corner of the house. Large windows were spaced evenly down the side. "I'm going to try and get a look inside." He pressed against the siding. He craned his neck around and eased his head over the glass. "It's boarded up," he grumbled softly. "I can't see a thing."

"I think I see a door down there,"

Lasaria said. "Come on." She bent over and ducked below the window frame. "I am so sick of creeping around. They either know we are here, or they will in a minute. I want in there." She dashed along the wall.

On the far end of the porch, a solid section of wood was inlaid with four elevated panels. The inner edge was secured to a white jamb with silver hinges. A brass knob was set on one side of the entry. Lasaria gripped the handle. She counted to three and turned her hand to the left. A metallic click resonated from the strike plate. The hinges screeched and the door cracked open.

"I don't like this," Alex asserted. He took the dagger from its sheath. It slipped in his palm. He took the blade with his thumb and index finger and wiped his hand onto his pants. "There could be a hundred people in there just waiting for us. Shouldn't we take it slow?"

Lasaria curled her fingers around the door. She tugged it opened a small amount. "I am done with all that nonsense," she said. She worked until there was enough space for her to slip inside. "You can come with me or not. At this point I will take care of it alone if I have too." She slid her shoulder into the opening and worked her way through. "Deuce is in here." She tilted to the side and disappeared into the house.

"Wait," Alex hissed. "Come on, wait." He looked around in disbelief. He was completely alone. He turned and stared at the doorway. "Oh man," he mumbled. "What was she thinking?" He bounced up and down. "Here we go."

Alex stretched his arm. He slipped his hand over the threshold and into the house. Cold air kissed his skin. Goosebumps formed at his wrist and crawled up to his bicep. He turned his head to the side and inched along. When the top half of his body was in, he popped his hips through the opening and lost his balance. He regained his footing and straightened the front of his jacket.

The side door entered in through the kitchen. A single slit of light penetrated the boards that blocked the windows. Dark flat tiles covered the floor. Exposed beams buttressed the ceiling. At the far end of the room, an oval kiln was built into the wall. The inner edge had crumbled into pieces. A layer of dust covered the hearth. Delicate snare webs came together at the center of the opening. A fat black spider waited motionless. A round wash basin was cracked in two. Flat copper strips had curled away from the wood at the seams.

"Lasaria," Alex whispered. He crept to the opposite end of the kitchen. A small archway led into another room. "Lasaria where are you?" He poked his head through the opening. "Come on, where are you?"

A hand reached out. Calloused skin clasped over Alex's mouth. "Hush," Lasaria whispered in his ear. She shoved him backwards. "There is someone upstairs."

"I told you," Alex scowled. He pulled her hand away and shook his head. "They are just waiting for us up there."

"Be quiet," Lasaria demanded. She leaned into the other room. "And put that dagger away. Whoever is up there, they are alone," she said. She looked to every corner of the second-floor landing. "It is Deuce. I know it is. So just be quiet and try not to do anything stupid." She turned her back to Alex. She put her hands out and crept away.

Alex followed Lasaria into the foyer. His eyes were fixed on the floorboards. Bucolic oak planks were faded to a dull, matte finish. A trail of petite footprints crisscrossed the open space. They tracked from one room to the other and back again. He lifted his head to check the way forward and gasped. The entrance to the house was a massive open room. Windows encircled a crystal chandelier. It dangled precariously above the front doors. It was broad at the top and tiered down into a single point. Elongated candles were spiked around the circumference of each level. Their wicks were scorched and melted into the wax. At the center of the room, a grand staircase ascended to the second level. Rich mahogany timber was hand formed into cascading steps.

Lasaria got to the base of the stairs. She wrapped her hand around the volute. Alex hustled to keep up. He positioned himself immediately behind her and ducked his head between her shoulder blades. They moved in tandem, one step at a time. When they reached the landing, Lasaria waited.

"What do we do now?" Alex whispered. His breath was hot on Lasaria's neck. "There are doors everywhere. I wouldn't even know where to begin."

Lasaria brushed her collar with the back of her hand and focused her attention across the landing. She didn't blink. "Deuce is in there," she said categorically. She lifted her finger and pointed. "I don't know if it is the Vitality Stones, or what, but I know Deuce is in there."

"Okay," Alex said, "but that doesn't answer my question. What are we going to do? This is clearly a trap. Right?"

"I am going in," Lasaria said. She bolted forward.

Alex jumped.

Lasaria was nearly to the door when Alex caught up. "Trap or not," she

continued, "we are going to be just fine."
She tried the doorknob. "It is open." She
smiled.

Alex touched Lasaria's arm. "Should
I get my sword out?" he asked. "You
know, in case we need it."

"Not yet," Lasaria insisted. She
leaned into the door and it opened. "If
anything, get the Vitality Stones ready to
go. You have your weapon close if you
need it. Until then, keep it away."

"Are you sure?" Alex moaned. He
felt around and found the bag of stones.
"I don't want to be caught off guard.
Maybe just the dagger."

Lasaria pressed her finger against her
lips. She lowered her shoulder and
bumped the door. When she turned, she
nearly fell over. Thick boards covered
the windows like bandages. Light snuck
in through cracks in the coverings. It
layered the room in streaks of color.
Deuce was positioned down the middle

of a four-post bed. His skin was taut against his jawbone. His arms were laid at his side. His outer layer of clothes had been stripped off. The jacket was folded neatly and set on top of the dresser. His scabbard had been taken from him and propped next to it. On the far wall, a deep cherry armoire was shut tight. Slender brown streaks were etched into the grain.

"Deuce," Lasaria puffed. She floundered and dropped to her knees.

Alex followed. "What is it?" he asked. He saw Deuce and the air escaped his lungs. "No. Please no." He stumbled and stopped. "The Vitality Stones," he exclaimed. "We can use the Vitality Stones."

Lasaria put her hands together and looked up. "They have powers," she said, "but the dead are gone forever. If they were not, I have a feeling your friend Leviticus would have told you otherwise."

"We don't know that he's dead."
Alex said cautiously. He went to the side
of the bed and placed two fingers on
Deuce's wrist. He was cold to the touch.
"I mean he doesn't feel alive," he said
softly, "but we don't know for sure that
he is dead. Why don't we at least try to
see if we can bring him back." He
dropped to one knee. A plank in the
floorboards was slightly beveled. It
creaked under the sudden strain.

Lasaria inhaled through her nose.
"You are right." She exhaled through her
mouth and got to her feet. "What was I
thinking? I never give up." She joined
Alex. "We are here for you Deuce. Hold
on for us."

Alex swept his jacket aside. He took
the knot and worked it between his
fingers. "Just give me a second buddy."
He closed one eye and poked his tongue
out of the side of his mouth. "I've almost

got it." The satchel came loose and he held it up. "We are going to get you back," he insisted. "I promise we are going to get you back." He uncinched the string and the bag came open.

"Just try everything," Lasaria said. She leaned over and investigated the bag. "Everything," she ordered.

Movement on the bed caused them to turn. Deuce bolted upright. Alex shifted his head and tried to move out of the way. He rocked forward and was struck in the throat. His eyes crossed. His vision blurred. The Vitality Stones slipped from his fingers and the bag crashed to the floor. Loose gems bounced off the fabric and scattered across the room.

Lasaria stumbled back. Her jaw dropped. "Deuce," she said loudly, "you are alive."

Deuce curled his fingers around Alex's throat. He leaned forward and tightened his grip. His eyes were hollow. A film glossed over his corneas. Alex squeaked. Air escaped his lips. His cheeks turned pink. He clawed at Deuces hands. He tried to wedge his fingers between his windpipe and Deuce's hands, but he couldn't get any room. After a few seconds, his head began to throb. His vision pulsated and started to fade.

"Deuce," Lasaria hollered.

Alex's eyes rolled back into his head.

"Deuce," Lasaria screamed even louder, "you are going to kill him."

2

Diego and Danice stood with their backs pressed together. They were at the center of the escalating standoff. A group of a dozen guards held their weapons at the ready. They formed an arc around the perimeter of their position. Plient braced his shoulder against a beam at the front of the house. He picked something from his teeth and held his fingers out. He examined whatever it was, lost interest, and flicked it away.

"Are we going to do this?" Plient groaned. He pushed off the wood and swung the end of the chain in a loop. "I was sleeping, you see, and would like to get back to it."

Danice stretched her arm out. She pointed the tip of her blade at Plient. "You kill my brother," she roared, "I kill everyone you love."

Plient chuckled. "You keep saying that," he mused, "but there you stand. Completely outmanned. I do not see this going well for you."

"Outmanned," Danice barked, "maybe. That is irrelevant. It is time you fought a woman with nothing left to lose." She lifted her saber over her head and rushed forward.

Plient flicked his wrist. The chain shot out and caught the middle of Danice's blade. The interlocking links curled around the steel. They wrapped until they were taut. He rotated his shoulder to the side and yanked. Danice's arm jerked at an angle. Her body lurched forward, and her toes dug into the grass. Strips of sod tore away in long, wide chunks. She fell and the chain went slack. Her weapon came free from her hand and she barely maintained her balance.

"You are lost in your rage," Plient told Danice. "You will never be able to defeat me if you do not learn how to control your anger. Come on," he urged, "get your weapon and give it another go. You can do this. I know you can. Just focus." He grinned. A gaping hole was where his bottom

431

teeth should have been.

Danice bent over. She snatched her sword and took a step back. "That was a mistake," she growled.

Diego glanced over his shoulder. "What is going on?" he hollered. He turned his attention to the line of guards. He held the dagger out. The tip trembled. The grip slipped in his hand. "Danice. What do we do?"

"You are not even going to live long enough to regret that," Danice said coldly.

Plient closed his eyes. He lifted his head to the sky and sighed. "You keep talking," he slowly exhaled, "but have yet to do a thing. Let me give you a little piece of advice. It will serve you well if you survive here today." He smirked. A low chuckle escaped his lips. "Keep your mouth shut." He dropped his chin and the smile vanished. "You come in here, screaming about your brother. It is like you want to join him in the afterlife. Next time just attack. Do not wait, do not hesitate, just attack."

"I will keep that in mind," Danice snarled. A grin spread across her face. Blood dripped from her brow. "For the next time." She bent her knees. She held the sword out and advanced.

Diego chanced another look. "Alright," he howled. He spun around and scanned the line of guards. "Time for us to kill them all." He put his right foot forward and waited.

Danice moved cautiously. She kept her elbow bent and her blade in front of her chest. Her eyes were focused straight ahead. Everything faded away. Her world closed in on a single point. Plient was all that remained. His skin had taken on a brilliant shine. Waves of air washed over his body. Muscles in his neck tensed. Light reflected off his corneas. It refracted through the sockets and his eyes sparkled.

Plient nodded. "Finally," he cheered. His grin returned. "It is about time we started this little party of ours." He put his arms out. "Maybe a hug first?"

Danice lowered the saber to her side. She gritted her teeth and turned pink. Her head trembled. Plient took aim. He flipped the chain out and snapped his wrist. Danice dropped to her left. A jagged steel link grazed the top of her ear and a thin layer of skin peeled away. She tilted her head and jolted forward. When she got close, she threw her legs under her body and slid between Plient's feet. She lifted her arm back and thrust the blade up. The edge of the weapon caught flesh and fileted it open. It sliced through the adductor muscles and blood poured over her face.

There was a deafening roar. Plient lost his balance and dropped to one knee. "Very nice," he groaned, "very nice." He slammed his fist into the ground and pushed to his feet. "You get one," he insisted. "Just the one."

Plient whipped the chain around. The strike connected. It hit Danice in the temple as she scrambled to her feet. Her eyes crossed and she fell to the ground. After a moment, her senses returned. She shook her head and blood flew from her hair. She wiped her eyes with the back of her hand. She pulled it away and the epidermis glistened cherry.

"I am really starting to like you," Plient said enthusiastically. "But you will not get another chance." He stepped back and his leg wobbled. "If I catch you again, I am going to end this."

Danice stuck her tongue out. She licked her lips and spit. "All of those muscles you have, and your brain is the smallest one of all," she taunted. She inched back until she was at the base of the steps. "And you are correct, you may catch me again. You might very well end it for me right now. But it is all over for you. No matter what happens, not matter what you do, you are a dead man. You are not going to survive the day." She grinned. Her teeth shined.

"Ha," Plient blurted. He vacillated but remained upright. "And how is that? I have caught you twice now. You have got me once." He looked down. Blood poured from his inner thigh. "It was a nice little move, impressive even, but it is not going stop me from killing you."

"You never learned that one?" Danice asked. She slid onto the first step. "No, not many people do." She got to the second step and sat up. "Our mother taught it to us. She thought it could help against people like you. You always remember to protect the head, but the legs, they are so easy to overlook."

Plient went pale. "What did you do

to me?" he rumbled. He put his hand over the wound. "What did you do?"

"Now let me give you a little piece of advice," Danice snarked. She got up and dropped her saber to her side. "It will serve you well if you survive the day." Her eyes bulged from her head. A wild sneer was set on her face. "Never underestimate your opponent. Size, strength, all that can work for you if used correctly. But it is knowledge that will save you."

"Knowledge," Plient yelled. His voice slurred. "Knowledge." He rocked backwards. "I want to see knowledge save you when my Daisy here is wrapped around your neck." He cracked the chain out.

Danice leapt from the porch. Steel struck steel and sparks showered the ground. She swept her arm to the side. She lunged in and just missed Plient's oblique. The blade slid along the side of his back and the skin slit open. Plient howled. He balled his hand and punched. There was a loud crunch. Danice's head snapped backwards. Knuckles connected with her unprotected septum and the bone caved in.

"What are you waiting for?" Plient roared. He looked at the line of guards behind him. "Get them." His voice was suddenly weak. He returned his focus to Danice and took another swing. She parried his attack and they locked in combat.

The guards looked anxiously about. One of them took a step. He took a second and the others followed. They moved in a staggered formation. Their weapons were matching longswords. The metal was tempered in the morning sunlight. Rust dotted the bulk of the blades. Large pits had formed along the length of the edges. Strips of leather hung off the grips. The ends curled away from the pommels in ribbons.

Diego shifted his feet. "Are you sure you want to do this, boys?" he asked. He took a stride and his foot slipped. "We have seen enough blood for one day," he said honestly. "Why make it any worse than it already is."

The guards advanced. When they were within striking distance, Diego lurched into an enemy. He snatched him by the cuirass that covered his chest. His fingers curled around the opening between the breastplate and the pauldron that protected his shoulder. He threw all his weight forward and lifted. The guard elevated off the ground. His arms flew above his head. He lost his grip on the sword and it launched into the air. It arced away and they crashed to the earth.

Nobody moved. The guard to their left shook his head. He spun to the side and swiped his sword down. Diego rolled his body. He continued until his back was flush with the soil. When he got completely over, he shoved the guard into the air. The strike hit the armor plating. It slid down a curve in the steel and jammed into the ground.

The detachment of guards swarmed. Diego released his hold and dropped his hands to the dirt. He dug his heels in and squirmed backwards. When his torso was exposed, he pulled his legs free and spun to his stomach. He got to his knees and scrambled ahead. Something solid struck him along the base of his spine. There was a loud crack and he toppled over.

"Diego," Danice squealed. She braced against the steps. Plient swiped his chain down and she parried. "This is it." She blocked a strike with her free hand. It struck her pinkie and the bone snapped.

Plient launched the chain

in at an angle. It coiled around Danice's neck. "Such a shame," he gasped. His breaths were shallow. "I really thought you would put in a bit more of an effort." He plucked the sword from her hand and tossed it to the side. "I am more disappointed than anything." He grabbed the opposite end of the chain and turned her around. "That is my fault. I expected too much from you." He pulled her close and their bodies pressed together. He yanked his wrist and the chain pulled tight.

Danice clawed at her throat. She tried to scream. A low grunt emanated from deep in her gut. It got to her lips and she squeaked. Plient stuck his knee in her coccyx. He arched his back and pulled his arms out. Danice turned pink. Her eyes rolled into the back of her head. All the color drained from her face. Her skin faded to a pale shade of blue.

"No," Diego roared. He kicked his leg out. His boot connected with a set of greaves. "Get off of me." He kicked again. A blade came down and punctured the back of his knee. He collapsed to his side. A horrifying shriek pierced the air.

"My, my," Plient snorted. He started to sway. "This was," his voice faded. "This was… what is wrong with me?" His elbow dropped. His fingers trembled. He tried to reposition his hands and the links slipped through his fingers.

The chain went slack. A wave of oxygen flooded Danice's brain. Her senses returned in a flash. Her hands shot to her throat. She pawed at the noose. When she couldn't get a solid grip, she flipped her hand around and forced her fingers through a gap between steel and skin. She worked until she had some room and tugged her head free.

"Not yet," Danice muttered. She stumbled down the steps. She looked over to Diego and hesitated. He was completely obscured by bodies. "Not yet," she repeated. She swiveled around and lunged for the nearest guard.

Plient snatched Danice by the hair. He yanked down. Roots peeled away from her scalp. "I am done playing with you," he snarled. "It is time for me to end this." He wrapped his fingers around the back of her neck and shoved her towards the ground. Plient raised his arm into the air. "Join your brother," he said coldly. He swung his hand towards the base of Danice's skull.

"No," someone wailed. "I want my mother." Archer jumped from the awning. He landed on Plient's shoulders and grabbed his wrist. "You know where she is," he hollered. "Give her to me."

Plient stumbled. His knee

gave out and he dropped. "Archer," he blurted, "is that you?" He flicked his arm out to shake him loose.

The guard's attention wavered. They caught sight of the attack and stopped. Diego eased from the pile. He crawled his way towards the edge of the field.

"Where is she?" Archer yelled. He curled his legs around Plient's neck. He crossed his ankles and applied pressure to his trachea. "You tell me right now or I will kill you."

Danice shuffled backwards. "Do it Archer," she hollered. "Kill him. Kill him now."

"He will not kill me," Plient slurred. He rocked back. His eyelids fluttered. "Will you Archer?"

Archer squeezed his legs together. "Yes, I will," he insisted. "You know I have killed before. I will do it again if you force me too."

"Do it," Danice pleaded.

"Finish this right now."

Plient tried to turn his head. "I know you have killed before," he acknowledged. He slumped over. "But patricide, that is something entirely different."

"Where is she?" Archer demanded. He bowed his back and hyperextended Plient's elbow. "This is your last chance. You tell me right now. Where is she?"

"Last chance," Plient grunted. He sucked in air. He exhaled and his body swayed. "I find that hard to believe. I mean come on now," he took a shallow breath. The vein in his neck throbbed. "Are you really going to kill your own father?"

Chapter 13

1

On the second floor of Lady Carol's estate a battle commenced. The bed at the center of the room lurched. Deuce twisted his legs under his body. He shifted his weight to the top half of his frame and threw himself forward. Alex toppled over. His head snapped back and smacked the bedframe. A gash tore open at the base of Alex's skull. Blood flowed from the wound. Bright viscous fluid stained the comforter red.

Deuce pushed down. He curled his fingers around Alex's throat and squeezed. Nails pierced the skin on the back of his neck. His thumbs dug into the jugular notch just above Alex's sternum. He shoved his knuckles upwards and applied pressure to his larynx. Alex gurgled. Pale pink spit bubbled on the tip of his lips. His eyes turned white and his arms dropped to his side.

Lasaria shifted around the corner of the bed. "Wake up," she pleaded. "Deuce, wake up." She ducked her head between Alex and Deuce. She threw her hands down and got a hold over Deuce's thumbs. "You are stronger than her." She peeled his grip loose. "You can beat this."

Oxygen seeped into Alex's lungs. He sucked in air and his eyes quivered open. He tried to turn his head, but it hardly moved. He tilted forward and felt an immense strain on his throat. His shoulders sank into a thick cotton blanket. His eyes popped from his head. The muscles in his arms started to spasm. A violent tremble went down the length of his spine. He jerked upright and his forehead connected with Lasaria's chin.

The group flopped to the side. They rolled over the lip of the mattress and launched from the bed. Lasaria was stuck between the two bodies. She tried to pull her torso free and her feet slid out from under her. As she fell, the heel of her boot caught on the edge of a wooden plank. Her foot stayed planted in place and her knee bent awkwardly. It snapped backwards. There was a deafening shriek and she crumpled.

Alex crashed onto his tailbone. A handful of stones scattered out from under his body. He grabbed Deuce by the collar and tossed his weight around. They spun across the floor clutched as one. Deuce struggled to maintain his grip. He clamped his fingers down and squeezed. His nails slid over Alex's skin. Long marks clawed across the side of his neck.

"Come on, man," Alex panted. He flipped Deuce onto his back. He extended his arms and got some separation between them. "Snap out of it." He reared his arm to the side. He flung it forward and smacked Deuce across the cheek.

Deuce glared back. A handprint flared on the side of his face. His pupils were lost amidst a cloud of smoke. He was void of emotion. After a moment he shot up. He wrenched his arms out and flipped over. Alex slammed the bottom of the armoire. It knocked back and hit the wall. There was a soft click and the door popped open.

"My leg," Lasaria said calmly. She

braced her hands on the floor and eased against the bedframe. "It will not move."

"Yeah," Alex huffed, "well, I kind of have my own problems at the moment." He dipped his head and slipped it under Deuce's axilla. He wiggled his shoulders, pulled his elbows in by his sides, and got his hands to the floor. He clenched his teeth and shoved.

Deuce flopped over. He fell back and his head hit the trim at the base of the armoire. There was a hollow clunk. The piece wobbled and door swung ajar. Alex shifted around. He scrambled on his hands and knees and threw his body over Deuce's torso. He pinned one of his wrists between his feet. He stretched the other arm out and held it under his body. Alex reached out. He found a loose Vitality stone and pressed it into the palm of Deuce's hand.

"Um, Alex," Lasaria said urgently. "There is someone else here." She reached to her ankle.

Alex bent forward. "I've almost got him," he puffed. "I can feel it." He felt around under the bed. "If I can just find a few more stones." He closed one eye and stuck his tongue out of his mouth. "Just a few more," he mumbled.

"No," Lasaria insisted, "someone is in the…" she trailed off. Her hand shot in the air. She gestured wildly across the room. "It is Lady Carol, she is here."

Pale brown fingers appeared from inside the armoire. Long white nails extended from the tip of each digit. They caressed the paneling around the opening. A hand emerged from the darkness. A linen sleeve hung loose off the wrist. The door creaked open and a slender woman stepped to the floor. A bright silver mane looped into a knot on the top of her head. Her eyes were a deep shade of violet.

Lady Carol looked at the commotion

and frowned. "My, my, how predictable," she said. She took two paces. The hem of her long white dress swept across the floor.

"Almost there," Alex said. He took the handful of vitality stones and ground them into Deuce's flesh. "If Archer was right, this should do it."

Lasaria pulled a dagger from her boot. She jabbed it out. "Why are you doing this?" she shouted. Her hand trembled. "What do you have to gain by working for Ulrich Flemming?"

"What are you talking about?" Alex asked. He glanced over and then looked back at Deuce. "I'm doing this because it was the plan to…" he stopped talking. He slowly turned his head around. "Oh, no," he blurted.

Lady Carol swept her arm to the side. An invisible force hit Alex in the face. His head snapped back, and he toppled over. "This is none of your concern," she insisted. "All I want is the girl." She turned her attention to Lasaria.

"Ulrich Flemming is a monster," Lasaria shouted. "How could you work with someone who killed so many of your own kind?"

"My sister was a nuisance." Lady Carol slunk towards the exit. "But that is not why we are here. I have absolutely no intention of handing you over to anyone." She turned and offered Lasaria her hand. "A woman like you should be free from the shackles of morality. The things you could do without that pesky little burden holding you down. That will be my gift to you. Take my hand, join my coven."

Lasaria thrust her dagger out and caught Lady Carol on the finger. It sliced open. "I am not a twin," she roared. "I have no powers for you to exploit."

Deuce groaned. He shook his head and color returned to his face. "Alex," he muttered, "Lasaria, where are we?" He reached up and rubbed his eyes. "What is going on?"

Lady Carol looked at the cut on her hand. "You may not have been born a twin," she agreed, "but there is a power inside you that no mortal can control." She lifted her eyes. "Leave them and come with me." She put her hand out. "This is your last chance."

"I would never join you," Lasaria spat. "You have no honor. You have no soul."

"No honor," Lady Carol mused, "no soul. Very well." Her hand shot out. Bright red strands wove around her fingers. "I gave you a chance." She spun towards the door and tugged. Lasaria's head jerked violently. Her neck cracked and she toppled forward. "Now it is time for the two of us to have a little fun."

Lady Carol secured the fistful of hair. She curled her wrist and thrust her hand down. Lasaria's body jerked. Her legs flipped, and she spun onto her stomach. Lady Carol floated over the floorboards. She slipped through the doorway and turned left. Lasaria's boots dragged behind her. They hit the threshold to the hall and caught on the frame. They stuck for a moment and were gone.

The room was quiet. Deuce got to his elbows and looked about. "Alex," he said frantically. "Alex, wake up. Something is wrong. I think someone just took Lasaria."

"Ughhh," Alex groaned, "what happened?" He brought his hands to his forehead and pinched his temples. "It is like my head is split open."

Deuce sat up. "We have got to go," he insisted. "That woman, I think it was Lady Carol. She has Lasaria."

"Of course, it is Lady Carol." Alex

reached around to the back of his head. His fingers grazed a round protuberance, and he winced. "But wait a second," he exclaimed, "you're alright. You're not a zombie anymore."

"Slow down," Deuce insisted, "just slow down." He turned his hand over and took a Vitality Stone from his palm. "So, you came here to save me? Why was it just the two of you? Where is Diego? Where is my sister?"

Alex turned to his side. He squeezed his eyelids together and blinked. "We split into groups," he said. "They're outside, We're inside." His nose scrunched. "Wait," he blurted, "where is Lasaria?"

Deuce shook his head. "That is what I was trying to tell you. Some woman took her. It must have been Lady Carol."

"What?" Alex exclaimed. "No." He jumped to his feet. "Where did they go?" he asked frantically.

"They just left." Deuce braced against the wall and worked his way up. "If we hurry, we can catch them."

Alex dashed towards the door. He got to the threshold and looked back. "We have to go," he shouted. "We have to save her."

Deuce took a step. His knees wobbled and he tripped. "Go," he insisted, "I will be right behind you."

"Are you sure?" Alex asked.

"Go," Deuce repeated. "Go now."

2

On the far side of Lady Carol's estate, time slowed to a standstill. The sun crept gingerly along. It neared the apex of its ascent and pulsed unobstructed. An azure sky stretched over the top of the trees. It enveloped the estate and extended far beyond the mountain peaks to the west. All the moisture evaporated from the air. The breeze dissipated and the temperature spiked.

"Archer," Plient wheezed, "the runt of my litter. What is your plan here?" He slumped over and propped his weight on his free hand. "Because where it stands, you are outnumbered three to one. Not the most promising odds, I would say."

Archer adjusted his grip. His fingers slipped and he nearly lost his hold. "You know what I want," he grunted. He wiggled his body down and slid his foot up his calf. He formed a triangle between his knees and his groin and positioned it around Plient's throat. "Where is my mother?" He clamped down.

"Just kill him," Danice hollered. She glanced to her side. A brilliant flare reflected off a steel blade. "We can find her when he is dead." She rolled over and scrambled for the weapon.

Plient rocked forward. "Did you think she would just let her walk away?" he managed. "After that little stunt she pulled, trying to run with you like that." His eyes drifted closed. He started to sway. "Look around you. There is nobody left. They tried to leave, and she killed them. She killed them all. It is only me, now."

"No," Archer snapped. He pinched his legs together as hard as he could. "She is alive, she has to be alive."

"Maybe," Plient said softly, "but you will never know." A smile crept onto his face. He laughed. "That will be your curse."

Plient wrenched back. His hand shot up and he snatched Archer by the throat. He brought his torso forward. He peeled him away from his shoulder and thrust his arm out. Archer launched into the air. He kicked out. His arms flailed around.

They groped for something solid to slow his momentum.

Archer cried out. He floated weightless before gravity finally took hold. His body plunged towards the ground. He put his hands down and slammed onto his tailbone. He bounced and his head snapped back. There was a tremendous crack. All his limbs went slack. His bones turned to rubber and he tumbled through the dirt like a ragdoll.

"Now you," Plient roared. He got to his feet and hobbled around. Blood poured down his inner thigh. It pooled in the grass and soaked the earth. He stuck his arm out and pointed. "Let us go to Elysium together, shall we."

Danice got to her hands and knees. "Elysium." She got to her feet and wobbled. "Elysium is for warriors who have earned the Gods' favor in life." She held her saber out. She closed one eye and pointed the tip of the blade at

Plient's heart. "Even Hades will not take you. You will spend your eternity imprisoned with the Titans."

Plient put his arm out. Dark blue veins ran up his forearm. He flexed and his bicep bulged. "If I find myself in Tartarus," he said, "I will break free and find you wherever you may be." He smiled and winked. "Because you, you I like."

"No more talking," Danice shouted. "It is time we finish this."

"Reluctantly," Plient moaned, "I agree. My time here is limited. So…" He tilted his head. "One last dance, if you please."

Danice tensed. She lowered her arm, stepped forward, and took off. Her mouth dropped open and she raged. Plient kept his arm low. He brought it back and snapped his wrist. The chain looped around. It hit the ground and deflected up at a sharp angle.

Danice timed her jump. She leapt above the attack and swiped her blade to the side. The razors edge sliced into skin. Pink flesh peeled open. She pulled her arm close to her body and twisted. A thick, meniscus organ was cut in half. It popped out of the laceration. Bile and gore spilled onto the soil.

Plient roared. He stumbled in a circle and swung the chain out. Thick steel links looped around. There was a tremendous bang. The strike caught Danice along the jaw. Her head whipped to the side. A hunk of flesh ripped away from her face. She kept her balance and coughed. Shattered bits of teeth disappeared into the grass.

"What should we do?" one of the guards hollered. He slowly advanced. "What should we do?" A guard approached Archer. He got close and kicked him in the side.

"Stay away," Plient demanded. He

started to sway. "This battle I fight alone." He turned to look at the guard. "And besides," he huffed, "you have your own problem to deal with."

The guard did an about face. He tried to shout out. Words escaped him and he squealed. Diego ran from the field. His arms were tuck in at his chest. His broadsword was perfectly vertical. He approached the bulk of the guards and roared. They turned in mass. He swiped his arms around and the blade caught someone just below the helm. It slipped through and sliced the bone clean in half. The guard's hands went to his neck. He staggered and collapsed.

Diego slid to his right. He repositioned his hands and lifted his weapon to his chin. When he had it elevated, he tipped it horizontally and whirled in a circle. The blade clipped the guard closest to him. There was a thunderous bang and he toppled over. He continued around and aimed his strikes. The tip nicked one guard on the jugular. He screamed and stumbled from the fight. He got a few paces away and crumpled to the earth.

"It looks like none of us are going to survive the day," Plient chuckled. He pressed his elbow against his side and winced. "It is better they die anyway." He motioned to his fallen minions. "Poor things. They would have no idea how to get along without me."

"What is wrong with you?" Danice slurred. She touched her face and cringed. "All of this death and you are still playing around."

Plient looked at his wrist. "Such is life." His breathing was labored. "It is all so absurd anyway. None of it truly matters." He peeled the chain away from his hand. "We live and we die. What happens in between those two events is irrelevant."

"How can you say that?" Danice scoffed. She glanced over at Diego. He parried a coordinated strike and cut two guards to pieces. "Everything we do matters. You think you can torture and kill without consequences?" She started to tremble. "In this life, and the next, you will suffer. I will see to it you never find a moment of peace."

Plient grinned. "I think I am in love," he sang. He belched and blood sprayed from his lips. "It is a shame we had to meet this way. We would have made a great pair, you and I. Even Ulrich Flemming would have bowed to us."

Danice marched forward. She switched her sword to her opposite hand and slapped Plient across the face. "You kill kids," she screamed. She slapped him again. "I would never be with a monster like you." Tears streamed from her eyes.

"Well," Plient moaned, "about that."

He looked away. "I might have lied about that one. The truth is I never even saw your brother. Alive, dead, who knows." He shrugged.

"Enough," Danice shouted, "just stop it." She swung her leg out and booted Plient in the side of the knee. He buckled and collapsed on all fours. "You are a coward. You will die with your face in the dirt."

Plient stretched his head out. "Make it a clean cut. Just below the base of the skull. One swift strike should do the trick." He reached his hand around and tapped the back of his neck. "Right here if you can. I trust you more than anyone to get the job done properly."

"Is this amusing to you?" Danice rubbed her eyes. She took her weapon and held it with both of her hands. "All of this death is just a joke?"

"I can accept what has happened here," Plient said. "Now send me on my way. I am anxious to see where I end up."

Danice's mouth dropped. She sneered and looked around in disbelief. Not far off, Diego stood over a fallen soldier. He lifted his sword above his head and angled the weapon down. He thrust his hands towards the ground. The tip of the blade sunk through the guard's midsection. His body twitched and was motionless.

"Danice," Diego hollered. "What is happening over there?" He braced his foot on the guard's cuirass. He tugged and his sword pulled free.

"Check on Archer," Danice insisted. She turned back to Plient. "Then go and find Lasaria. I will take care of this one." She looked down and glared. "We are almost done here."

Diego limped over to Archer. He knelt and put his hand on his shoulder. "Come on buddy," he said softly. He rocked him back and forth. "Wake up. We can go and find your mother now."

"How pathetic," Plient said. He looked up and started to say something else.

Danice lifted her weapon into the sky. She bent her elbows and brought her hands down. At the last moment she curled her wrists over. She shifted her weight to her arms and screamed. The razor's edge sunk into flesh. It tore through muscle and tendons and cut deep into the earth. Plient's body slumped forward. His elbows wobble and gave out. He hit the ground and his head bounced. It rolled to Danice's feet and struck her in the boot. His eyes were fixed open. A grin was spread across his face.

Danice shuddered. "Let the birds feast on your corpse," she growled. She shut her eyes and shook her head. After a moment she looked up. Lady Carol's estate dwarfed everything around it. "We are coming Deuce," she said. "Alive or dead, we will find you."

3

Alex dashed out of the bedroom. He passed through the doorway and skid onto the landing. Minute particles wafted high into the air. Dust passed through a streak of light and swirled in intricate patterns. A set of prints curved around the banister. Duel lines trailed behind. They cut through a thin layer of dust. He took off after them. At the stairs, he didn't stop. He bounded down four steps at a time. When he hit the bottom, he followed the tracks through an archway at the rear of the foyer. He got to a dividing wall and came to a halt. He stood at the beginning of a long corridor. A black and purple checkered runner covered the length of the floor.

The far end of the hall was completely decimated. A stack of wooden planks had been torn loose from the floorboards. They were splintered in pieces and piled off to the side in a heap. A void in the floor was ripped open between the walls. A spiral staircase plunged into the depths. It went underneath the house and disappeared into the darkness.

Alex hurried over. He placed his toe on the first step. He put his weight on the one leg and bobbed up and down. The stairs didn't budge. He stepped down and waited. The sheath of his karabela tilted back. It hit the metal rail and a hollow ping resonated into the abyss below. When nothing happened, he took off.

At the bottom of the descent the light vanished. The temperature dropped. The stench of rot and decay overwhelmed the air. A cool breeze brushed over Alex's skin. The hairs on the back of his neck stood on end. In the distance, an orange speck stood out in the abyss. It flickered and then disappeared.

"Wait up," Deuce panted.

Alex jumped. "You nearly gave me a heart attack," he huffed. He put his hand over his heart and clenched. "How did you even get down here? I didn't hear you coming down the stairs."

Deuce leaned in. He put his lips next to Alex's ear. "I am just that good," he whispered. He slipped his arm around his shoulders and pulled him close. "What should we do now?" he asked. "My mind is still a little foggy."

"I'm not sure," Alex confessed. He moved his hand to his belt. His fingers caressed the hilt of his sword. "I guess I am just going to run in there and fight. I don't know what will happen, but I have to do something."

"I am not sure why you are helping us," Deuce uttered, "but I have to say, I really do appreciate it." He hugged Alex tight.

Alex kept his eyes straight ahead. "You are my friends," he said. "Your fight is my fight." He slid the karabela free and held it at his side

Deuce chuckled dryly. "Well," he said, "I hope you know what you are getting into." He relinquished his grip. He took his scimitar and held it out. "Oh, I almost forgot," he added. "I grabbed a few of the Vitality Stones off the floor before I got my gear."

"Thanks," Alex said quietly. He tapped down the side of his arm until he found Deuce's hand. They exchanged the Vitality Stones and he tucked them into his waistband.

Alex stuck his hand out. He swept around from side to side and made contact the wall. He leaned over and pressed his weight down. Cold, pliable earth scratched away underneath his nails. The smell of mud and clay filled the air. He stopped and stuck his ear out. Everything was silent. After a moment, he reached back and tapped Deuce on the leg.

"Come on," Alex said. His voice boomed in the darkness. "Let's go," he said softer. He kicked his foot and started ahead.

Deuce reached out. He grabbed the back of Alex's jacket and held the fabric in his hand. "I am right behind you buddy," he whispered. "Right behind you."

They crept along. The passage continued in a repetitive line of nothing for some time. After a while, the circular glow swelled in intensity. It warped from a speck in the distance to a vertical fracture of light. They neared the obstruction and the path was suddenly awash in a muted orange hue. The walls narrowed into a point. They merged and formed a space just wide enough for a single person to pass through. Alex turned his torso. He put his arm through the gap and inched between the rocks. When his chest got to the middle, he sucked his gut in and slipped through the opening.

On the opposite side of the barrier the light erupted into a brilliant radiance. The corridor opened into a cavernous space. A large chamber was studded with marble columns. Thick wooden sticks were wrapped with rags. They were set ablaze and mounted to the wall every few feet. A small ledge was elevated around the perimeter of the room. It jutted out of the stone and wrapped the circumference of the space.

Alex clamped his eyes shut. He waited until they had adjusted to the sudden change. "No," he gasped. His eyes swelled from his head. "What is going on here?"

Lasaria was tethered to the ceiling at the center of the room. Her head was slumped over her chest. A hexagon bolt was hammered into the stone above her head. A thin piece of wire was secured around the threads. The cord was pulled tight. It ran in a line and cut into the flesh on Lasaria's wrists. Streams of blood flowed down her forearms. They passed over the points of her elbows and dripped to the stone below.

"My, my, you are an annoying little thing," Lady Carol moaned. She moved along the ledge and stopped. "Through all of this, I never imagined you would be the one to give me trouble. Such a tiny creature. What am I going to do with you now?"

Alex took a step. "Let her go," he shouted. He stuck the karabela out and took another step. "Just let her go, you hear me?" His hand shook.

"I hear voices," Deuce said. "What is going on." He slipped through the gap and stopped. "Lasaria," he wheezed.

Lady Carol moved closer. "A threat," she said, "how cute. And there are two of you. Whatever shall I do," she said sardonically.

"Lasaria," Deuce repeated.

"I am warning you," Alex barked, "one last time."

"No," Lady Carol snapped back, "I will warn you one last time. This is no game. If you do not leave here now, you will not leave here at all." She opened her arms and put her palms towards the ceiling. "I have lost time and, more importantly, my patience. This is it. Go, now, and forget the girl from your memory."

Alex glanced at Deuce. They locked eyes and he turned to Lady Carol. "I warned you," he yelled. "Now let her go." He thrust his karabela out. He bounced on his toes and charged forward.

Lady Carol pulled her hands towards the middle of her chest. She clenched her thumbs together, an invisible current charged in her palms. The energy glowed purple. She thrust them out and the air split in two. The blast hit Alex in the face. It penetrated through his bones and knocked him backwards. He collided with Deuce. He tumbled over and smashed onto his side.

"What were you thinking?" Lady Carol wailed. She grinned and her teeth glistened. "I am standing 10 feet above you. You were never going to hit me."

Deuce shook his head. He got on one knee and huffed. "What is the end goal here?" he shouted. "Even if you do kill us, her father will never let this go."

Lady Carol frowned. "Let me worry about what comes next," she said. She curled her fingers into a ball. She clenched her fist and it glowed. "You are just children," she lamented. "You will die quickly." She jammed out and a wave sailed from her knuckles.

Alex threw his weight to the side. He rolled behind the closest pillar and covered his head. The blast flew passed his ear. It crashed into the wall and tore a scar in the stone. Chunks of soil and rock rained down around him. He clambered onto his knees and tucked his body into a ball. Lady Carol hurled another blast of energy. It struck the pillar and burst. A brilliant blue light tore up the length of the column. There was a tremendous jolt and the support splintered.

Deuce ducked over. He barreled towards the center of the room and launched ahead. He slammed into the ground. He tumbled forward and smashed into a marble column. A blast hit the floor at his feet. Dirt spewed into the atmosphere. A large depression sunk into the earth. The column started to shake. There was a loud belch and it buckled.

"Alex," Deuce murmured. "Alex." He picked up a stone and tossed it towards Alex. It hit him in the hand. He looked over and scowled. "Distract her," Deuce mouthed. He pointed towards Lady Carol and then to Alex. He tapped his own sternum and pointed to Lasaria.

Alex nodded. He crawled to the stone and squat behind the pillar. "I'm coming to get you," he hollered. He took a deep breath and exhaled. He took another, held it in his lungs, and raced into the open.

A blast of energy tore across the chamber. It hit the marble and deflected away. A second and third wave followed in rapid succession. The first missed. It hit the ground and a gouge split the room in two. The second clipped Alex on the right ankle. His feet flipped out from under him. He slammed onto his left deltoid and crashed to his back.

Deuce ran from cover. He weaved behind an intact column and dove towards the one near the center of the room. He pushed his back against the stone and poked his head out. Lady Carol glanced over. She whipped her hand and a wave of energy cut through the room. Deuce pulled his head back. The blast struck his cover. The foundation lurched. It dropped on a slant and a pair of columns snapped.

"My home," Lady Carol snarled, "look what you have done to my home." She stalked down the ledge. She got to a better position and shot a wave of energy at Alex.

Alex tucked his arms in.

"What we did?" he screamed. "You did this to yourself." He dropped his hand to his belt. He pulled the Manrikigusari free and held it at his side. "I've already warned you," he said sternly. "Now I will tell you. This is your last chance. I don't want to hurt you, but I will."

Lady Carol screeched. She lifted both of her hands over her head and clutched them together. Her body trembled. A pale aura manifested to life. It seeped from her skin and shimmered all around her. Her silver hair glowed. All the oxygen was sucked from the room. The candles flickered and the light faded away.

Visibility was reduced to a bare minimum. Alex counted to three. He held the Manrikigusari out to the side and ran from cover. He angled towards the base of the wall. He adjusted his trajectory and curled around so he was below Lady Carol. He drew near and heaved. The chain flew out. It stretched as far as it could and snapped tight. The counterweight flung to the side. It coiled around Lady Carol's ankles and she fell back into the wall.

Deuce pivoted from cover. He brought his arm back and thrust it forward. The sword slipped from his fingers. It arced through the air and clipped the wire just above Lasaria's hands. The steel cord sliced clean. The tension was suddenly removed, and it snapped towards the ceiling. Lasaria plunged to the floor. Her body rotated as she fell. Her feet hit and she smashed onto her hip.

Lady Carol brought her hands down. The ground rumbled and buckled out in a wave. Energy surged away from her position. The floor tore up in mass. The columns at the center of the room broke free from the ceiling. There was a tremendous whine. The earth jerked in a massive fit. The supports broke free from the foundation and sank.

Alex threw his arms out. He adjusted and tried to maintain his balance. The earth rippled beneath his feet. He teetered and toppled over. As he fell, he wrenched back. Lady Carol's legs slipped out from under her. Her shoulder connected with the ledge. She was pulled from the catwalk and her temple smacked the stone. Her momentum carried her over and she plummeted to the ground.

"What happened?" Deuce shouted. He dashed to Lasaria and hoisted her up.

Alex slunk over to Lady Carol. "She is out cold," he yelled. He looked around. The ceiling on the far side of the room bowed. There was a rumble and it caved in.

"We are about to be buried alive."

Deuce put Lasaria over his shoulder. "We have to go," he stated. He limped towards the exit.

Alex twisted his head around. "What about her?" he asked. He looked to Lady Carol. "We can't just leave her here. She will die."

"There is no time," Deuce said. He got to the void in the wall and maneuvered Lasaria's lower extremities through the opening. "Do you think she would save you?"

Alex shook his head. He dropped to one knee and removed the Manrikigusari from Lady Carol's legs. He tossed the weapon around his neck and grabbed her by the wrist. The air suddenly cracked. Another column snapped and the walls sunk inward. Alex clenched his teeth and heaved. Lady Carol lurched. She moved a foot and got caught on a chunk of stone.

"I can't do it," Alex

grunted. He wrenched with all his might. "I am so sorry," he cried. He pulled his hands away and she fell to the earth. "I am so sorry." He peered down. Her skin was caked in grime. Her eyes were closed tight. "I am so sorry," he repeated. There was a deafening boom. The remainder of the supports crumpled. "I really tried," he muttered. He sniffled and turned away. "I really tried."

4

High in the sky a bird screeched. It watched the disturbance below. It looped the plantation in concentric circles. When the commotion ceased, a second flew in low over the top of the trees. It swooped down and scanned the whole of the clearing. Near the epicenter of the carnage, it rolled to the side. Its beak opened wide and it wailed a long, somber note. At the far side estate, it veered up on a steep trajectory. It curled back and joined the other in flight.

Danice stepped over Plient's body. She slid her sword into its sheath and walked a few paces. At the edge of the battleground, she stalled. A soldier was crumpled over onto his chest. His arms were folded under his body. His legs were locked in a V. To her right, a second soldier was motionless. His neck was sliced just above his cuirass. His head was severed clean. The helm had rolled a few feet before it finally came to a rest.

Farther away a group of combatants were piled together in a heap. Their armor was completely battered. Every inch of the steel was peppered with large pits. Sizeable gaps were accessible between each individual piece of gear. The flesh beneath was shredded into bits. Blood pooled beneath them. It soaked into the dirt and started to coagulate.

Danice smacked her face. She smacked herself a second time and a faded print formed over her cheekbone. In that moment, her mind snapped into focus. She scoffed, shook her head, and took off. She veered around the mass of bodies. She jumped a dark stain. At the perimeter of the field, she pivoted. She planted her feet and barreled along a row of crops. Thick stalks clawed at her jacket. She dropped her head. She sprinted into the open space between the two pastures and skid through the grass.

Danice dug her heels in and dove to the side. "Oh man," she hollered. She whirled on her toes.

"What the?" Diego swiveled. He grabbed Archer by the shoulder. "Danice," he shouted. "I could have killed you."

"You should be closer by know," Danice said sternly. "Why are you walking?" She put her hand up to her jaw. She tapped the bone and winced.

Diego backed down a small embankment. "Both of us can barely walk," he said. He got to the center of a long culvert. He patted his feet and water splashed over his boots. "And I feel like half of my internal organs are crushed."

"Who cares about any of that?" Danice barked. She turned and shuffled ahead. "My entire face is broken. But none of that matters. We need to find Deuce."

"And we will," Diego insisted. "But we will never survive another fight like that." He put his thumb up and motioned over his shoulder. "We need to be smart about this. We need to give Lasaria and Alex a chance."

Danice made a fist. She wrapped her

fingers over her knuckles and squeezed. "I am not going to wait," she said carefully. "You can stay here with the kid for all I care. But I," she paused. She looked into Diego's eyes. "I am going."

"That is not fair," Archer snapped. He looked at Diego and back to Danice. "You are supposed to help me find my mother. You promised."

"No," Danice said. "We find Deuce, then we find your mother. That was the deal."

Diego laid his arm around the middle of Archer's back. "She is probably in the house," he said. He slipped his hand under his arm and eased him off the ground. "Danice, you go. I will get Archer to the back porch. When I know he is safe, I will find you."

"But," Archer protested.

"We will find her," Diego interrupted. He adjusted his hold and propped Archer on one leg. "She has got to be in the house."

Danice turned towards Lady Carol's residence. "Deuce," she yelled out, "I am com–"

A thunderous explosion cleaved the calm in two. The ground surrounding the structure started to rumble. All the vegetation within a radius to the north tore from the soil. There was a piercing whine. The house belched and tipped to the side. A large beam along the center of the roof snapped. The frame bulged out and the second-floor veranda buckled inward. A series of pops fired off in rapid succession. Shards of glass burst from the windows. The floor joists gave way and the second level collapsed in on itself.

"By the Gods," Danice said breathlessly. She stumbled a few feet. Her world shrunk into a singular tunnel of vision. She took a step, paused, and bolted towards the house.

Rubble and debris billowed from the devastation in a haze. Massive sections of foundation were fractured into pieces. The cement slabs that remained were crushed under the weight of the ruins. Splintered lengths of timber poked out from the pile like spikes. A lone pillar stood intact. A swatch of floorboard teetered awkwardly on the point. It tipped over and the column snapped at the base.

"How did this happen?" Archer shouted. He sprinted passed Danice and stumbled. "How did this happen?"

Something moved along the outer perimeter of the structure. Repetitive actions stood out amongst the shifting wreckage. After a moment, a silhouette slowly materialized. Deuce hobbled from the cloud of dust. He bounced on the balls of his feet and changed the position of his arms. Lasaria was slumped over his shoulder. Her vibrant auburn hair was muted to a dull shade of red.

Deuce wiped the grime from his face. He leaned forward. "Danice?" he asked. "Danice, is that you?"

Danice stopped in her tracks. She put her hands in front of her chest and turned her palms to the sky. She lifted her head and clamped her eyes shut. All the energy surged from her body. Tears streaked down her cheeks. They cut through the blood and exposed the light pink flesh underneath. Her legs trembled. They wavered and she collapsed to her knees.

"Lasaria," Diego shouted fervently. He threw his arms open and ran towards Deuce. "What happened to her? Is she alive?"

Archer ambled over to the remains of the house. "Mom," he cried. He looked around frantically. "Mom," he choked.

"Lasaria is alive," Deuce assured. He

dropped and laid her in the grass. "But there was no one else in the house. Just the four of us. Alex tried to save Lady Carol. I grabbed Lasaria and got out of there." He started to cough.

Danice slumped back. "Deuce is alive," she mumbled, "Deuce is alive, Deuce is alive, Deuce is alive," she repeated softly.

"I am alive," Deuce agreed. "But we have to go back in and find Alex. I cannot just leave him in there. He is the only reason we got out at all." Deuce looked to his sister. "Even if he is dead, we still have too..." his voice trailed off. He got to his feet "You are hurt," he said breathlessly. "Like hurt really bad."

"Oh no," Danice smiled. The teeth on the bottom side of her mouth were missing. "This is nothing. What," she asked, "am I not pretty anymore?"

Deuce knelt beside Danice. "Oh no," he moaned, "I think the battered face will make you more appealing. Maybe even Anika will finally notice you."

Danice chuckled. "Who knows. She will not tell me if she does. But she will probably like the scars." She sat up and put her arms around Deuce. "I am so glad you are here." She hugged him. "Mom never would have forgiven me if you got to see her first."

"Could you imagine," Deuce hooted. "You would have spent all of eternity listening to her complain." He clamped his hands together and pulled his sister tight. "She would have been happy to see us though."

"Yes," Danice said softly, "she would have. But not yet. She would not want to see you yet."

Someone grunted in the shadows. "What about me?" Alex asked. He sauntered from the ruins and put his hand out. "Do you think there will be anyone who wants to see me again?"

"Alex," Diego shouted. He spun on the ball of his foot. "You are alive." He rushed forward. He snatched Alex by the shoulder and wrenched him in. "You saved her," he said, "you saved my princess."

Alex blushed. "Group effort," he insisted. He put his arms around Diego's midsection and they embraced. "What happened to you guys?" he asked. "It looks like you went to war."

Diego bobbed his head. "How did you get out of the house? Deuce said you tried to save Lady Carol. Is that true?" He smiled.

"What about my mother?" Archer shouted. He turned around and stomped towards the group. "You are all so proud of what you have done here, and I still have nothing." His skin turned bright red. "What about my mother?"

Alex pulled from Diego. "She wasn't out here?" he asked.

Archer took another step. "No," he shouted. He curled his fingers into fists and started to shake. "She was not out here. Did you see her in the house?"

"No," Deuce admitted.

Diego put his hand out. Archer swatted it away. "We can still try and find her," he said. "It might just take some time, is all."

"Liars," Archer screamed. "You are all liars. You were never going to help me find my mother. You lied to me and now I have nothing."

Alex lowered his head. "We will find her, we will. But you need to calm down."

Archer cocked his fist back. "Calm down," he shouted frantically. "Calm down. My mother is still missing, and that one just killed my father." His eyes glassed over.

"Father?" Alex turned to Diego.

"I will show you what I do to liars,"

496

Archer screamed. His voice cracked. He snapped his arm forward and his knuckles caught the side of Alex's face. He followed through on his punch. Before anyone could react, he took off. He sprinted away and vanished into the remains of Lady Carol's estate.

Chapter 14

1

A stiff gust blew in over the top of the mountains. Parallel clusters of fat cumulonimbus clouds came in from the north and the south. They formed in mass above the tallest peak in the area and blotted out the horizon. Brilliant orange light shrouded the upper ridge of the cloud cover. An assortment of warm colors exploded across the valley. Streaks of pink and red saturated the sky. A static charge built through the atmosphere and the world glowed amber.

There was a persistent breeze. The trees swayed and leaves drifted from the canopy. Diego hacked his sword through a tangle of vines. He turned the blade to the side and sliced the vegetation along the undergrowth. When he had a space wide enough for two people to get through, he rotated the pommel 180 degrees and cut up.

Diego did an about face. He lifted his head and looked to the sky. "It is going to be dark soon," he said. "We should rest here for a little bit before we push on." He looked down. He pinched the tip of his blade between his thumb and finger and ran them along the edge. "Just like the last few nights." A bright green sludge collected on the side of his digits. "We stay on the move until we get to Atina." He flicked the excess buildup away. "And even then, we will not be stopping for long."

"You really need to slow down," Lasaria said in jest. "I can barely walk here." She slid her arm from Alex's shoulder and hobbled forward. "I am fine," she said softly. She reached out and put her hand over Diego's wrist. "Really, I am."

Diego pulled away. "It is not even that," he said. He put his weapon into the scabbard and pivoted around. "With everything that has happened to us, I don't want to take any unnecessary chances." He grabbed vines with both of his hands and tore them free.

"I don't know," Alex wheezed. He put his hands on his hips. "I kind of agree with Diego here. The faster we go, the faster we get out of here."

Lasaria glanced over her shoulder. She scowled. "We have been going for two days," she pleaded. She looked to Diego. "We need rest."

"And we will," Diego countered. He ripped a tangle of foliage from the mass. "But we leave before nightfall. I am not certain we could survive another attack."

Alex stepped forward. "I barely survived the first time," he nipped. "I will be the first one to die if we are ambushed again."

The shrubbery rustled behind them. "Oh, you will be fine," Danice snarked. She limped in propped up on Deuce's arm. "It is the rest of us that need to worry. You have that armor to protect you."

"The armor doesn't really help when you get shot in the shoulder," Alex whined. He spun around and glared at Deuce. "Or choked out." He said seriously. After a second, he grinned.

"Yeah, yeah," Deuce said with indifference. He bent over and helped Danice to the ground. "I am never going to live that one down, am I?"

Alex shook his head. "Never," he insisted.

Deuce chuckled. "You were the one with the Vitality Stones and apparently I still got the best of you." He flipped and plopped next to his sister. "You could have told me any outlandish story you wanted to. I would have had to believe you. Instead you go with the truth," he laughed. "An amateur move, if I do say so myself."

"Lasaria was there," Alex said. He kicked a rock through the dirt. "She would have eventually told you what happened."

"I suppose." Deuce shifted back and leaned against a tree. "I would have done it differently, that is all I was saying."

Danice snorted. "You mean you would have lied," she stated.

"Call it what you will," Deuce said, "but I would have come out of that fight looking like a mighty warrior. Bards would sing songs of my glory."

"You would have done something like that." Danice smiled. She reached around and smacked Deuce on the leg. "Wouldn't you?"

Deuce scoffed. "Are you calling me a liar?" he blurted. He leaned up and tapped his chest. "Are you calling me a liar?"

"I suppose I am," Danice said snidely. "What are you going to do about it?"

"Diego," Deuce said sharply. "Diego. That attack is about to happen right now." He seized his sister by the hair and tugged her back. "How dare you call me a liar," he laughed. He wrapped his arms around her. "This is what you get."

"That is enough," Diego blurted. He spun and dropped his hands to his side. "We need to get some rest."

Everyone fell silent. Deuce looked at Lasaria. She rolled her eyes and shrugged. After a moment, he relinquished his grip. He lifted his hands into the air and scowled. Danice slid to the side. Her elbows sank into the soil and she turned around. She moved away and made a gap between her and her brother.

"Fine, fine," Lasaria relented. She put her arm out and Alex helped her sit. "Wake us up when it is time to go."

"Before it is time to go," Diego snapped. He turned his back to the group. "We will not be here very long."

Lasaria huffed. "Semantics," she said sharply. She laid in the soil and shivered. "You know I really do not like this side of you." She stretched her arms, locked her fingers, and slid her hands beneath her head.

"I don't know," Alex said. He dropped to his knees. Rocks were scattered about. He picked one up and tossed it aside. He grabbed another and cleared a patch of earth. "I kind of like it. Very decisive."

There was an audible grunt. Diego slipped his cloak from his shoulders and turned it over in his hands. He secured the bottom corners and stretched them out as far as they would go. When it was fully extended, he sank to his knees. He laid the coat over the bushes and ran his finger along the stitches. A thin gash sliced the spine of the garment. Small punctures were grouped just below the left lapel. Dark patches stained the ends of both sleeves. He tapped the blood and the fabric clung to his finger.

Diego laid on his side. He took a deep breath and closed his eyes. The air caressed his skin. Small bumps formed at the back of his neck. A bird chirped from the brush. Another joined along and they flew off. He rolled to his side and wiggled his hips. The long leather sheath was caught under his body. He adjusted the weapon to the front of his body. He dug into the jacket and rolled onto his back. After a second, he rolled to the side. He shifted again and flopped to his back. Diego opened his eyes. He sucked in through his nose and exhaled out from his mouth. He closed his eyes a second time. His mind went blank.

The light faded away. Diego bolted upright. He whipped his head around and blinked frantically. His companions were still there. Lasaria was on her back. Swooping curls draped over her face. Her nose was just visible through a part in her hair. Alex was turned onto his side. One arm was bent under his head. The other was outstretched. Two of his fingers held a swatch of Lasaria's jacket. Deuce's legs were curled to his chest. His eyes were closed tight. The delicate skin on his lids fluttered. Danice was completely motionless. Her eyes watched a point deep in the trees.

"What is it?" Diego asked.

Danice brought her finger to her lip. "Something is out there," she whispered.

"Another ambush?" Diego got onto his belly. He wormed his way over to Lasaria. "Wake up," he whispered.

"I do not think so," Danice said. She put her hands down and eased up. "It sounds like something else." She wacked Deuce on the leg. "Like an animal… a dog maybe."

Lasaria rubbed her eyes. "Time to go?" she asked.

"Please mama," Deuce pleaded playfully, "just let me sleep for a little while longer." He smiled and stroked his throat.

Danice took Deuce by the arm. "Something is coming," she said sternly. "I am not certain what it is, but it is coming."

Alex leaned on his elbow. "Everything okay?" he asked.

"Something is coming towards us," Diego said. He crawled to his jacket. "Danice thinks it could be a dog. I am not sure. Either way, I want to get on the move before it gets here."

"I like dogs," Alex said. "I have only met just the one, but he seemed to really like me."

Danice put her hand up. "Quiet," she shushed. She lifted her head. "It is too late," she said flatly. "Whatever is coming will be on us before we are gone."

The group got to their feet. They gathered at the center of the clearing and waited. Diego snatched his sword. He clasped it with both hands and stood with his feet shoulder width apart. Danice did the same. She tugged her saber from its scabbard and put her right foot in front of her body. She bounced on the ball of her foot and back onto her heel.

Their immediate vicinity fell silent. All the creatures scattered far from the uninvited intruders. In the distance, a clawing noise closed in on their position. It approached rapidly and its movement became more distinct. A deep, drawn out howl reverberated through the forest. It died away and another quickly followed.

"I know that bark," Alex said. He paced towards the boundary of the clearing. "A kid at the orphanage came back to visit once. He brought his new dog with him. It was a tiny little thing, but it had a great big voice. He said it was a beagle." He put his ear out. "It sounds like something is wrong, though."

The sound faded away. The vegetation rustled and the branches parted. An animal burst through the trees. It leapt onto a fallen piece of

timber and launched through the air.
Alex was paralyzed. The dog's front
paws struck him just below the stomach.
He lurched and his feet gave out. His
knees buckled and he toppled to the
ground.

"He got me," Alex moaned. "He got
me good."

Deuce laughed. "Now that was
funny," he hollered. He slapped his head.
"I like that thing already."

The dog landed on his side. He spun
to his back and his legs kicked the air.
He rocked back and forth and threw his
weight to the side. His entire frame lifted
off the ground. He bounced and rolled
back into the same position. On the
second attempt, he gathered more
momentum and flipped completely
around.

The animal got to his feet. He shook
his head and wiggled his rump. A rotund
belly was covered with fine white fur. A

dark brown coat was covered in a solid black overlay. His ears fell down the side of his head. They hung low and nearly scraped the ground. His tail was covered in coarse, tricolored fur. It was thick at the base and tapered off towards a solid white tip. Halfway up, it bent at a dramatic angle.

"Who are you?" Deuce asked. He put his hand down and slowly approached the dog. "What are you doing all alone out here?"

The dog popped his hindquarters into the air. He put his paws out and lowered his head to the dirt. His jaw opened wide and his tongue flopped out of the side of his mouth. He lifted his head and howled.

"I suppose that is an answer," Deuce laughed. He stood and turned to Danice. "Can we keep him?" he jibed playfully. "I promise I will take care of him."

The dog trotted to Alex. He pawed at

his leg and howled.

"What do you want from me?" Alex demanded. He reached out and pet the dog's head. "I am all out of food."

A whirling hiss penetrated the surrounding forest. Deep in the trees, the amber glow of twilight sliced in two. A wave of energy rippled out from the center point of a projectile. It streaked through the air and came into the clearing.

"Deuce," Danice screamed. She wrapped her arm around Deuce's shoulder and pulled him to her chest. She forced him to the ground and arched her back.

There was a hollow thud. Danice lurched. She tipped forward. Her knees wobbled and she swayed. A long wooden cylinder pierced her tunic. It cut clean through just below her left shoulder blade. A small portion remained visible. Three dark feathers were fashioned to the end. Blood pooled at the heart of the puncture wound. It soaked through in a ring.

Deuce put his hands up. "No," he trembled. "What?"

The dog howled. Alex grabbed him around the chest and dragged him between his knees. He ducked his head and bent his body over the animal.

A second hiss matched the first. Danice twisted her head. "Lasaria," she screamed. She threw her body to side and shoved her hands out.

Lasaria tumbled over. An arrow tore through Danice's wrist. Her arm whipped around and she spun in a circle.

"Danice." Diego's eyes bulged from his skull. "Are you alright?" he yelled. He tore his sword out. "Where are they? I do not see anything."

Danice pulled her arm in. "Go," she wheezed. She rocked forward and stepped towards the edge of their camp.

"Get everyone and get out of here." She took shallow breaths.

"What are you talking about?" Deuce reached for Danice's leg. "We will not leave without you," his voice cracked.

There was movement near their position. A branch snapped and the sound punched the silence. It fell away and the air hissed. Danice threw her weight over. Her shoulder slammed into the center of Deuce's chest. A sickening crunch perverted the serenity of the forest. She staggered but managed to keep her balance.

"Go," Danice coughed. Blood poured from her lips. A shaft punctured the left side of her torso. It ran through her body and came out below the breastbone. "Please." Her head lagged and her legs gave out.

Lasaria got to her stomach. "I wish I still had my bow." She clawed her way over to Danice.

"What can I do?" she asked her.

"Keep them distracted," Diego demanded. He crouched and waddled into the bushes.

Danice rolled to her side. An arrow flew in and hit the ground behind them. "Distract… them," she choked out.

"Deuce," Lasaria shouted, "get over here."

Deuce got on his hands and knees. He hurried over and maneuvered around Lasaria. "You will be alright," he said desperately, "you have to be." He took Danice by the hand. "You have to be," he pleaded.

Lasaria scrambled to the base of a large tree. She sunk her fingers into the dirt and pulled a stone free. "Stay with Danice," she said. "I am going to help Diego."

"Please," Deuce cried. His hand trembled. "Stay with me." He reached down and cupped his sister's cheek. "Stay with me," he cried.

Danice shifted to her back. The arrow in her chest caught on the ground. It tugged and she winced. "Come on," she coughed. Her chest heaved. Blood coated her lips. "You need to get Lasaria and Diego and go."

"I will not leave," Deuce wept. He bent over and put his forehead to Danice's shoulder. "I will never leave." Tears saturated the fabric. "Never, never, never." His voice was muffled.

Danice lifted her arm. She laid her elbow around the back of Deuce's neck and pulled his face to hers. "I love you brother," she said softly, "you know that. But it is time."

There was a tremendous racket. Someone wailed in horror.

"I got him," Lasaria hollered.

Danice coughed violently. Blood spurt from her lips and her eyes glossed over. "Oh, Deuce," she moaned. Her lips twitched into a smile. "Elysium."

"No," Deuce wept. "Please."

Diego came into the clearing and faltered. "No," he gasped.

"It is absolutely beautiful," Danice said quietly. Her arm went slack. It fell over her brother's shoulders. "The flowers, they are everywhere. You will love them."

Lasaria returned. "How is Danice?" she asked Diego. She saw Danice and her mouth fell open. She put her hand to her face. Tears fell down her cheeks.

"Wait," Danice said, "I think I see someone." She strained to lift her head, but it didn't move. "Mother," she asked, "is that you?"

Duece sat up. He leaned on his heels and put his hands over his face. "Danice," he sobbed. He shuddered violently.

"I am older than you are." Danice smiled. She seemed to laugh. "I know," she agreed solemly. "I will be quick. I need to say goodbye first." A glow flickered in her eyes. "Deuce," she said, "Deuce. I am sorry but I have to go now."

Deuce collapsed. He took a deep breath and slowly exhaled. "I know," he said stoically. "It is alright. You were an amazing sister and I will always love you. But the fight is over. Go. Rest."

"What a brother," Danices murmured. She looked content. "I love you so much." The light faded from her eyes. Her chest rose and fell. It didn't rise again.

2

The group made it to Leeds at midday. Thick, dark clouds roared in from the west. They dropped over the mountains and swelled into a single mass. The sun slowly faded to a subdued glow. A static charge built in the atmosphere. There was a deafening boom. The ground shook and flashes of light cracked through the clouds. Fat drops began to fall. Another burst of thunder quickly followed, and rain poured down in sheets.

The front entrance to the city was sealed tight. A guard at the top of the wall saw them approach. He leaned between a crenellation in the stone and motioned to someone below. The outer portcullis rattled open. It ascended and a deafening screech eclipsed the sound of the storm. It elevated to a high-pitched squeal and the center gate started up.

Deuce walked ahead. His head was slumped forward. His arms hung at his side. He pulled a wooden cart behind him. A blanket of hay covered the bed. A pair of wheels at the rear propped the conveyance up. Danice was laid in the center. Her weapons were set at her side. White linen sheets covered her body. Water saturated the fabric and it hugged her like glue.

Diego took massive strides to catch up. "Let me help you," he offered. He laid his hand on Deuce's shoulder. "You have been carrying her since the forest. You do not have to take her the rest of the way yourself."

"I have brought her this far," Deuce said. Rain streamed through his eyes. It streaked down his face and soaked his clothes. "I will bring her the rest of the way home."

"You do not have to do this alone," Diego said. "We are family. We will be here for you until the end."

Deuce kept his eyes straight ahead. "My family is dead," he said, "and so is yours. You are kidding yourself if you think otherwise."

"We are all family," Lasaria said delicately. She trotted up to the cart. She looked at Danice and her chest throbbed. "We choose to be here for one another. We live and die together because it is what is in our hearts. Danice sacrificed herself for all of us. If that is not family, then I will never know what is."

They fell quiet and continued through the front gates. Inside the city, the bulk of the populous had dispersed from the streets. A group of women gathered under a thatched awning. They chatted merrily amongst themselves. When they caught sight of Lasaria they smiled. They saw the devastation on her face and the levity vanished. They continued in silence. A man in a burlap tunic passed by. He moved to the side and bowed.

"Listen," Diego finally said. He put his hand on the crook of Deuce's arm and eased him to a halt. "Let me take her to the castle. You should go and be with Sai. She would want to know that you are alright. Plus," he paused, "she would want to know about Danice."

Deuce lowered the cart. He closed his eyes and shook his head. "I have to be there," he said quietly. "She would have done the same for me."

"Yes," Lasaria agreed, "she would. And you will be. But let us take her to my father. He will send her off with the farewell she deserves."

"I," Deuce muttered. "I."

Lasaria moved passed Diego. She put her arms around Deuce and brought him in. "Go," she urged "be with Sai. Come to the castle when you are ready. Then we will send Danice off together."

Deuce buried his face in the nape of Lasaria's neck. "I am just so angry," he cried. "I am just so angry."

"You have every right to be angry," Lasaria said softly. She clasped her hands together and hugged him close. "But right now, it is time to mourn for Danice. The anger will still be there. Let the sorrow of your loss have its moment."

"It – is – so – hard – " Deuce was barely audible over the storm.

Lasaria relinquished her grip. She stepped back and took Deuce by the hand. "We will be waiting for you at the castle," she assured him.

Deuce lifted his head. He wiped his eyes and nodded. "Sai would want to know," he agreed. He put his hand to his cheek. "I will not be long.

Tell Alex I will get his Vitality Stones for him. I know how valuable they are."

"Never mind any of that." Lasaria pulled away. "The Vitality Stones can wait. Just grieve for your sister. That is all. This war can wait."

Deuce stared into Lasaria's eyes. His face scrunched up and he nodded. "You are my family," he said. He did an about face and walked off. He rounded into an alley, glanced back, and was gone.

Diego watched Deuce go. When he was a distance off, he grabbed the wooden handles and lifted them into the air. He corrected his grip and trudged forward. Lasaria followed. Her right knee was bent askew. She hobbled near the rear of the cart. Alex was farther back. He maintained a healthy distance between himself and the rest of the party. The pup jogged at his heels. His mouth was open wide. His tongue hung over his canines.

Alex hustled to catch up. "Are you sure it wasn't Archer who did this?" he asked. He balled his hand into a fist and hammered it towards the ground. "Because if it was, I am going to kill that little –"

"Not Archer," Lasaria cut in. She shook her head from side to side. "It was a member of the Kai'tu Tai. I killed him and took his payment for Charon as proof."

Alex furrowed his brow. "The what?" he asked. "For whom?"

"Kai'tu Tai," Lasaria repeated. "They are a group of assassins who work for Ulrich Flemming. I am not sure why they were after that dog, though."

The pup bounced on his front paws. Mud splashed onto his fur. It covered the end of his ears and his snout. He barked jovially.

"Okay," Alex said, "but who is Charon?"

Lasaria sighed. "Charon is the gatekeeper to the Underworld. The coin is a payment for safe passage across the River Styx."

"Does Danice need a coin?" Alex asked. He reached down and patted the side of his trousers. "What about Leviticus? I never gave him any sort of payment to take with him. Or me for that matter. Will I need a coin?"

"Danice is in Elysium," Lasaria answered. "She has no need for anything as trivial as a coin." They went passed a large stone building. A woman hollered from the doorway. Lasaria gestured somberly. "I cannot speak for Leviticus," she continued. "As for you, it all depends on how you live your life. Do good things, and Elysium will be your reward."

Alex lowered his eyes. He focused on the ground and followed the trail of footprints. They went deep into the city. Massive structures of timber and stone replaced the more modest buildings on the outskirts. Those who had remained out during the storm were dressed in colorful robes. A man was draped in golden chains. They encircled his stomach and dangled from his wrists. Three people galloped by on horseback. Dark indigo robes were pulled over their heads. They hung loose around their shoulders and shrouded their features.

Farther in, the street curved in an arc. It narrowed and started up a steep incline. Water ran down the slope in droves. Dirt slid away under Diego's feet. His fingers slipped from the cart. He adjusted his hands and tightened his grip. When he regained control, he stomped his heels into the earth. He tipped forward and pressed on.

At the top of the rise, the rain let up. The temperature increased and a swarm of microscopic insects descended into the street. Diego rounded a bend and a fortified stone wall emerged through the fog. They approached and a set of doors swung open. A dozen soldiers hustled through. They split into two groups and took up position on either side of the entrance.

Diego pulled the cart through the procession. He got to the threshold of the castle courtyard and paused. "I will see to Danice," he said, "for Deuce." He walked on.

Lasaria adjusted her coat and ran her fingers through her hair. "Well here we go," she huffed. "It is time for you to meet my father."

Alex turned around. "Hey. Boy," he hollered to the pup. "Get over here." The dog had stopped. He stood at the edge of the street and stared into the distance.

"Get over here," Alex repeated sternly. The dog looked back. He howled and trotted over.

"It is time," Lasaria sighed, "for you to meet the King of Sparham."

3

King Wasagowi's castle was perched atop a rise in the center of the city. Massive granite blocks encompassed the estate. They were stacked five high and fastened together with dark grey mortar. Squat stone towers were built into the outside ring of the fortification. They were spaced in even increments along the top of the wall. A series of openings were chiseled into the front of the battlement. A bronze glow emanated from the closest one. Silhouettes danced in the shadows. A copper helmet popped out from one of the gaps. It watched the activity for some time and slunk inside.

Lasaria lifted her head. She took a commanding breath and walked through the outer gate. A swatch of gravel led into the estate. It weaved through a dense grove of brush and disappeared. Alex followed at Lasaria's heels. He positioned himself directly behind the princess. He hunched over and dipped his head below her shoulders. The pup trotted at their side. His eyes were open wide. His head swiveled from side to side.

"Follow me," Lasaria said. She stopped suddenly. Alex looked up and his forehead collided with the back of her head. "Not that close," she said sternly.

There was a tremendous thud behind them. Alex jumped. He threw his hand to his waist and wrenched his head around. The portcullis was shut tight. The wooden doors slowly closed. A pair of soldiers were assigned to each. They worked in unison. There was a three-count and they heaved. They repeated the movement and the entrance gradually closed.

"Come on," Lasaria demanded.

Alex turned back. "Sorry," he said. "With everything that has happened, I am just a little nervous is all."

Lasaria walked on. "I am sure my father has gotten the news about Danice," she said. "He will have some questions for us."

"Questions?" Alex dashed to catch up. The pup barked. His tail wagged as he ran along. "Like what kind of questions. I don't think I have it in me to –"

"There is no reason for you to worry," Lasaria interrupted. She put her hand in the air and pointed to the sky. "There is only one rule with my father. When he speaks, you listen. If you do that, you will be fine."

"Okay," Alex started, "but –"

Lasaria made a fist. "How about you start right now," she snapped. "Stop talking, start listening."

Alex rolled his eyes. "Fine," he conceded. "Just tell me when I can speak again, will you."

"I can do that," Lasaria said. "Better yet, wait until my father asks you to speak."

Their voices died away and they continued in silence. The courtyard was quiet. Short, thick, trees covered the grounds. They twisted at the top and opened into a canopy of brilliant emerald foliage. Wooden planks were secured to oblong rocks along the edge of the path. Thin strips of braided rope looped under the supports to create seats.

They moved through the courtyard. The path veered to the left. It cut back to the right and opened into a vast clearing. Alex stumbled to a halt. The castle was a single solid structure. Shaded squares of brick lined the wall of the fortification. Steele bards covered the outer perimeter of the roof. A pair of doors were perched open at the center of the building. A pale figure waited just beyond the threshold. Black fabric swathed his body.

A set of marble figures stood watch over the entrance of the castle. Luminous cerulean streaks cut through faded white stone. On the right, a slender man was draped in layers of robes. His face was fixed with a solemn expression. A single strip of gold circled the top of his head. On the left, a young woman beamed. Her eyes leapt from the stone. Her nose was slender at the top. It tapered down and angled up at the tip. A long veil fell over her shoulders. Her arms hung at her side. Short, plump fingers held a rotund belly.

"My father favors defenses over opulence," Lasaria said.

She moved passed the figures. "It looked much different when my mother was alive," she added cynically.

Alex paused. He looked at the statue of Lasaria's mother. "She seems nice."

Lasaria went inside. "She was," she said. She paused in the antechamber. The room was devoid of luxury. "Is my father waiting?" she asked.

The man stepped to the side. "He is," he said softly. He looked at Alex and scowled. "This one is not allowed in the throne room." The man motioned to the pup. "I will take your…" he cleared his throat, "…pet, to your room."

Alex shrugged. "I guess I will see you later then," he said. The pup threw his head back and howled. The sound echoed off the chamber walls. "It will be fine," Alex assured him.

The pup snarled. One eye closed part

of the way and he tilted his head. He howled and turned his back.

"You will see him soon enough," Lasaria reassured. She reached over and took Alex by the arm. "Are you ready?" she asked.

Alex nodded. "What is that expression," he said, "as ready as I will ever be."

Lasaria smiled. She pat Alex on the hand and led him across the foyer. They went down a short corridor and came to a door. The wood was faded to a dull shade of beige. Gaps had formed between the planks. A thick, black substance was smeared in the cracks. It expanded and dried into a hardened shell. A single iron handle was mounted on the left side of the frame. The tarnish was rubbed down to the base metal.

"I thought it would be more dramatic," Alex admitted.

"It used to be," Lasaria

said quietly, "when my mother was alive. Now this is where my father holds court."

Lasaria held her breath. She locked her arm around Alex's elbow, and pushed the door ajar. They huddled together and went in. The room was an oval chamber no larger than a bedroom. Soft candlelight gently illuminated the space. The walls were bare. Most of the furnishings had been removed. A dark carpet covered the floor. A single seat was bolted to the center.

King Wasagowi was alone in the room. A black robe shrouded his figure. It caught under his backside and pulled tight over a bulbous belly. He sat slumped forward. A wisp of lengthy, grey hair hung over the side of his face. It receded into a horseshoe and clung to the back of his head. His elbows dug into his knees. His hands were clasped together over his mouth.

"Lasaria," the King said. He heard the door open and stood up. "I am glad to see you are home in one piece."

"Father," Lasaria said. She tugged Alex forward. "I am sure you have heard about Danice."

The King closed his eyes. "Yes, yes," he said softly. "Diego has already come and gone. Poor Deuce. How has he managed?"

"I told him he could take his time coming up here to say goodbye," Lasaria said. "But I imagine he is already on his way."

"I suspect the same." The King approached. He touched Lasaria on the shoulder. "Preparations have already been made. She will have a sendoff befitting her life."

Lasaria slipped her arm from Alex. "There is so much I must tell you." She put her hand into her coat and pulled a coin from her pocket. "Ulrich Flemming is on the attack. I took this from the Kai'tu Tai I killed. What he was doing so far from the Barrens, I could not say."

The King put his hand in the air. "We will have time for all of that later," he said softly. "Right now, I would like you to introduce me to your friend."

Alex focused on his feet. "I am Alex," he said. He looked up and put his hand out. "It is nice to meet you."

"Diego told me you helped Lasaria escape from Lady Carol." The King stared at Alex's hand. He did nothing. "For that, I will always be truly grateful."

Alex pulled his arm in. "We all worked together," he said. "It was Deuce who got her out of the house before it collapsed. I don't even really know how I got out."

There was noise in the hallway. Muffled voices conversed in frantic tones. The King looked up. Lasaria and

Alex turned towards the door. Sai Lee walked into the room. Her eyes were solid red. Creases formed at the side of her face. A film crusted her cheeks in streaks. She swept to the side and Deuce entered.

"Deuce," Lasaria said startled. "You did not need to come up here so soon."

The King took a step. "Oh Deuce," he sighed, "I am so sorry my son."

"I told Sai what happened," Deuce said flatly. "We both agree that Danice would want us to get this over with."

Lasaria touched his cheek. "Are you certain?" she asked. "We can wait."

Deuce slowly rotated his head. "I am done waiting." His voice was cold. "Danice is dead. Her body is all that is left. We will see it on its way. When that is done, we kill anyone who had a hand in this."

Sai Lee snorted. Her chest heaved. She started to cry. "Danice would not want that," she blurted. Tears poured down her face. "I cannot lose you too."

"It is all I have left," Deuce said.

The King glanced at Lasaria. He looked to Sai Lee and then at Deuce. "Come," he insisted, "I have something to show you." He took Deuce by the hand. He led him through the doorway and into the hall. "I am not certain that everything will be ready just yet, but we have prepared Danice for her journey ahead."

Lasaria hooked Alex about the elbow. She put her free arm around Sai Lee and directed them into the corridor. They trailed behind. Alex fixed his gaze ahead. He located a small indentation in the wall and focused his attention on the defect. Sai sniffled. She hiccupped and cried.

"Danice is gone," Deuce said bluntly. "I saw her on her way. This is nothing."

The King pulled Deuce in. "You said goodbye," he said kindly, "but there are those of us who will miss Danice dearly. We did not get the same moment as you. Let us have our goodbye."

"I suppose," Deuce grumbled. "For you."

"Not only me." The King smiled weakly. "There are others who asked they be allowed to join us tonight as well."

Deuce lowered his head. "I am not going to wait until tonight," he said sternly. "When this is over, I am going to the Blood and Dagger. If anyone wants to find me, that is where I will be."

They descended a small set of stairs. The corridor curved away before it hit an intersection. King

Wasagowi steered them to the left. They went through a stone archway and approached a thick wooden door. The King stopped. He let Deuce free and turned to face him.

"A loss such as this is a terrible thing," the King said. "It is how we face the loss that determines who we are as people. Do you have the strength to carry on? Or do you curl up and die. The choice is yours, and yours alone."

The King took his hands away. He turned towards the door and grabbed the latch. He looked to Deuce. He nodded and leaned in. The door opened a pinch. It hit something solid and bounced back. The King furrowed his brow. He used his weight and shoved. The door opened a bit. It hit something else and snapped back.

"Wait," someone insisted. "I will get it."

There was a brief uproar. The volume

swelled and quickly fell away. The door lurched. There was the sound of shuffling and it slowly opened. The sun flooded the corridor in warmth. Deuce shut his eyes. He waited for his vision to adjust and stepped outside. The plaza was packed. People stood shoulder to shoulder. They surrounded a stone slab. Brush was piled at the center. A figure was set atop. Bright linen cloth wrapped her body.

A slender woman stood near the base of the pyre. Long, black hair flowed over olive skin. A man to her left shared the same complexion. He leaned in and whispered in her ear. She nodded. She pulled a stick from the pile of kindling and walked to Deuce. When she was right before him, she held it out. They locked eyes. Deuce nodded and took the stick. She returned the gesture and turned away.

"Today we say goodbye to a

warrior," Deuce said loudly. He held the stick out. Someone leaned in and a flame flickered up from the end. "A warrior and the best sister a guy like me could have ever hoped for." He started forward. The group separated. He approached the pyre and leaned in. "Rest easy dear sister," he said softly. He laid the flame upon the stone slab and it jumped to the pile. "I will see you soon."

4

Alex stood before a stone hearth. He clutched a long iron rod in his hand and poked the charred remains of log. It crumbled to ash and the center of the fire caved in. Flames leapt from the grating. They flickered and stained the flue black. Above the mantel, a square of shaded brick covered the wall. Small silver hooks were placed on opposite ends of the discoloration. A thin metal wire hung from one of the mounts. It uncoiled and the end started to fray.

There was a loud pop. A burning ember soared from the fire. It floated away and drifted gently to the floor. The pup jumped. He stood at the end of the bed and tilted his head. After a moment he howled. His voice was deafening in the chamber. He stared at Alex and howled again. He howled a third time.

"I hear you," Alex said emphatically. "Man, you are loud." He dropped the poker. It banged to the floor and rolled away from the fire.

The pup hopped down. Alex did an about face and walked towards the bed. He knelt and scratched him behind the ear. The room was a large, symmetrical space. A musty odor permeated the air. Adjacent to the fire, a large copper basin was secured to the floor. Steam wafted up from inside the tub. The windows were filled in with brick. Pale green shutters were set against two of the walls. The others were completely bare. At the far end of the space, a bed was made up. Dark grey linnens were folded and stacked near the headboard. A small wardrobe was directly next to the only door. Dark blue and black robes hung neatly on wooden hangers.

"What is your name?" Alex asked the pup.

The pup howled. He leaned his head into Alex's hand and closed his eyes.

"Yeah," Alex said sheepishly, "I really like you too." He stroked the pup's neck. "We will think of something to call you. I bet a name will just come to me."

Alex stood. He peeled his tunic away and walked towards the tub. The pup dropped his head and scowled. He jumped up and howled. Alex swiveled around. He narrowed his eyes and growled. The pup howled again. Alex laughed. He dropped his trousers and dipped his finger in the water. He put his entire hand in and swept it from side to side.

Alex propped on the rim of the basin. He put his feet in the water and eased into the bath. The world faded away. He submerged his head and scrubbed his scalp. He worked his way down to his feet. When he felt clean, he tipped back. He closed his eyes and slowly exhaled. Alex fell into a trance. His skin turned red. His hands withered into prunes.

There was a gentle rap on the door. The pup lifted his head. His lip curled and he howled. Alex bolt upright. He shook his head and rubbed his eyes. The fire had dwindled to a faint glow. A small flame flickered from the remains of the embers. A gritty haze filled the water. Goosebumps covered Alex's skin. He got up and stepped out of the tub.

"One second," Alex hollered. He grabbed his trousers and walked to the door. "Who is it?" he asked. He got his pants on and put his ear to the wood.

"It is the King," a raspy voice answered.

Alex cracked the door. "Hello sir," he said. He moved back and the entrance swung open.

"May I come in for a moment?" King Wasagowi asked. He put his hands over his stomach and waited.

Alex scrunched his face. "Um," he stammered, "of course, sir," he finished. "This is your home. I just appreciate having a place to stay."

The King grinned. "How is the room?" he asked. He lumbered in. "It is not much, I am afraid, but I am happy to have you as a guest in my home."

Alex checked the hall. Everything was quiet. "It reminds me of the place I used to live," he said. He shut the door behind him. "But the bed and the bath make all the difference."

"I wanted to have a moment alone with you," the King said abruptly. "It was not the proper time for us to discuss the matter earlier."

Alex turned. "I just tried to stay back," he admitted. "I didn't know Danice like all of you did. It looked like there were a lot of people who wanted to say goodbye."

The King bowed. "She was a remarkable woman," he said kindly. "More so than any of us will ever know."

"I really liked her," Alex said.

"Me too," the King agreed. He lifted his head and strolled to the center of the room. "My daughter has told me a little bit about you," he continued. He looked at the pup and smiled. "About the circumstances around how the two of you met," he continued. "About your friend Leviticus."

Alex slunk over. "I didn't know," he stammered. "He was so nice to me."

King Wasagowi put his hand in the air. "I believe that everyone should have a chance at redemption," he said kindly. "Maybe Leviticus found his redemption in you."

"I," Alex stuttered. He suddenly realized his torso was exposed. He crossed his arms over his chest. "Let me grab my shirt really quick," he said. He pivoted and his feet slipped.

"Wait," The King exclaimed. He reached out and snatched Alex around the shoulders. His fingers dug into his flesh. "What is this?"

Alex tried to pull away. "It is nothing," he said defensively. He wiggled but couldn't break free. "It is just a scar or something."

"This is no ordinary scar." The King trembled. He placed his finger to Alex's shoulder and traced the outline of the flaw. "This is a royal brand," he said breathlessly. "But there is no way it is possible," his voice faded away.

"Leviticus said I belonged to someone," Alex snarked. "I don't care what anyone says, I will never be a slave."

King Wasagowi turned Alex around. "You misunderstand," he said eagerly. He pulled him in. "This is the symbol for your family. Your real family." He tightened his grip. "Alex," he murmured, "my dear boy, you are a King."

TO BE CONTINUED

CPSIA information can be obtained
at www.ICGtesting.com
Printed in the USA
LVHW010733080820
662689LV00001B/22

9 780578 729343